More Praise for the Novels of Julie Ortolon

"Julie Ortolon takes her wonderfully colorful and appealing characters on an unexpectd journey of discovery. Be prepared to laugh."　　—Christina Skye

"Ortolon's protagonists must overcome some tough emotional issues before thay can set their sights on the future, but their journey is laced with humor. . . . Earnest and endearing, Ortolon's newest is a heartwarming and at times heartrending read."
　　　　　　　　　　　　—*Publishers Weekly*

"So romantic it will make you melt!"
　　　　　　　　　　　　—Virginia Henley

"This is an author on the rise! An endearing, emotional, romantic tale."　　　—*Romantic Times*

"As long as Julie Ortolon is writing books like this one, romantic comedy is in good hands."
　　　　　　　　　　　　—All About Romance

TOO PERFECT

Julie Ortolon

A SIGNET ECLIPSE BOOK

SIGNET ECLIPSE
Published by New American Library, a division of
Penguin Group (USA) Inc., 375 Hudson Street,
New York, New York 10014, USA
Penguin Group (Canada), 90 Eglinton Avenue East, Suite 700, Toronto,
Ontario M4P 2Y3, Canada (a division of Pearson Penguin Canada Inc.)
Penguin Books Ltd., 80 Strand, London WC2R 0RL, England
Penguin Ireland, 25 St. Stephen's Green, Dublin 2,
Ireland (a division of Penguin Books Ltd.)
Penguin Group (Australia), 250 Camberwell Road, Camberwell, Victoria 3124,
Australia (a division of Pearson Australia Group Pty. Ltd.)
Penguin Books India Pvt. Ltd., 11 Community Centre, Panchsheel Park,
New Delhi - 110 017, India
Penguin Group (NZ), 67 Apollo Drive, Mairangi Bay,
Auckland 1311, New Zealand (a division of Pearson New Zealand Ltd.)
Penguin Books (South Africa) (Pty.) Ltd., 24 Sturdee Avenue,
Rosebank, Johannesburg 2196, South Africa

Penguin Books Ltd., Registered Offices:
80 Strand, London WC2R 0RL, England

First published by Signet Eclipse, an imprint of New American Library,
a division of Penguin Group (USA) Inc.

First Printing, November 2005
10 9 8 7 6 5 4

Copyright © Julie Ortolon, 2005
All rights reserved

To Friends

For filling my days with laughter,
for three-hour lunches (when we should be writing),
for enabling my Chico's shopping addiction,
for unquestioned support, sympathy,
whining, and wining,
for champagne celebrations (anytime, any reason),
and for e-mailing in the face of deadlines!

Chapter 1

Big things often begin with a simple dream.
—*How to Have a Perfect Life*

Amy Baker's worst nightmare had come true. She was stranded. Left behind on a tropical island with no way to get home. At least not a way that wouldn't prove humiliating.

Yesterday, after watching the cruise ship she'd been on literally sail off into the sunset without her, she'd agonized over what to do. Being stranded was only half her problem. She'd been traveling with an elderly couple as a nanny to their three grandchildren, and just before being left behind she'd been fired.

It was all her fault, of course. She'd taken the children ashore on the French island of St. Barthélemy and hired a taxi to get to one of the beaches. As had happened on other shore excursions, she and the children became wrapped up in one of her games of make-believe. They were pirates searching for buried treasure. After a mock sword fight ranging up and down the white-sand beach, she'd glanced at her watch and realized she'd lost track of time. Again! She was an hour late getting the children back to the

ship for afternoon snack time with their grandparents.

With the grandfather's health failing, that was the one
time of day set aside for him to spend with the children.

Amy had arrived at the landing frazzled and frantic to find a very angry grandmother standing on the
dock tapping her foot with impatience. Naturally, the
three children—who'd been having a blast all day—
picked that moment to break into a full chorus of,
"We're tired. We're hungry. We hate this trip."

If Amy hadn't committed several other similar
transgressions, perhaps the incident would have been
forgiven. As it was, the grandmother had had every
right to chew Amy out right there in front of several
passengers while loading the children on the tender
boat that ferried people back and forth from ship to
shore. Embarrassment had swamped Amy down to
the soles of her tennis shoes. She'd turned and
headed blindly away from the dock—and succeeded
in getting lost.

Considering the tiny size of Gustavia, the island's
capital, she was sure only she could accomplish such
a feat.

By the time she found her way back to the landing,
the last tender had come and gone. She'd stood there,
at the end of the harbor, watching in disbelief as the
sun sank into the sea and the ship grew steadily
smaller on the horizon. As much as she'd been
dreading getting back on board, getting left behind
was a thousand times worse.

All she had on her was a beach bag with her emer-
gency stash of money, a half-empty tube of sunblock,
snacks for the kids, her autographed copy of *How to*

Have a Perfect Life, and a wet, sandy beach towel. She didn't even have a change of clothes, or underwear so she could take off the swimsuit she wore beneath her T-shirt and shorts. Everything else she'd brought on the trip, including her credit cards and passport, were on their way to St. Thomas.

Calling her grandmother to wire her funds would only earn her a lecture about her absentmindedness, but the thought of turning to her friends Maddy and Christine was out of the question. They'd move mountains to help her, but then she'd lose the bet that had sent her on this trip in the first place.

She refused to be the only one of the three who failed to fulfill the challenge they'd made nearly a year ago. Maddy had faced her fear of rejection to get her art in a gallery, and Christine had faced her fear of heights to go skiing. Now it was Amy's turn to face her fear of strange places to take a trip by herself. So far, she'd accomplished only half of that feat. She'd gone somewhere on her own. Now she had to get back—on her own.

And the more she thought about it, the more she realized that turning to her friends for help wasn't the only thing that would make her a failure. Arriving home a week early with her tail between her legs would do it too. She had to figure out a way to finish her full vacation time. Okay, so it had been a working vacation, but it was still a two-week break from her regular life and everything familiar and safe.

That was the real challenge, wasn't it? Staying away from home for the full two weeks. Facing her fears and dealing with them. She had to do this or lose her self-respect.

That night, though, as she lay awake in a hotel room that had wiped out most of her cash, her options looked bleak. Not only was she stranded on an island, she was stranded on St. Barts—one of the most expensive islands in the Caribbean. Even when she sorted out the problems of getting replacement credit cards, how could she afford a week here? Why couldn't she have done something reasonable, like get stranded on an island that had a budget beach hotel and a discount department store for her to buy some clothes? No, she had to get stranded on a chichi island—where the locals spoke French, no less!

Tears started to fill her eyes, until she remembered her mother insisting that giving into despair never accomplished anything. "There's a bright side to everything," her mother had said more times than she could count. "You just have to find it."

Swallowing the lump in her throat, she closed her eyes and prayed for an answer.

The following morning, she found a travel agency to help her contact the ship and arrange to have her things packed up and sent home. That seemed wiser than having them sent to St. Barts, since she didn't know how long she'd be on the island. The agency also solved her passport and credit card problem. Within minutes she was picking up a cash advance at a local bank.

Next on her list was the enormous problem of finding a place to stay that she could actually afford. That was when she found the answer to her prayers.

As she stood on the street contemplating her options, her gaze fell on a sign in the window of an employment agency: IMMEDIATE OPENING FOR A LIVE-IN HOUSEKEEPER.

Her breath caught at seeing the perfect solution. Okay, maybe it was wrong to apply for a job when she knew she'd be quitting days later, but as the idea took root, she realized she actually had four weeks before she absolutely had to be home.

Four weeks. In the Caribbean.

It was terrifying. It was thrilling.

Four weeks. Could she really do that?

The worrywart inside her battled with the part of her that had always longed for freedom to go and do and see.

She beat it back by realizing that yes, she had things organized enough back home; she could stay away that long. She would work for two weeks—assuming they hired her—give two weeks' notice, and be home a whole week before the bridal shower she was throwing for Maddy's and Christine's double wedding on the one-year anniversary of their challenge.

She entered the employment agency shaking with both excitement and doubt. An hour later, she was heading for an interview.

Her spirits lifted with every step as she climbed the footpath that led from Gustavia to the mansion perched on the cliffs overlooking the bay. Her mother was right, she decided. Rather than a catastrophe, life had given her an adventure. A real, live adventure, not the imaginary kind she usually took.

Needing to catch her breath, she stopped and shaded her eyes to take in the view. And, oh, what a view!

Dozens of sailboats and fabulous yachts bobbed at their anchors in the bay while their owners explored the tropical paradise. Farther out, a cruise ship sat like an enormous luxury hotel floating on the sparkling water of the Caribbean Sea. The sky and water held every shade of blue from azure to indigo as a light breeze sang through the palm trees around her.

As she'd done so often during the trip, she wished her mother could have seen this. The Caribbean was one of many places they'd visited a thousand times in the stories they made up together, traveling on the ocean or through the air on their magic flying ship. *Do you see it, Momma? It's even more beautiful than we imagined.*

The sweet pain of memories filled her heart in a rush.

Fearing she'd cry if she stood there much longer, she resumed her climb, catching glimpses of a stone structure through the dense, tropical growth. As she got nearer, though, a new worry edged aside some of her enthusiasm. The structure at the top of the trail didn't look like a house. It looked like an old fort, the type that would have guarded the island during the time of pirates.

Before her mind could take off on some flight of fancy about swashbuckling buccaneers, she wondered if she'd taken a wrong turn. She glanced at the cover sheet to the application she'd filled out. The job description and directions were written in French, but the woman at the employment agency had definitely pointed to this path and told her in English to follow it to the top. As talented as Amy was at taking wrong turns, even she couldn't have messed this up. Could she?

She ducked past the last curtain of palm fronds and found herself facing a very tall, bracken-covered rock wall. Staring way up at the crenellated battlement that lined the top of the wall made her almost dizzy. On the corner toward the sea, a square tower jutted up even higher.

How wonderfully fascinating. Like ancient ruins in some secluded rain forest far away from civilization.

The path split in two directions: one heading uphill and around to the inland side; the other path headed to the side that faced the sea. Choosing the seaside path, she let her imagination conjure a story of exploring forgotten ruins: *The intrepid archaeologist Amelia Baker battles her way through the jungle to unravel the secrets of a mysterious fortress. What has become of the soldiers who once walked the battlement? Do their ghosts still haunt the old stone walls?*

A delicious shiver ran down her spine at the thought.

She found a door in the base of the tower, but it definitely didn't strike her as the main entrance, so she continued on along the edge of the cliff with the bay far below. The moment she cleared the tower, her eyes widened with delight. One whole section of the outer wall had been removed, exposing an inner courtyard to the view of the sea.

Inside lay a garden gone wild. Tropical flowers exploded with color, struggling for space and spilling past their borders. Bougainvilleas climbed the trunks of giant palm trees while bromeliads and orchids dripped down to meet them. Small songbirds and butterflies added a kaleidoscope of music and life. Through the dense tangle she glimpsed a second-floor gallery with louvered shutters bracketing dozens of doors. Apparently someone had converted the old bastion into a private residence some years back, but the place looked abandoned now.

As she ventured forth through a tunnel of vegetation, the perfume of flowers and damp earth nearly overwhelmed her senses. Very little sunlight reached the ground, and the darkness added an eerie layer to the garden's atmosphere. Reaching out, she moved the leaf of a banana tree. A small monkey shrieked in her face. She screamed as well, which sent the long-tailed monkey scurrying up a tree trunk where it frightened a red macaw into flight. The ruckus echoed about her in a chain reaction of bird cries.

"Oh, my goodness." She pressed both hands over her racing heart and laughed at herself. "Sorry," she called to the brown-and-white monkey who scowled down at her from his—or her—perch high in the trees.

When Amy's pulse settled, she resumed her search until she found another door. This one didn't look any more welcoming than the one to the tower. The solid panel of aged wood hung from massive wrought-iron hinges. At eye level, a snarling gargoyle—who looked a great deal like the vexed monkey overhead—held a large round knocker in its mouth, its lifeless eyes daring her to knock.

What sort of person would live in such a strange place?

In spite of her fascination, a sense of foreboding

crept up the back of her neck. She had plenty of experience dealing with wealthy eccentrics, but this place went beyond odd into the realm of the bizarre. Maybe she should toss her pride to the wind and buy a plane ticket home. Thinking of the challenge, though, stopped her from retreating. If Maddy and Christine could complete their challenges, she could do the same.

She ran a quick hand over her hair to be sure her riot of corkscrew brown curls was still neatly confined in a braid down her back. As for her attire, there wasn't a thing she could do. She was stuck with the white shorts and striped "crew shirt" she'd purchased from the ship's store as a souvenir. It was neat enough, even if this was her second day to wear it.

Okay, no more stalling. Squaring her shoulders, she lifted the circle of gnarled iron and knocked three times. The banging echoed through what sounded like a vast, empty space, evoking visions of Gothic mansions from old horror movies.

No sound followed.

She stood in uncertainty, wondering again if she'd taken a wrong turn. An eternity later, the panel began to creak open on rusty hinges. She braced herself, half expecting to see Frankenstein's Igor smiling evilly and bidding her to enter.

For Amy, the reality proved nearly as frightening. The man who answered the door was quite possibly the sexiest man she'd ever seen in her life.

Tipping her head back, she stared into a tanned face surrounded by sun-streaked hair that fell in waves to broad shoulders. A rumpled tropical shirt hung open to the waist, revealing a very fine chest. As if startled to see her, he ripped off the earphone to an MP3 player strapped to the waistband of his khaki shorts. He looked like the poster version of an expatriate American who should be sipping rum in a beachside bar listening to Jimmy Buffett.

"*Bonjour!*" he said with obvious delight.

Okay, expatriate Frenchman, she corrected.

While he continued speaking in rapid-fire French, he ran a hand over his reddish-brown goatee as if to be sure he was presentable. He would be better served to button the shirt—which would spoil the view of his sculpted abs but keep her tongue from rolling out of her mouth.

At least she didn't have to worry about her shorts and T-shirt being too casual for the interview.

"I'm sorry," she finally managed, feeling dumbstruck, the way she always did around attractive men. Although "attractive" was an understatement. He looked like he'd stepped out of a travel brochure that had beyond-gorgeous people enjoying the tropics. "I don't speak French. They said that was okay."

"*Mais oui. Pardon.*" Laughing, he waved his own words away. "I say you get here very fast. The agency, they just call. When you knock down here, I am not even certain I hear correct."

"Oh." She tried not to gape as she stared into his yummy chocolate eyes. Long lashes—surprisingly dark for a man with light brown hair—made the eyes even dreamier. "Would you like me to come back?"

"No!" Panic flashed across his face. "*Entrez, s'il vous plaît.* Please, you come in."

She sidestepped past him, clutching the beach bag in front of her, painfully aware of her dumpy body. Looking about, she found herself in a square entryway with no hallways or doors other than the one she'd just come through. Stone stairs led up through an opening in a wooden ceiling. A rusty, wheel-shaped chandelier hung from a chain directly overhead with a spider industriously spinning its web between the dust-covered candles. The sound of squeaking hinges preceded an ominous thud as he closed the door, shutting out all the light except what came from the top of the stairs. She squinted to adjust her eyes to the darkness as dank air engulfed her.

"You have trouble finding the front entrance?" he asked.

"What?" She turned in time to see him lowering a bar to lock the door. "Oh. I thought—" Her cheeks heated as she realized she should have taken the other path up the hill to the inland side. Did she always have to pick the wrong direction? "I wasn't sure which way to go. Are you Lance Beaufort?"

"*Oui.*" He turned to face her. "You are Amy?"

"Yes, Amy. Amy Baker from Texas." As if he couldn't tell from the accent.

"I am most relieved to meet you." He held out his hand. She accepted it and his fingers closed about hers in a brief, business like handshake that shouldn't have made her heart flutter. But did. "Let me show you up."

She followed him up the stairs, taking in the iron sconces holding torches. From the smoke on the walls, they looked as if they'd been used recently. "Don't you have electricity?"

"On this level, no. But someday. Maybe." He glanced back at her over one of those broad shoulders. "The man who start this project, he want the atmosphere to be—how do you say?—*authentique*. We will keep, to a point."

They topped the stairs and Amy blinked in surprise at finding herself in a bright, open space with high ceilings. Scaffolding stood against the walls while drop cloths and buckets of plaster littered the floor. The double doors with beveled and stained glass told her this was the main entry hall. She could glimpse a road or driveway through the doors. On the wall facing the courtyard, louvered doors led to the gallery. They stood open, letting in a nice breeze and glimpses of the sea through the palm trees.

"As you see, everything is the mess now, and will stay until I find a new crew."

"What happened to the old crew?" she asked as they picked their way across the drop cloths.

"This is a good question." Passing through an archway, they entered a long, unfurnished room with more signs of abandoned construction work. The fort formed a giant U with doors lining the inner wall but solid rock for the outer wall. Bars of sunlight slipped through the louvers, striping the dusty wooden floors. "We hire many workers. All quit without notice. Same with the housekeepers. We are most desperate to find someone who will stay."

"Oh." She bit her lip, grappling with guilt.

They passed through another long room, this one with half-finished bookshelves from floor to ceiling on three walls.

"You said 'we.' Are you doing this project with

your wife?" she asked, hoping he said yes. A wife would be so much less intimidating than dealing with a gorgeous bachelor.

He merely chuckled as he led her into a much smaller room. She entered behind him, finding a makeshift office. The shutters on the glassless windows had been flung open to an unobstructed view of the bay and the sea beyond. They must be in the tower, she realized. A long folding table sat in the middle of the room covered with blueprints, tile samples, paint chips, and a stack of how-to books.

Moving around the table, he took a seat in the swivel chair with his back to the window. "Please, sit."

"Thank you." She perched on a straight-back chair that faced him. Nerves twisted in her stomach as she handed him the application and watched him read.

Hoping for distraction, she looked about. The room held little furniture. Only the table and chairs and a battered old buffet that sat next to a closed door. Unlike the gallery doors, this door was made of solid planks that hung from black hinges. Above the buffet was an odd square panel flush against the wall. The walls themselves reminded her of a medieval castle. Oh, the stories she could conjure in a place like this . . .

Curious about what plans they had for converting it into a residence, she turned her attention to the table. Among the clutter of blueprints and books she found something that seemed out of place: a copy of *The Globe*. She never bought tabloids, but their covers frequently amused her when she stood in line at the grocery store.

This one had a close-up shot of a dark-haired man wearing black sunglasses and ducking his face away from the camera. The headline read: MISSING MOVIE MIDAS SPOTTED IN PARIS.

She assumed they meant Byron Parks. She'd never understood why they called him the King Midas of Hollywood. He didn't produce or direct. In fact, as far as she could tell, he didn't seem to do anything other than attend parties, go to premieres, and date movie stars. Maybe they called him that because of his wealth. When his face showed up on a cover alongside some beautiful woman, the caption usually reported that so-and-so had been seen with billionaire Byron Parks. She'd flipped through just enough tabloids to know he was the son of legendary producer Hamilton Parks and former French fashion model Fantina Follet. Articles on him claimed he'd received the best both parents had to offer: a hefty trust fund from his father, and his mother's photogenic looks.

Amy agreed he always did look suave dressed in European designer clothes and sunglasses. He also looked bored as all get-out in every picture she'd ever seen, even in the flood of photos that had dominated the tabloids during his most recent romance with Hollywood's newest sweetheart, Gillian Moore. The couple's much-photographed dates usually showed the fresh-faced Gillian with both her arms wrapped about one of Byron's, beaming for the camera as if she'd just won the biggest prize at the carnival. Amy had shaken her head at that, since she didn't see a world-weary party boy as a particularly grand prize. Apparently, Gillian had agreed in the end. The couple split in an extremely public fight that included Gillian slapping Parks in the face before a barrage of cameras. The photos had been splashed across every tabloid cover. Immediately after that, Byron Parks had disappeared from Hollywood and no one had seen or heard from him since.

Apparently, six months later, people were still speculating on his whereabouts.

"I see your last employ is with Traveling Nannies," Lance Beaufort said.

"Hmm?" She tore her gaze away from the magazine.

He lifted his eyes just in time to realize where she'd been looking. With a frown, he glanced down, saw what was on the table, and pushed the tabloid under a blueprint. His expression lost a great deal of its friendliness. "Your last employ?"

"Oh, yes. It was with Traveling Nannies." She squirmed at the half lie since she didn't "work" for Traveling Nannies. She owned the franchise, which specialized in placing experienced nannies with the traveling elite. If he learned that, he'd know she didn't intend to stay on long term.

"Have you experience in other domestic duties?" he asked.

"Not professionally." Truth was, she'd never even worked as a nanny until this one doomed-from-the-beginning assignment. "I've managed my grandmother's house for the past eleven years, though, since she's in poor health. I assure you, I'm very capable. I can cook and clean and—and run errands if you want." What was she saying? Run errands when the mere thought of wandering a strange town sent a streak of terror to her heart? "I'm a really good cook."

"*Oui?*" His eyes glinted as he took in her generous figure. Maybe for once, being plump would work to her advantage. A lot of people followed the faulty logic that overweight people knew more about cooking than skinny people. In her case, though, the assumption proved true. He looked back at the application, and his enthusiasm dimmed. "Hmm, I see you have no work visa."

"The woman at the employment agency said she'd help me get one," Amy assured him. "She seemed very eager to help."

"I'm sure she was." Laughing, he kicked back in his swivel chair, the picture of the relaxed, confident male. Oh, how she envied that sort of self-assurance. "I wonder, did she tell you why we have much trouble to fill this position? Or rather, to keep it filled?"

"No." Amy frowned. "Is there a problem with the job?"

Smiling mysteriously, he swiveled the chair and a beam of sunlight slanted in on his face. The contrast of glaring light and harsh shadow turned his handsome features almost ghoulish. "I suppose that depends on how easily you frighten at things that go bump in the night."

"Excuse me?" Trepidation returned—full-blown this time. "What sort of 'things'?"

He studied her with narrowed eyes. "I see she did not tell you. And you are new to the island, *non*?"

"Very new."

"Ah." His expressive brows drew together. "Some of the locals, they have a silly notion."

"Silly notion?"

He looked about the room, as if seeing the whole fortress. "They believe the new owner of this monstrosity is himself a monster." His gaze came back to pin her in place. "I can assure you, Gaspar is quite human."

"Gaspar?" Curiosity warred with apprehension.

"The man you are to work for."

"But I thought I'd be working for you."

"Oh, no. I do not live here." His tone implied that nothing on earth would make him live in this place. "I am Monsieur Gaspar's personal assistant." He gestured to the sketches and blueprints cluttering the tabletop. "I hire for him workers to finish this place. Not an easy task when so many of the islanders think the fort is haunted."

"Haunted? By ghosts?" Beneath the fear, she felt a stirring of interest. Ghost stories always intrigued her—at least fictional ones did. "People don't really believe that, do they?"

"But, of course." He spread his arms wide, as if he believed it too, and found the notion grand. Then he let his arms drop with a sigh. "Unfortunately, the ghost stories, they grow worse now that Gaspar has arrived. The islanders, they call him *La Bête*, The Beast."

"Why would they do that? Is he mean?"

"He is . . . tormented. A man cursed with a face he cannot bear to show the world. He came here to find privacy. With his money, he can afford to be a recluse."

"Is he disfigured?" Empathy filled her at the thought.

Lance Beaufort gave a noncommittal shrug. "As the only one allowed to see him, I will say only that I understand why he would prefer solitude to company. Some days, I can barely stand to look at him myself."

She stiffened at his words. What a terrible thing to say! And what would this man, with his handsome face and perfect body, know about the anguish of feeling ugly? She fought the urge to give him a good-size piece of her mind. "I see," she said instead.

Her chilly tone must have betrayed her thoughts, because he shrugged. "I assure you, I say nothing Monsieur Gaspar does not say about himself. His face, it is why he purchase this fortress to live away from those who would gawk. Unfortunately, the place need much work, so for now, no solitude."

"How awful." And how insensitive of this man to say it so offhandedly.

He gave her a curious look, as if finding her sympathy odd; then he waved it aside. "You need not concern yourself with that. You need only to cook, clean, and honor Gaspar's privacy. In time, he may grow comfortable enough to allow you to see him. Until then, he has strict rules to insure that your paths do not cross. Are you willing to follow these rules?"

"Are you offering me the job?"

"*Ma chère.*" A charming smile flashed behind his goatee. "The job, it was yours the moment you knock on the door. Will you take it? The salary, it is most generous and includes room and board."

Relief rushed in when she realized he wasn't going to ask any questions that would be awkward to answer, like a request for references and a phone number for her last "employer." The job was hers! Just like that! "Yes! Yes I'll take it!"

He looked equally relieved. "How quickly can you move in?"

"Is today too soon?"

"Today would be perfect."

Chapter 2

Adversity can bring opportunity.
　　　　　　　　　—How to Have a Perfect Life

Amy's relief dimmed when Lance stood abruptly, his expression going from congenial to intense.

"And now, for the rules," he said. "The most important is that door." He pointed to the closed door next to the buffet.

"Yes?" She rose as well.

"You must never, under any circumstance, go through that door."

Her eyes widened as she stared at the forbidden door. "What's behind it?"

"The stairs to Gaspar's private quarters in the top of the tower."

"Oh." She looked up at the wooden ceiling. An odd feeling, part intrigue, part fear, brushed her skin with the knowledge that the man was up there now. What did he do all day? "Doesn't he want me to clean his room?"

"He would prefer to tend to himself." Lance came around to her side of the table. "Until the construction is complete, you will mostly cook his meals and deliver them here." He moved to the buffet and slid open the panel above it to reveal a wooden box dangling from a rope inside the wall. "It is the dumbwaiter."

"Really?" She moved closer. "I've never seen one. How does it work?"

"You place the tray here, then pull this rope. The tray goes up. When Monsieur Gaspar finish, he send the dishes down."

"I see." She frowned at the ceiling again. "He stays in the tower all the time? Is he ill?"

"Not physically," Lance said, as if that would reassure her somehow. All it did was raise new concerns to battle with her empathy. "Now come," he said. "I tell you the plans for the fort on the way to the kitchen." He led her back the way they'd come. "This wing was many small rooms. I think for the officers' quarters. We gut it to make two big rooms. This one is the library."

"Look at all these bookcases." Sawhorses sat in the center of the room with a pile of lumber ready to cut into shelves. "I can't imagine having so much shelf space for books."

"You like to read?"

"I *love* to read."

"Then you and Gaspar have something in common," Lance said as he continued walking.

She followed, noticing the rough beams holding up the ceiling. Even when finished, she imagined the place would retain a rugged, masculine energy, an echo from the past when uniformed soldiers resided here. What had their lives been like?

"This will be the living room," Lance said.

The room had a massive stone fireplace against the

outer wall, which seemed odd on a tropical island, but she supposed the weather dipped enough to need it on occasion. And it gave the room a nice focal point.

"So much space," she said, picturing the doors thrown open, allowing in light and breeze. The definition between inside and outside would be wonderfully vague. People could wander in and out, from room to room. And from what she'd seen of the gallery, it looked wide enough to hold lots of outdoor furniture. "Goodness," she said, "think of the parties you could throw here."

He cocked a brow in amusement. "Ah, but the point of buying a fort on an island is to escape people, not invite them over."

"Yes, of course." She pulled in some of her enthusiasm. "It just seems like a lot of house for one person."

"We have not so many rooms."

"But they're so big!" They picked their way back through the construction mess in the entryway and turned into a long room with a high, beamed ceiling. "Let me guess," she said, grinning broadly. "This will be a bowling alley?"

"The dining hall," he corrected with a chuckle, looking surprised by her sense of humor.

"Wow." What a shame Mr. Gaspar didn't like people. She envisioned a long table filled with laughing friends sharing good food and stories. "You could feed an army in a room this size."

"I believe that is what they did."

She laughed, realizing he was right. "So is this the

only floor you're using besides the tower? What's on the other floors?"

"Below us are many small rooms I think for storage, a stable, animal pens, and a prison."

"A prison? Really?" She couldn't wait to see it.

"Above us is the soldiers' barracks," he explained as they walked through the long dining hall. "They are untouched."

"What will you do with them?" She forced herself to walk straight rather than turning in circles like a gawking tourist.

He shrugged. "Hire a crew to clean is all."

What a shame, she thought. The fort had two whole floors of unused space. They could easily be turned into guest rooms for a bed-and-breakfast. Wouldn't that be the ultimate lifestyle? Running a fabulous inn on a tropical island, having a steady stream of fascinating people come through your door with tales of where they'd been?

Reaching the far end of the room, he opened a swinging door and swept his arm for her to enter ahead of him. "And now, for your domain, *mademoiselle*."

Her breath caught as she stepped into a spacious kitchen that provided a startling contrast to the neutral-toned masculinity she'd seen so far. Here color abounded in a style that blended French country charm and tropical motifs. The aged-wood floors made a nice anchor for pale yellow walls and light green cabinets. A few of the cabinets had glass doors to show off the brightly colored dishes that combined cobalt blue, earthy red, and mustard yellow.

Hand painted tiles depicting flowers and fruit as boldly colored as the dishes decorated the backsplash while a ceramic rooster cookie jar sat crowing on the counter next to the sink. The window over the sink and door to the gallery offered a stunning view, but for now her attention was all on the commercial-grade oven, the side-by-side refrigerator/freezer and the center island that had a grill and cooktop on one end and eating space with bar stools on the other. Pots and pans hung from the wrought-iron rack overhead. The range of tones and textures couldn't have been more cozy in spite of the room's size.

"I love it," she said, turning about to take it all in.

"I am glad you approve."

"I do." She smiled. "At least the crew finished this before they disappeared."

"Actually, no. I do most of it."

"Did you?"

"With the trouble we have with workers, I am learning much about building." Pride shone on his face.

"Well, you did a great job. Did you pick the colors?"

"*Oui et non.* Yes and no." He looked about in satisfaction. "They are the same as my *grand-mère's* kitchen in Narbonne."

Well, that explained the French country feel, although she doubted his grandmother's kitchen matched this in size. She could easily cook for that dinner party she'd imagined, or that inn full of guests. Instead, she'd be cooking for a solitary recluse and herself.

"Here, I show you the rest." He crossed to a door

that led to a small hallway. A Dutch door at the far end led to the outside. "That is to the carport. I will get you keys for the car."

That statement had her eyes going wide. If she could get lost on foot, how much more lost could she get with a car? Knowing her, she'd head for Gustavia and wind up on the opposite side of the island.

"The laundry room is there." He pointed. "And that is a storeroom. Your room is here." He opened the door directly across from the kitchen. "It is not large, but perhaps you will like it."

She moved past him to find a room with the same welcoming colors as the kitchen. Wicker furniture held cheerful cushions, creating a sitting area. Then her gaze went to the bed, and she gave an *ooh* of delight.

The four-poster rose nearly to the ceiling to hold the mosquito netting. She knew the netting served a practical purpose on a tropical island, especially with no glass in any of the windows, but she thought it was the most romantic thing she'd ever seen.

Lance crossed to the gallery doors. "You want to keep these closed when you are not in your room, or the monkeys, they steal anything that sparkles. But when you are here, the view, it is *magnifique*." He opened the doors and moved back.

She went out onto the gallery and discovered her room sat directly opposite the tower, with each at the far end of its wing. Looking down to the side, she saw the rocky shore of the cove far below. A gentle wind came up the cliff side, kissing her cheeks. The dizzying height made her think of her friend Christine, who would have heart failure if she stood so close to a sheer drop like this. Amy, though, loved the thrill of it. Breathing in the salty air, she looked out at the sea. "It's so incredibly beautiful here."

"I am happy you think so." He joined her at the rail. "Hopefully, you will stay longer than the others."

Guilt nettled her but she bit her lip against any confessions.

"And now for the other rule."

"Yes?" She faced him.

"You are free to roam the house and grounds during the day when others are about. But after you deliver Gaspar's supper, you are not to go beyond the kitchen until morning."

"Can I sit out here?" She looked up, imagining the stars at night.

"Here, *oui*, but not the courtyard after dark. Gaspar often walk the grounds at night. If you see his face before he is ready, I promise you will be dismissed *tout de suite*."

"Oh." Well, she thought, getting fired might be one way out of the job when the time came. But did she really want to suffer that kind of humiliation again?

"You will follow the rules?"

"Yes, of course," she assured him.

"*Bon*." He gave her a smile so dazzling, she felt light-headed. She knew the smile came from his relief that she'd taken the job, but how would it feel to have a man like him smile at her because he found her attractive? Even her active imagination couldn't conceive of that. "If you are to move in today, I will drive you to town and help you collect your things."

"Oh." She did a quick mental scramble for how to explain her lack of clothes. "Actually, I, um, have very little to move. I can walk down later and get everything."

"You are certain? I am happy to assist."

"No, really." She forced a smile. "I'd rather spend some time poking about the kitchen. Besides, it's nearly noon. Won't Mr. Gaspar want lunch?"

"Another reason to drive to town. I will buy lunch at one of the restaurants."

"Why do that when you just hired a cook?"

One of his brows lifted. "If you are able to find enough food in the kitchen to make a meal, you are capable of miracles."

"Well, why don't I look around and see what I can find?" She smiled at the prospect since she loved spending the day amid the comforting smells of food simmering and baking. He followed her back to the kitchen. A quick search of the pantry, refrigerator, and freezer revealed just enough staples, canned goods, and frozen food to make a few meals if she kept them simple. "Oh, I can handle this, no problem."

"You are certain?"

"Absolutely. Lunch will be a snap. I assume I should make enough for you as well?"

"*Oui.*" He still looked doubtful that she could actually pull this off. "If you have no questions, I will return to my work."

"Yes, go on." She made a shooing motion with her hands. "I'll have lunch in no time."

A sigh of relief escaped her when he left. Now maybe she could relax and absorb everything that had just happened. She couldn't believe she'd found a way to stay on this gorgeous island for the next four weeks! It really was terrifying and thrilling at the same time. And she couldn't wait to tell Maddy and Christine. They were going to be very impressed with her bravery.

The pride that came with that thought burst when reality crashed in. Her laptop was on the ship. Which meant she wasn't merely away from home, she was well and truly cut off.

Panic squeezed her chest.

The main thing that had helped her cope with her fear of traveling was knowing she could stay in touch with everyone back home. She could check in every day and have the reassurance that nothing horrible had befallen anyone in her absence.

With some steady breaths, she reminded herself that she'd taken measures to insure that everything would be okay. She'd hired Elda, one of the older nannies, to run the office while she was gone and—more importantly—to take care of her grandmother. Since Amy worked and lived in the converted carriage house behind her grandmother's house, the two jobs went hand in hand.

How long could she expect Elda to handle things, though? Running the office didn't require much, but taking care of Daphne Baker, or Meme, as the family called her, would try the patience of a saint.

The minute Meme heard that Amy wasn't coming home on time, she'd go off on a worry-fest that could trigger a heart attack or stroke. Amy could already hear the thousands of outrageous concerns: What if Amy's new employer is a rapist or ax murderer?

What if Amy catches some tropical disease and dies? What if Amy is kidnapped by terrorists?

For as long as Amy could remember, Meme had been obsessed with worry that if her granddaughter left the house, something terrible would befall her. The fact that Amy had no sense of direction only added to Meme's fears.

Ironically, it was far more likely that something horrible would happen to Meme, like she'd fall and break a hip and Amy wouldn't be there to help her. The two women's fears had fed off each other until two years ago, when Amy decided it had to stop. They—or at least she—couldn't keep living in stark terror every time she needed to go to the grocery store. She'd been making steady strides in that direction, and this trip was one more step, a big step, to prove to both of them that Amy could go away from home, manage on her own, and return safely to a living grandmother.

Except . . . what if she proved the opposite? Since she'd gotten lost, getting home would take longer than she'd planned. What if something happened to Meme?

Her stomach churned, giving her the familiar impulse to eat anything she could get her hands on to make the nausea go away.

No, she told herself. Eating never stopped bad things from happening. It only set off more worries and lectures from her grandmother about her weight, which made her eat even more. She pushed away the urge to binge by concentrating on more important things.

Her immediate problem was getting in touch with

her friends as well as with Elda. Since Maddy had moved to Santa Fe, they'd developed a habit of e-mailing each other every afternoon around four o'clock Texas time so they'd all be online together. She hadn't checked in at all yesterday and had little hope of finding a computer to get online today. They'd be worried to death if she didn't find some way to contact them.

Would Lance Beaufort let her use his phone to make an international call and deduct it from her first paycheck? Or surely he had a computer somewhere in this fort that had Internet access. Everyone did these days. Well, except for Daphne Baker, who was sure computers caused cancer. Maybe Lance would let her use his computer. That, however, seemed like a very personal request to make of a man she'd just met.

Oh, well, she'd just have to think of something. And since cooking helped her think, she turned her attention to that.

The man who called himself Lance Beaufort left the kitchen twitching his mouth back and forth to ease the irritating itch of the glued-on goatee. As exasperated as he was over having the workers not show up that morning, he'd actually been looking forward to a day without donning his disguise. Wearing a wig in a tropical climate made his head hot, and the colored contacts dried out his eyes.

He'd gladly tolerate it, though, if this new housekeeper worked out. He needed food! For the past two weeks, he'd dreamed of having a meal without driving to town or suffering his own feeble attempts to cook—both of which took time away from working on the building project.

Passing through the entryway, he felt a surge of eagerness at the thought of strapping on a tool belt and MP3 player so he could spend the afternoon working up a good sweat to the beat of driving rock. Construction work was a new and unexpected pleasure born out of desperation. He'd never done anything remotely like it in his life, yet he found he had an innate knack for building things. Who would have guessed that he, of all people, would or even could do blue-collar work—and enjoy it? Nothing beat the pride, though, of admiring something he'd done with his own hands.

That was the one thing about his life before coming to St. Barts that had given him pleasure: his ability to bring a vision in his head to life—but in a very different kind of way.

Before he could tackle the plastering, though, he had a phone call to make.

Reaching the makeshift office where he'd interviewed Amy, he pulled a set of keys from his pocket, unlocked the door to the tower, and jogged up the spiral steps to "Gaspar's" apartment. Of course there was no Gaspar. Or Lance Beaufort, for that matter. He often shook his head in amazement that people never clued in to the names. "Lance Beaufort" meant *assistant at the beautiful fort*. And Gaspar was French for *Casper*, as in Casper the Friendly Ghost. How did no one ever get that? Not that he wanted them to. The whole purpose for the alter egos was to keep people from guessing who actually lived here.

He emerged into a spacious living room and office,

which he'd furnished himself. Since he couldn't hire
a decorator without risking his secret, he'd come up
with his own idea and rummaged through the shops
in town with an enthusiasm that surprised him. He
wound up with a room that looked like Hemingway
meets Techno Geek. The furniture mixed Stickley an-
tiques and heavy rattan with an entertainment center
that would make any audiophile or movie addict
weep with envy. Shelf lights backlit some small vases
and statues he'd found in one of the local galleries.

People said a lot of things about him, but no one
had ever questioned his taste or style.

Since the room lent itself to low lighting, he adjusted the shutters to let in small bars of light, then
picked up the remote control from the computer desk
in the corner and pointed it at the entertainment center. In addition to the wide-screen TV in the center
of the unit, a row of small monitors lined the top,
each one hooked to a different surveillance camera.
Apparently the man who had started converting the
fort into a residence back in the seventies had been
as paranoid as the imaginary Gaspar. The surveillance and sound system throughout the fortress had
been the only modern amenities besides plumbing.
Everything else had clearly been someone's attempt
to play pirate lord in a crumbling pile of rubble.

As the monitors sprang to life, his gaze went to
the screen that showed the kitchen. Seeing Amy
Baker busily at work, he dropped into his favorite
armchair and reached for his mobile phone. Since
he'd purchased it after coming to the island, it had
none of his old numbers programmed in. He had to
think a minute before remembering the number he

wanted. Had he been in hiding that long? That he'd forget a number he used to call so often?

Finally it came to mind. He hesitated, though, before punching it in. This would be his first contact with anyone back in LA since leaving that world. With a breath, he placed the call.

The answer came on the second ring. "Whitman here."

"Guess who?" he said in his normal American accent.

"Good God," Chad Whitman said. "Could this really be the Incredible Vanishing Byron Parks?"

"As I live and breathe," Byron answered.

"And apparently you do, contrary to speculation in the tabloids."

"Speaking of, that's why I called." A weight pressed down on his chest, but he kept his voice casual. "I saw the story in *The Globe*."

"You mean the issue that has you on the cover dodging the camera clickers in Paris?"

"That would be the one." Byron settled back in the chair.

"So is that where you're hiding out?"

"You think after successfully dodging the paparazzi all this time I'm going to answer that?"

"Looks to me like your luck ran out."

"I don't think so." Byron chuckled. "That picture is three years old."

"Really? So where are you?"

"No comment."

"Hey, it's me. I won't give your hiding place away, even if the price on your mug shot has gone up at least three times since you disappeared. Some of the more resourceful parasites have started offering to split the take with anyone who will betray your whereabouts."

"This is supposed to encourage me to confide in you?" he asked dryly.

"No," Chad said, "but it keeps us from talking about the article on me."

"Is it true?"

"Sadly"—Chad sighed—"the rags are actually right this time. About some of it anyway."

Shit, Byron thought but said nothing. Instead, he sat forward with an elbow on one thigh as he dropped his forehead to his hand. Chad and Carolyn Whitman were getting a divorce? He'd known the couple for eight years, ever since he'd bought the film rights to Chad's first novel, which changed the course of all their lives.

Byron had grown up in LA. As Hamilton Parks's son, he knew everybody who was anybody, but he'd never used those connections as anything other than entrée to the hottest parties. Then he'd read Chad Whitman's suspense thriller that relied more on emotional dilemma than action to suck the reader in. He'd mentioned to several friends that he thought the story would make a good movie. No one showed a shred of interest.

Something about the story had grabbed him, though, to the point he couldn't leave it at that. So he'd bought the movie rights and put up his own money with an independent studio to see the film made. A collective gasp went out throughout Hollywood. "Never put up your own money" was the mantra of the industry. He did it anyway. And wound up with a blockbuster hit.

In the process, he'd made Chad Whitman and his wife millionaires practically overnight. The refreshingly upbeat couple from Idaho had moved to LA during the filming, and Byron had introduced them around. They'd quickly embraced the whole Hollywood lifestyle, becoming more and more part of its center as Chad switched from writing novels to brilliant screenplays. All the while, Byron had sat by, silently watching, as Chad grew obsessed with his success and Carolyn grew derisive and brittle.

He'd watched silently, but inside he'd felt at least partially responsible—and not just about Chad and Carolyn, but so many other writers and actors who'd gotten their first break in a film due to him. That first taste of success had turned Byron into an instant addict for bringing stories he liked to the screen. Not as the money man—once was enough for that—but as a packager.

He had an unsurpassed talent for reading a novel or script, buying the rights, getting the right actors to commit, then selling the whole deal to a studio for many times his original investment. Everyone said, "If Byron Parks says it's good, it's a sure bet."

As the years passed, he'd felt more and more like the King Midas people called him. Everything he touched turned to gold—hard, cold, lifeless gold. It gleams in the sun and buys any object a person can desire, but it doesn't give sustenance when you're hungry, and it doesn't give the warmth of a human touch.

The King Midas of legend realized this quickly and, regretting his gift from the gods, washed it away in the river Pactolus. The daughter he'd killed with a hug came back to life, his food was once again edible, his wine drinkable.

Sitting in his tower, a world away from LA, Byron wondered if he could reverse any of the damage he'd done with his Midas touch. But what? Stop hand-picking movies that entertained millions and provided jobs for thousands? Give up the thrill of watching a story come alive on the screen? That seemed backward.

He rubbed his face to scrub the tension away. "I'm sorry to hear that," he finally offered and started to leave it at that. He never got involved in other people's personal problems. Life always tramples those who care.

But Chad and Carolyn were two of his closest friends. He cleared his throat and ventured into unfamiliar territory. "So . . . what happened?"

"I don't even know where to begin." Chad sighed. "Caro stopped taking her antidepressants about a year ago. Without telling me or her doctor. I love her, man—you know that—but, Jesus, how much am I supposed to take? Anytime I left the house, I never knew what I'd find when I got home: Caro the happy bouncing ball or Caro the despondent zombie who could morph into Caro the hysterical drama queen in a heartbeat."

Byron listened with growing discomfort as Chad described the deterioration of his marriage. Some part of him deep inside kept thinking, *Carolyn went off her meds and it took you a year to notice?*

Was he any better, though? His friends' marriage had been breaking up for a long time, and he hadn't bothered to notice. Well, perhaps he had subconsciously, but he hadn't said anything. When Chad finally wound down, he asked, "How are the kids holding up?"

"I don't know." Chad sighed. "I haven't seen them since she kicked me out of the house. I've got so much going on, what with the director of my latest project asking for script changes every time I turn around, I don't have time to think about the kids."

At those words, something inside Byron stretched taut. Chad didn't have time to think about his kids? A whole tirade of words he didn't even know he had—words about how the kids should be Chad's number one priority right now—reached the base of his throat, and stopped. To keep them from coming out, he got up and paced. "I'm sorry to hear that."

"Yeah, well, you know how insane things get in the middle of production."

"I know." He turned and paced the other way, picking up speed. "The business really bites sometimes. I understand."

He circled the coffee table, ready to explode from the pressure building up inside of him. Memories of his own parents' divorce, of how he'd felt watching from the sidelines pretending he wasn't hurt, swelled unexpectedly up from his gut and punched the words free.

"Actually, strike that. I don't understand. And you have *no* excuse for shoving the kids aside until it's convenient for you to deal with them. Do you know how hard divorce is on children? Caro kicked you out two weeks ago, and you haven't even talked to Jade and Micha? You've left them alone with a manic-depressive mother who's in God only knows what state of mind, wondering when and if their father's coming home? What is wrong with you?"

"What's wrong with *me*?" Chad sounded incredulous. "What's wrong with *you*? Since when do you care about anything other than finding the next party or script to package for profit?"

Byron flinched from the sting of that well-aimed jab but forged ahead. "Are you going to go see Jade and Micha? Sit down and explain that none of what's happening is their fault?"

"Yeah, yeah." Chad sighed. "When the movie's in the can, I'll take them to Disneyland or something."

"Oh, right, that'll make up for everything." He let his trademark sarcasm drip into his voice even if the words were more passionate than normal. "And when Micha turns sixteen, you can buy him a Ferrari and he'll forget all about how much it rips up everything inside you when your parents are so wrapped up in their own lives they forget you even exist."

"Look, I haven't forgotten about Jade and Micha."

"Then how come in your whole soliloquy about you and Caro and *your* pain, you didn't mention them once?"

"What is up with you, man? I feel like I'm talking to a pod person. I think you've been away from the action too long. It's warping your brain."

"Maybe I haven't been away long enough," he shot back and realized his body was vibrating with things he'd never felt before. "There is more to life than drifting from one party to the next and being bored when you get there."

"But being bored and cynical is what you do best, Byron. It's who you are."

Was it? The thought stopped him. Had he played the role of "I'm Byron Parks and I don't give a damn about anything" so long, he'd actually become that? And if it was a role, who was he really?

Who the hell was Byron Parks?

Were the roles he played here, of Beaufort and Gaspar, any more or less the real him than the role he'd played his whole life?

A movement on one of the monitors caught the corner of his eye. He glanced over to find Amy's image moving from one screen to the next carrying a serving tray. She'd already finished fixing lunch and was headed for Beaufort's office.

He remembered the tabloid he'd left lying on the table downstairs, the one she'd shown interest in during the interview. The last thing he needed was for her to take a good look at the photo on the cover and notice any similarities to his face. He'd learned the hard way to never underestimate people's compulsion to snoop when they thought no one was watching.

"Chad, I have to go." He watched Amy enter the library. "Go see your kids, though. They're more important than any movie."

After disconnecting, he hurried downstairs and slid into the chair behind the table. A quick check of the goatee and wig assured him everything was in place.

Like a method actor, he took a deep breath and cleared his mind. As he exhaled he became Lance Beaufort: open, happy, and easygoing.

Everything Byron Parks wasn't.

Chapter 3

Amy peeked through the open door into the office and saw Lance Beaufort sitting at the table. He finger-combed his shoulder-length hair as if he'd been pulling it in frustration while he worked. Coordinating a renovation of this magnitude must be very challenging, especially when the workers didn't show up.

"Knock, knock," she said since her hands were full and she didn't want to just walk in.

"Ah." His face lit with a smile and her heart fluttered at the sight. *"Entrez vous."*

She carried the tray in carefully since it barely held the two plates and glasses of ice tea.

"Let me help." He rose and hurried over to take the tray from her. How had she forgotten in just a few minutes how incredibly good-looking he was? He still hadn't buttoned his shirt all the way, and the sight of his well-muscled chest flustered her.

"I'm afraid I wasn't able to do a salad, and the vegetables are frozen. Well, they're not frozen now.

I mean they're from frozen." She caught herself babbling and told herself to stop. "Hopefully this will do until I go shopping."

"Anything is appreciated." His accent caressed the last word, drawing it out slightly.

Her hands felt empty and awkward when he took the tray from her. "Should I send Mr. Gaspar's lunch up on the dumbwaiter?"

"No, I carry it to him."

"Oh." She frowned in disappointment since she'd been looking forward to trying out the contraption. "All right."

"This looks delicious." He studied the dishes with obvious surprise. "What is it?"

"Bronzed chicken breast," she told him proudly, "with white wine sauce over rice pilaf."

"You're kidding!" He sounded almost American the way he said it. His eyes flashed upward as if he'd said something wrong. When he spoke again, the accent came out thicker than ever. "If this taste as good as it look, I am your slave for life."

"Well, taste it," she encouraged, smiling as she waited for his verdict. She didn't have confidence about many things, but she knew she could cook.

He lifted one of the plates, cut off a tender, juicy bite of meat with the fork, and placed it in his mouth. His eyes rolled back. "Oh, mmm, mmm, mmm!" He stomped his foot as if overcome with pleasure.

"You like it?" A grin bubbled up inside her.

"*Mademoiselle*, a moment, *s'il vous plaît*. I am having *la petite morte*."

A startled laugh escaped her at the French term for sexual orgasm. *La petite morte*, the little death.

After swallowing, he took her hand and kissed the back of it lavishly. "I am yours, *chérie*. If that is not enough, you shall have whatever you desire. Ask me for the moon, I will fetch it, if you promise to cook for me the rest of our lives."

A fit of giggles seized her so quickly she couldn't speak.

"You are a culinary queen." He kissed her hand again, this time twining their forearms together, which brought her body closer to his. Her giggles ended with a squeak of surprise as she looked up at him. "A goddess," he continued, gazing into her eyes. "And I your humble devotee. Name your price. What can I do to make you stay forever?"

Her heart beat so wildly, she couldn't even breathe. She just stood there, wide eyed, staring into his warm chocolate eyes surrounded by long, dark lashes. Never in her life had she been this close to a man like him. One so tall, so gorgeous, so thoroughly male. The few boyfriends she'd had had always been on the decidedly dorky side. They certainly hadn't exuded charm, confidence, and a boatload of sex appeal.

When she didn't speak, his smile faded. His expression went from flirtatious to confused as he studied her face. It was the look of a man noticing something for the first time and finding it curious that he hadn't noticed it before. "You have very pretty eyes."

Her eyes went even wider at that, and the lack of breathing made her head spin.

"Are you all right?" he asked in alarm. "You look faint."

"I'm fine," she managed weakly.

"I have frightened you," he realized with a start.

"I—I—" Her vocal cords refused to work with her heart in her throat.

"Forgive me." He took a hasty step back, dropping her hand. "I only mean to tease."

She sucked air into her lungs. "Of course."

"I apologize—"

"It's okay!" Her cheeks went up in flames. "I knew you were just playing. That you weren't, you know, coming on to me. Of course you weren't." She laughed. "I'd be silly to even think that you— Well, obviously *you* would never—" *Come on to someone like me*, she finished in silent misery.

Byron frowned in bafflement as color flooded her previously pale face. He really had frightened her. How strange. He'd invented Gaspar to frighten people, not Beaufort. Most people liked the friendly Frenchmen, a role he found surprisingly easy to play. Being Beaufort was simply a matter of not playing Byron the Bored all the time. He gave her a genuinely sheepish look. "I do apologize."

"No, my fault. I just get . . . flustered . . . around people . . . sometimes."

People, or men? he wondered. "I will try to not fluster you."

She laughed—at herself, he was sure—then dipped her head and smiled up at him in such an artlessly alluring way, he stared. How on earth had he not noticed earlier that she was pretty? Okay, so she didn't have the kind of beauty that would stop traffic, but if a man bothered to look, she was really cute. No, not cute. Cute wasn't the right word.

"I'm fine now." Still blushing, she patted her hair. The braid looked painfully tight and did nothing to enhance her face since she scraped her hair straight down against her head and started the braid at the nape. "I'll just be going, so you can take Mr. Gaspar his lunch."

He felt an odd stab of disappointment at the thought of her leaving. It was the first time since his self-imposed exile that he hadn't welcomed the thought of solitude.

She hesitated at the door. "There is one thing, though."

"*Oui?*"

"I need to go to town, to the grocery store and to find an Internet café, but I don't know my way around very well. Since you offered to take me earlier, I was wondering . . . would you mind driving me?"

"I am delighted," he said and pushed the wall-plastering project back even more.

"Thank you." The smile she sent him made her even prettier.

"We can stop on the way to collect your things," he said.

"Oh." The smile vanished. She bit her lip and her eyes shifted—the same way they had earlier when he'd mentioned getting her things so she could move in. "Yes. All right. I'll just wait for you in the kitchen."

He frowned as she left. Something wasn't right. She seemed so sweet and guileless on the surface, but women were never as simple as they seemed. The only thing he knew for certain about Amy Baker was that she could cook. Lord, she could cook!

Taking the tray, he carried it upstairs and set it on

the coffee table before the entertainment center. He carried the untouched plate over to the window that looked out on the courtyard. Having the housekeeper cook two lunches for only one man created a slight problem since he had to dispose of it somehow. The monkeys had seemed like the perfect solution—until he'd been between housekeepers and was faced with two very demanding pests who still expected to be fed every day.

Opening the shutters, he leaned out. "Okay, guys. Chow time."

Two spry animals scrambled up the nearest palm tree and leapt onto the windowsill. He started to put the plate down, then hesitated. He looked at the juicy, sauce-drenched chicken with the succulent flavor of it still in his mouth. Looked at the monkeys. Looked back at the chicken.

He shook his head. "I can't believe I'm going to give this to you."

They shrieked in protest at his delay, lifting their greedy little hands.

"Give me one good reason why I should keep feeding you when you've done nothing but cause me grief." They were the ones, after all, who had run off the other two housekeepers and caused so many islanders to refuse to work on the renovation.

Since the fort had no glass in any of the windows, a traditional security system wasn't an option. At first he'd thought maybe that wasn't necessary. St. Barts wasn't exactly a high-crime area. Then he'd learned that a common dare among the kids on the island was to sneak up to the haunted fort in the middle of the night.

So he'd had the seemingly brilliant idea to build on the islanders' belief that the place was haunted. He'd produced a soundtrack of scary ghost noises, then hooked the fort's outdoor speaker system to motion detectors. The idea worked beautifully to frighten the kids away. Unfortunately, the motion detectors couldn't tell the difference between mischievous kids and monkeys.

After waking up in the middle of the night a few too many times to the sound of moans and anguished screams, he dismantled the motion detectors. By then, though, the first two housekeepers had already hightailed it back to town, carrying stories of a demented monster living in the tower.

"You know," he told the monkeys. "If I had half a brain, I'd let you two go back to fending for yourselves."

The male jumped up and down, screaming his demands while the smaller female folded her humanlike hands under her chin and stared up at him with pleading brown eyes.

Oh, man. Byron sighed. How was he supposed to resist a look like that? For all he knew, she had babies or something. "I am such a sucker."

And wouldn't that shock everyone back home?

He set the plate down and watched the monkeys pounce on it. The female grabbed the chicken breast and hissed at the male when he tried to take it from her. The male, being no dummy, let her have it and settled for the rice and mixed vegetables.

"Let that be a lesson to you, my friend." Byron shook his finger at the male. "Women never are as sweet as they look."

With the monkeys appeased, he went back and sat in the chair that faced the entertainment center to eat his own lunch. Movement on one of the monitors caught his eye. He glanced up to see Amy in the kitchen washing pots and pans with her back to the camera. He started to return his attention to his meal since he wasn't in the habit of staring at the screens like some twisted voyeur. He merely glanced at them now and then to keep track of who was where. But something in Amy's body language made him look closer.

Was she talking to herself?

Since he had no intercom in that part of the fort, he had no way of hearing her. When she turned to hang a pot from the hooks over the center island, he realized she wasn't talking. She was singing. She wiggled her body inside that giant striped shirt she wore. What a terrible clothing choice for a woman on the short and plump side. Horizontal stripes made any woman look larger than she really was.

That thought made him tip his head to study Amy more closely. Maybe she wasn't as heavy as he'd first assumed. She certainly moved well, but that didn't really mean anything. He'd watched more than one well-endowed woman dance away at nightclubs around the world. Healthy women with healthy attitudes about their bodies had always appealed to him more than skinny sticks who obsessed over every pound. As he watched, Amy got gradually more into the rhythm of her song, shifting her shoulders and her upper torso. She added a sexy little hip wiggle.

He raised a brow. Oh, yeah, she could definitely move.

Taking up a dish towel, she danced about the kitchen, wiping down the countertops. Then she took the towel by one corner and twirled it about.

His eyes widened when she dipped at the knees and wiggled her way back up in an arousing-as-hell bump and grind. "Cute" definitely was not the right word. Give her a feather boa and she could hold her own against any stripper.

An image popped into his head of a voluptuous female body strutting about a stage—and his own body reacted in a predictable way. He straightened abruptly. Good God, he was ogling his housekeeper. He brought a hand up to shield his eyes.

She had no clue anyone could see her.

Thinking about how much he hated cameras pointed at him, he dove for the remote control. The instant the screen went blank he breathed a sigh of relief, then assured himself nothing too embarrassing had happened. Okay, so he'd felt a twitch of arousal; men had to deal with that at awkward moments all the time. He'd simply put it from his mind.

Glancing at the blank screen, he laughed. Like he'd ever forget that!

Cute? Oh, no. Amy Baker was hot!

He just hoped he didn't give that thought away when he took her into town. With the way she'd reacted to a little platonic flirting, she'd take off running if she knew she turned him on.

Lance Beaufort drove an Alfa Romeo. And he drove it with style. With the top down, he had one hand on the leather-covered steering wheel and the other on the gear shift. The screaming red paint sparkled in the sun as they zipped down the narrow road toward town.

Tipping her face to the wind, Amy pictured herself as Grace Kelly with a scarf about her perfect blond hair and big sunglasses hiding her movie-star eyes. Or maybe Sophia Loren. She'd always thought Sophia was one of the sexiest women who ever lived. As Sophia, she'd let her hair go free to dance about her. And she'd wear cat's-eye sunglasses with tiger-stripe frames.

The idea made her laugh.

"What is that?" Lance asked as he downshifted for a tight turn.

"Nothing?" Blushing, she ducked her head. "I was just enjoying the drive. And your car. I've always wanted something like this."

"It is Monsieur Gaspar's."

She ran her palms over the fine leather seat. Oh, how sinfully good that felt. "He has nice taste."

"And the money to indulge it." Lance took his eyes off the road long enough to send her a smile. A pair of sunglasses hid his eyes, but the smile still made her pulse jump. "You know what they say. Money, it does not buy happiness."

"True, but it buys nearly everything else." She grinned, then thought of Mr. Gaspar trapped in the tower by his fear of showing his face. Lance was right. Money didn't buy happiness. "What's he like?"

Lance kept his eyes on the road as the wind ruffled his long, wavy hair. "Private," he said at last.

"I didn't mean for you to tell me anything too personal. I just wondered, you know, what's he like in a general sort of way?"

"He liked the lunch you cook."

"Did he?" Pleasure blossomed inside her. "I'm glad."

"So is he. And relieved to have you cook for him."

"Have you worked for him long?"

"Since he come to the island six months ago."

"You were already living here?"

"I arrive the same time."

"Oh." She thought a minute. "What's his first name?"

He concentrated on driving a while before he answered. "Guy."

"Guy Gaspar?" She turned the name over in her mind, and found it strong and intriguing. A good name for a medieval knight. She pictured a battle-scared Norman warrior who hid his face behind a his helmet visor. Standing in the back of some great hall, he'd ache for the damsel he could admire only from afar. Would he stay forever her secret champion? Or would she draw him out of the shadows with a love that didn't care about the scars on his face? A love that could heal the wounds in his heart?

She sighed to herself at the thought.

The daydream dissolved, however, as they reached the bottom of the hill. Lance turned onto the main street through town, with shops running down one side and the harbor on the other.

The town dazzled Amy all over again with its cleanliness and colorful architecture. Each of the islands she'd seen had its own personality. Most were populated by dark-skinned descendents of slaves who spoke English with an accent that blended both British and Creole inflections. Here the population was predominately French. A slice of Europe in the Caribbean where celebrities and the ultrawealthy came to relax away from the crowds.

As they drove, she tried not to gape at the row of mega yachts moored so closely together that a person could likely walk from one end of the harbor to the other without any danger of getting wet. The vessels bore the names of ports from around the world. A uniformed cabin steward moved about the back deck of one of the yachts, setting fresh flowers on the dining table. In the berth next to it, a crew member polished brightwork, making the brass gleam in the afternoon sun.

"Goodness," she breathed. "Can you imagine living like that? Having personal servants on board your own private sailing ship?"

He chuckled, apparently amused by her awe.

In her line of work, she dealt with quite a few celebrities and people with money, but nothing like this. "Why, I wouldn't know how to relate to people like that."

"They are not so different than other people."

"Except that they say things like, 'Darling, wherever shall we be off to next?' " she said in her best Katharine Hepburn imitation, then switched to Cary Grant. " 'I don't know, dearest. I hear the Joneses are sailing over to Aruba. Perhaps we should join them.' 'Oh, yes, let's. Aruba should be lovely this time of year.' "

Lance laughed loudly at that, a burst of sound that had her smiling.

"*Très bon!* Very good," he said. "You do voices well."

"Thank you." She smiled in pride.

"Do you like old movies?"

"I adore them," she said with feeling. "You?"

He seemed to consider her question before answering. "Gaspar is more the movie junkie. He say movies and books, they are what make life bearable."

"Yes, exactly," Amy agreed. Gaspar's words struck close to home and sparked a sense of kinship. "Is that what he does all day? Watch movies and read?"

"It is a good way to pass the time, *non*? Without the escape of entertainment, the world would be a sadder place."

"I agree." She thought of her mother, who'd been trapped in a paralyzed body, and how the two of them used to make up stories together. Imagination had turned what could have been a tragic life filled with self-pity into something magical.

Meme had understood back then, but since Amy's mother died from complication connected to her paralysis, Meme seemed bent on scolding Amy for her constant daydreaming—as if daydreaming and early death were somehow connected.

At least Amy's fears—that something would happened to Meme in her absence—were logical. Meme's stress level always escalated out of control when Amy wasn't there, triggering all kinds of ailments. No telling what this news would do to her.

Feeling a renewed surge of need to contact home, she looked over at Lance. "You said Gustavia has an Internet café."

"All the port towns do."

"Could we stop there first?"

"Certainly. I have things to do as well. I will drop

you off, then go to the nursery to see if I can hire a landscape crew to take care of the courtyard. We can meet at the market in"—he looked at his watch—"two hours?"

Drop her off? As in leave her to find her own way to the grocery store? Her breath shortened at the thought. *Don't panic*, she told herself. Gustavia was a very small town. She'd already learned a bit of it. Besides, if he dropped her off, then she could duck into one of the stores, buy a few souvenir T-shirts and some shorts, and tell him she'd gathered her things on her own.

With that in mind, she struggled to memorize landmarks as he drove around the back side of the harbor through a maze of narrow streets. The town definitely didn't lack in shops, but they all looked frightfully expensive.

He pulled to a stop on the far side of the harbor. "The Internet café is just there."

She spotted it a few shops down, then took in the rest of the stores. "How do I find the grocery store?"

"It is over there." He pointed across the water. "You need only to walk back the way we come. You cannot miss it."

"Right." She looked in the direction he pointed and saw a small market directly across the harbor. Cheerful bushels of fruit lined the sidewalk out front. The place was so close as the bird flies, she could almost read the signs in the window. Surely she could find it on foot. "Okay." She nodded. "I'll meet you there."

The moment she climbed from the car and watched him drive away, though, her confidence wavered.

Yesterday she'd stood at this same harbor and watched the cruise ship vanish over the horizon. An echo of the panic she'd felt then tried to return, but she refused to give in. She could handle this. She would handle this.

No panic attacks allowed.

Chapter 4

When faced with a challenge, the first step is to stay calm.

—*How to Have a Perfect Life*

Amy had often wondered about the term "Internet café." As she passed through the metal-and-glass door she found it more curious than ever. To her, the word "café" evoked images of people sitting around bistro tables, eating fancy sandwiches, decadent desserts, and sipping cappuccino served by waiters wearing black pants, white shirts, and long white aprons. Conversation and laughter would mingle with the music from a singer sitting on a bar stool in the corner playing a guitar.

This café was nothing like that.

The place smelled of body odor. Fluorescent lights buzzed overhead, and the scuffed linoleum floor needed a good mopping. Crew members from the various ships appeared to be the main clientele. They crowded together, shoulder to shoulder along the narrow counter that ran along three walls.

In spite of the obvious downsides, the place fascinated her. What would it be like to work on one of the cruise ships or freight vessels? How much of the world had the people in this very room seen?

She felt a bit worldly herself as she approached the clerk behind the counter. He wasn't much cleaner than the floor, and the game on his PlayStation held his full attention.

"Excuse me?" she said, hoping he'd hear her through the earphones. When he didn't respond, she raised her voice. "Excuse me. Can you help me, please?"

He spared her an irritated look.

"I've never done this before," she confessed. "How do I use one of the computers to send an e-mail?"

Heaving a sigh, the clerk slid off the bar stool and helped her sign on to one of the few computers not in use. When he ambled off, Amy stared at the unfamiliar keyboard, which had extra keys she didn't recognize. She quickly discovered some of the keys stuck in the down position or refused to go down at all. Fumbling along, she managed to get on the site for checking her mail away from home.

Scanning the new posts, she saw her friends were already worried about her since she hadn't checked in yesterday. She typed in her response, using symbols to make up for the letters that didn't work.

Subject: *I'm Ok@y*

Message: *I'm sorry I worried you. I re@!!y @m @!! right, but the !@st two d@ys h@ve been @n @dventure.*

She went on to explain what had happened.

Maddy answered back right away: *Amy! My God! You must be freaking out. What can we do to help you get home?*

The instant offer for help squeezed her heart. She tried not to get teary eyed as she answered: *You don't* need to do @nything. I'm fine. @nd I'!! m@ke it home in time for the brid@! shower. I'!! h@ve E!d@ send out the invit@tions—@ssuming she @grees to st@y on unti! I get home. I don't think th@t wi!! be @ prob!em, though. She seemed very excited @bout running the office @nd !ooking in on Meme. I do h@ve one prob!em, though, @nd th@t's how to te!! Meme I won't be home on time. I'm sc@red to de@th she'!! worry herse!f into @ he@rt @tt@ck when she he@rs @bout this. I wish Christine w@sn't in Co!or@do so she cou!d bre@k the news in person. Except, Meme is sti!! m@d @t Christine for c@!!ing her a hypo-chondri@c right before we !eft for S@nt@ Fe to see you. M@ddy, m@ybe if you c@!! her, @nd re@ssure her th@t I'm fine, she'!! h@nd!e it better.

Maddy: *Of course I will. You know that. But forget about the bridal shower. You don't need to worry about that on top of this.*

Amy: *No, I w@nt to do it. Just t@!k to Meme for me. I wi!! e-m@i! @g@in tomorrow to see how she's doing.*

Maddy: *I'm sure she's fine. But what about you? What about your luggage? Good heavens, Amy, call me, collect if you need to, so I can help you sort this out. I mean it!*

Amy worked on her answer, growing frustrated by the keyboard. Finally, she had a well-worded as-surance typed out, only to have it vanish from the screen before she hit send. She stared in disbelief. Suppressing a growl, she tried again to explain why she didn't want them to help her, but the computer ate that response as well. She nearly screamed.

Giving up, she typed, "I'm going to be fine. I'!! be in touch," and hit send before anything else could go wrong. Seeing her time was almost up, she hurried through a quick exchange with Elda. The woman, who personified calm, promised to stay on and assured her that, aside from a few theatrics, Meme was doing just fine. Amy should relax and enjoy herself.

Amy's time expired in the next instant. The screen went blank. Panic streaked through her.

A "few theatrics"? What did Elda mean by that?

Amy pressed a hand to her racing heart and thought about buying more time. What was she going to do, though? Stay online all day saying, "Are you sure Meme's okay?"

Elda had said Meme was fine, and Amy would come back tomorrow and check on things.

Besides, the terror rioting through her right then lay at the heart of the fear she'd promised to face. She wasn't afraid to travel because she thought something bad would happen to her, but rather she feared something horrible would happen back home while she was gone. Getting lost always intensified that fear.

She had to stop letting it rule her life, though. Yes, Meme was old and frail, and, yes, Amy would continue looking after her when she returned home, but she had to prove to them both that she could leave the house without anything tragic happening to either one of them.

But what if something awful did happen?

Stop it, Amy, stop it! she ordered herself. Several deep breaths helped to calm her down.

Determined to conquer her fear, she left the café and contemplated her next priority: buying some clothes. With luck, she could do that on her way to the grocery store. She shielded her eyes and looked

across the harbor at the little market Lance had
pointed out. To get there, all she had to do was make
her way around the end of the harbor, keeping the
water in sight and on her left. How hard could that
be?

A lot harder than she hoped, she quickly realized.
A dockside restaurant forced her to head uphill into
a jumbled maze of narrow streets. Cars and motor
scooters zipped by carrying locals and tourists. The
shops were just opening back up, since they closed
everyday from noon until two thirty. She saw clothing stores advertising every designer name imagin-
able: Prada, Versace, Hugo Boss, DKNY. Other store
windows glittered with a fortune in duty-free gold,
diamonds, and precious gems. She passed art galleries, gift shops, shoe stores . . . Good heavens, did
women really walk on heels that tall? And look at
the prices! Who paid that much money for a tiny
strap of leather to hold on five-inch spike heels?

Why couldn't she have gotten stranded on one of
the islands where local women sold cheap tropical
shirts in souvenir shops along the dock? An island
that catered to ordinary folk like her?

That thought made her realize that the people
around her fell into two categories: the stylish ones
who looked like they actually belonged in such an
exclusive setting, and those who were gawking and
gaping just like her.

She conjured a fantasy in which she was one of
the former. A resident, she decided. On her way to
the market to pick up some produce, a bottle of wine,
and a freshly baked baguette, of course. Every ro-

mantic movie with a grocery shopping scene had to have a baguette sticking out of the bag. And a bundle of flowers.

As she wandered the streets, she imagined herself nodding to her neighbors as they sat and sipped coffee, watching the gawkers with smug amusement. The shop owners would call out her name and wave—since she patronized all the stores regularly.

She nearly laughed out loud when she realized that, except for the last part, her fantasy was actually true. She *was* a resident of this tropical paradise, albeit a temporary one, and she was on her way to the market. As for the clothes shopping, she needed to get serious about that before she ran out of time.

Even as she thought that, the fragrant aroma drifting from a nearby restaurant made her stomach rumble. The only thing she'd eaten all day were the kid snacks she'd had in her beach bag. After fussing at herself to not binge-eat while fixing Mr. Gaspar's lunch, she'd wound up not eating anything. That was never a good idea, because skipping meals always made her gain weight.

What to do about it, though?

She ruled out sitting down at one of the sidewalk cafés. That would take too much time, and she only needed something to tide her over until she returned to the fort.

A cheerful red-and-white beach umbrella shading an ice cream vendor's pushcart caught her eye. Her stomach leapt with joy. She tried to squelch the craving, but . . . well, she had had a stressful two days. Didn't she deserve to splurge a little? She hadn't allowed herself to have ice cream in eons. How much damage could one little serving do?

As if in answer, she watched one of the stylish people—this one a tall, willowy woman with long, dark hair and a killer tan—stop to buy a frozen treat. *See*, she thought, *you can eat ice cream and still be skinny.*

She marched up to the ice cream vendor and told him she wanted whatever the other woman had ordered. He handed her a vanilla ice cream bar covered in chocolate and nuts. She nibbled at the chocolate coating as she continued her search for clothes. It tasted heavenly!

The window of a boutique with trendy island fashions caught her eye. Still enjoying her fantasy of being a real local, she stopped to admire the outfit on the wicker mannequin. The tiny miniskirt and midriff-baring top would look chic and sexy on the woman who had just visited the ice cream vendor.

Amy had the amusing notion that if she ate enough ice cream bars, she'd become just like the other woman: slender and graceful, with the unbelievably thin thighs that every woman on the island seemed to have. Maybe that was the key to a perfect figure; live on an expensive French island and eat nothing but ice cream.

She grinned at the idea, until she caught her reflection in the window.

Her fantasy burst in an instant.

With her standing exactly even with the mannequin, her reflection and the outfit lined up perfectly. Her bulky outline spread well past the skimpy skirt and top. Lifting her eyes to her own face, she watched her smile drop away.

As if in tune with her mood, a cloud passed over the sun, dimming the island's brightness.

A painful pressure squeezed her chest. Who was she kidding? Some women were born to be thin no matter what they ate. She was not one of them. She was born to struggle against every pound. An ice cream bar made a nice little treat for a woman with the right metabolism. For her, it put an instant inch to her waist.

Angry at herself for forgetting that, she tossed the half-eaten bar into the nearest trash can. Her stomach rumbled in protest, but she ignored it. She'd buy some lettuce and nonfat dressing at the grocery store. But . . . which way was it?

A glance at her watch told her she wasn't just out of time. She was now late. Half an hour late. How had that happened? Great. Just the way to start a new job. She stood looking up and down the street, praying for divine intervention.

The cloud overhead opened up and dropped rain with the force of someone dumping a bucket over her head. Fabulous. Now she was fat, lost, and drenched. Could she possibly feel any worse?

Clutching her beach bag to her chest, she took off at a jog, heading for the nearest overhang, but tripped on a crack in the sidewalk and went down hard. Pain shot up from her palms and knees. For a moment, she couldn't even breathe. When she could move, she gingerly turned and sat on her bottom on the wet sidewalk. The rain plastered her hair and clothes to her body.

After two days of bucking up her spirits, of telling herself everything was going to be fine, of looking on the bright side, she dropped her face in her scraped hands and cried.

Sitting in the car with rain drumming on the convertible top, Byron wondered if a third housekeeper had run out on him. He'd been waiting for her for half an hour. If she'd been on time, she would have missed the cloudburst. Hopefully, she was merely standing in some shop to wait it out. But what if she wasn't? What if his description of Gaspar had already frightened her off? He'd tried to tone it down this time, to make *La Bête* just scary enough to keep her on her side of the fort at night. Maybe he'd still overdone it, though.

That thought added to the irritation still simmering inside him from his conversation with Chad. Beneath the anger directed toward his friend lay a sense of bafflement. Had he really shown concern for others that rarely?

I feel like I'm talking to a pod person.

All right, so maybe he normally kept his emotions, along with his opinions, to himself. That didn't mean he didn't have any, did it?

Bored and cynical is what you do. It's who you are.

Six months ago he would have shrugged that off. Why did it bother him now? What did it matter that people thought that about him?

Tired of sitting and stewing, he decided to look for his missing housekeeper. He drove the streets, ducking his head to peer through the rain into the shops. The gray deluge did little to dim the colorful town.

Flowers bobbed and swayed, dancing to the beat of the rain.

Then he turned a corner and saw her.

On the sidewalk up ahead, she sat with her face in her hands, soaked and sobbing. His heart lurched at the sight. He whipped into a parking space along the curb and leapt from the car. Rain poured over him as he rushed to her. "Amy! What happened?"

She lifted her head and stared up at him with big green eyes that widened in surprise.

"Are you hurt?" he asked over the sound of storm hammering the sidewalk.

"I tr-tripped," she explained, wiping her cheeks, which did little good in the rain. "I'm o-okay, though."

He frowned at the scrapes on both her knees. "Let me help you up."

Rather than accept the hand he held out to her, she scrambled up on her own, wincing as she did so.

"How badly are you hurt?" He bent to examine her knees. Blood ran down her right shin.

"Only a little." She tried to step away from him and nearly collapsed. He slipped an arm about her waist to steady her. Panic flashed across her face. "Really. I can walk."

"Let me help you."

"No, I'm okay."

Ignoring that ridiculous claim, he swept her into his arms.

"Oh, my God!" She pushed against his chest. "What are you doing? I'll break your back!"

"Be still." With her struggling he nearly dropped her to the sidewalk. She threw her arms about his neck, which brought her face a mere breath away from his. Her eyes went even wider.

For one brief instant, a heartbeat that seemed to last forever, they stared at each other while rain ran down both their faces. Some part of his brain registered that she had flawless skin—the kind that comes from nature, not makeup—and there was a lot less of her than he'd expected.

"You can't carry me," she protested in a small voice. "I'm too heavy."

"I have you," he insisted, striding to the car. She had a few extra pounds on her frame, but it was a small frame that fit easily in his arms. Her bare legs draped over one of his arms and her soft breasts nestled against his chest. Shifting her, he wrestled the door open.

"Lance, no!" she protested. "The leather seats. I'm all wet and dirty."

"And more important than a car," he growled, incredulous that she'd care. Did everyone in the world have their priorities screwed up? Setting her in the passenger seat, he closed the door on any more foolish protests. Going around to the driver's side, he climbed in, then swiped water from his face with his hands, pressing the goatee to keep it in place. Fortunately the wig was of good enough quality to take a little rain and still look real.

He bent to get a look at Amy's knees. "How bad is the cut?"

"Not too bad." She inched away from him. "I'll be fine."

He looked at her in exasperation. Twice in one day he'd showed concern to a fellow human being, and he'd been slapped back both times. Why bother caring when apparently no one wanted that from him? He straightened away from her. "Why did you not come to the market?"

"I'm sorry I was late." She bit her lower lip, drawing his gaze to that cupid's-bow mouth of hers. He knew women who would pay plastic surgeons a hefty sum to have a mouth like that. She didn't strike him as the type.

"What happen?" he asked.

"I . . . I got lost."

"You got lost?" He stared at her in disbelief. "In Gustavia?"

She nodded and dropped her gaze, shielding her eyes with her long, wet lashes. His own eyes narrowed in speculation. Maybe that wasn't fear he sensed from her. Maybe it was guilt. But guilt about what?

The rain drumming on the roof stopped as quickly as it had started. No doubt the sun would reappear in a second or two, making the whole island sparkle.

He sighed. "Since you cannot walk, I will buy the groceries while you wait in the car."

"I can walk," she insisted.

He scowled at her. For someone who seemed shy and sweet, the woman had a definite stubborn streak. He remembered her dancing around the kitchen and wondered if the sweetness was all an act. With the memory came the same twinge of arousal. He scowled at his body's inappropriate response.

"You cannot walk about the store, bleeding on their floor," he insisted. "Tell me what you need."

Her shoulders sagged in defeat. "Very well. I'll

need to make a list." She looked about searching for paper and pen. Realizing that the armrest was a console, she started to open it.

"No need." He laid a hand over hers. She jerked away from his touch, but not before he realized her skin felt as smooth as it looked. Was she that silky all over? Okay, definite inappropriate response to that thought. "Tell me what you need. I will remember."

"But I need so much," she said in distress. "And when it comes to produce, I never know what I want until I see what they have. And I don't know what sort of canned goods they sell here. I've never shopped for groceries anywhere but back home."

"Then we do this." He put the car in gear and drove back around to hunt for a parking place closer to the market. "Tell me what you would buy if you are home. I will do my best."

"All right." A frown of concentration creased her brow as she began listing items.

He listened in fascination as she became gradually less nervous and more animated.

"Oh," she said as if a thought had just occurred to her. "Does Mr. Gaspar have a sweet tooth."

"He has a most definite sweet tooth." Seeing a car pull away from the curb, he snagged the free space before anyone could beat him to it.

"Okay," she said. "See if they have kiwi and berries. I'll make crèmes brûlées for dessert."

His mouth watered at the thought. "All right. Is that everything?"

"Let me think." Her brow puckered adorably. "This is so hard. Ideas usually just come to me while I'm going up and down the aisles."

She clearly had a passion for cooking. He caught himself wondering if she would be as passionate in bed. Not that he'd ever find out. First, she was his housekeeper, and he didn't want to mess that up. Second, if she really was afraid of him, she'd probably faint if he made a pass at her. And third, if he did somehow get past her fear, what would he do if the goatee and wig came off in the middle of having sex?

Besides, wasn't there something innately wrong with pursuing a woman while pretending to be someone he wasn't?

That thought brought him up short.

Hadn't he been pretending on some level his whole life?

Okay, clearly the roles of Beaufort and Gaspar were causing an identity crisis. He didn't even know who he was anymore.

She let out a sigh. "If you see something you think Mr. Gaspar would like, grab it and I'll figure out something to do with it."

"I will do my best. You wait here. When I am done, we will go to collect your things."

Her guilty look returned. "We don't need to do that."

He lifted a brow. "You do not wish to collect your clothes?"

"I . . . I'll come back tomorrow and get them."

"What will you wear until then? The clothes you wear now are dirty and wet."

"I can wash them out."

"Why do that when we need but a moment to stop and get your things?"

"Because . . . my knee!" She wrapped both hands around it, her eyes pleading for him to believe her. "It's starting to hurt more than I realized. I think you're right. I shouldn't walk on it."

He narrowed his eyes. "I am happy to pack whatever you need."

"No, really. I'm not up to it. Can we just go back to the fort after you buy the groceries?"

"If that is what you want."

"It is. Thank you." Her shoulders sagged in relief.

He climbed from the car and headed for the grocery store, his anger mounting. The woman was definitely lying about something. Could she possibly know who he was and be hoping to snap a few pictures to sell to the tabloids? But how had anyone figured out his hiding place? He'd been careful to cover his trail.

Or had he turned so cynical, he saw liars and opportunists everywhere? He had to admit, the thing that stirred his distrust the most was her sweetness. She couldn't really be that nice. Could she?

The fact that he even wanted to give her the benefit of the doubt surprised him. And pissed him off on some level he couldn't begin to understand.

Chapter 5

Trying new things is never comfortable at first.
—How to Have a Perfect Life

Relief flooded Amy when they finally reached the fort. All the way back, Lance had radiated anger, making the short drive unbearably long. Finally they turned into the driveway and passed the impressive portico that marked the front entrance. The columned facade helped the place look more like a residence— albeit a very large, imposing residence. The driveway continued on to the far side of the structure, where a temporary metal carport sat amid piles of construction debris.

Lance parked beneath it and set the brake with a hard jerk. "Wait," he said when she reached for the door handle. "I will help you."

She puzzled over his mood as he stalked around the car to her side. She hadn't been late meeting him or hurt herself on purpose. And he was the one who'd insisted on doing the grocery shopping. Why was he so mad at her? He opened the door and held his hand out to her. She looked at it, then up at the hard angles of his face. "I can walk in by myself."

He scalded her with an impatient look. "A few minutes ago you are in too much pain to sit and wait for me to get your things."

"Oh, well—" She pasted on a smile. "Now that I've been sitting, I'm feeling much better."

"Fine." He stepped back.

She swung her legs out and stood, wincing as she put weight on her right knee. Then she gasped as he swept her into his arms. "Lance! I can walk."

He glared at her as he kicked the door closed. "Are you always so stubborn?"

"I'm not stubborn," she insisted indignantly. She had no choice but to put her arms about his neck, which brought her breast against his chest. Heat rushed through her from both embarrassment and arousal, which made her even more embarrassed. With her head nearly resting on his shoulder, the scent of warm male filled her senses. She ignored the urge to nuzzle her nose against the bare skin of his neck as he carried her into the back hall.

"Okay, you can put me down now." To her relief he lowered her legs. Unfortunately, he held one of her arms in place over his shoulders and kept an arm about her waist.

"Try to put only small weight on it," he said.

She nearly pointed out that with her, there was no "small weight." Taking a tentative step, she found the knee didn't hurt as badly as she'd feared. She had to pretend, though, or he would start up again with his questions about why she'd insisted on returning here without stopping for her clothes. She limped down the hall, painfully aware of her body pressed up against the whole length of his.

Oh, God, did he have to wrap his arm so far about her that his hand rested on her poochy belly?

Entering the kitchen, she gave thanks when she saw the bar stools at the center island. All she had to do was reach them; then she could sit and he wouldn't have to touch her. When they reached the island, though, he turned toward her, put both his hands on her waist, and lifted her off the floor! She barely had time to shriek before she found herself sitting on the counter.

"Let me see the knee," he said, bending to examine it. She put her hands over her dimply thighs in a vain attempt to hide them. "The bleeding, it is stopped, but we need to clean the cut."

She started to say she could do that if he'd help her down so she could hobble over to the sink, but that would require him touching her again. "Will you bring me a bowl of water, some soap, and a clean dishcloth?"

He gathered the items she'd requested, then started to clean the knee himself.

"I can do this," she insisted, twisting to avoid his hands. "You need to bring in the groceries."

"They can wait."

"No, they can't." Getting a hold of the cloth, she tried to tug it out of his hands. "We have dairy products, meat, and frozen food melting in a hot car out there."

Giving in, he let her have the cloth, then stomped off.

She frowned in the direction he'd gone, and irritation joined confusion. If he was so angry with her, why was he trying to baby her? Although *why* was he angry with her?

He returned with all the plastic groceries bags hanging from his fingers in two massive, awkward bundles.

"You know," she said, "it's acceptable to make more than one trip."

"But not necessary." Cans clunked as he dropped all the bags on the counter.

"Careful!" she scolded. "You'll break the eggs and squish the bread."

"Oh." His anger dimmed a bit as he looked inside a few bags. "I think everything survived."

"You need to put the cold stuff away," she told him as she dabbed at the cut.

He looked ready to argue, then examined the contents of several bags. Grabbing two, he stuffed them in the refrigerator, bag and all.

"What are you doing?" she asked.

"What you tell me to do." After glancing through the remaining bags, he repeated the process with the freezer.

"You don't do it like that." She sighed in annoyance.

"Why not? Is done." He pulled a bottle of peroxide from one of the bags and came toward her.

"Thank you." She reached for the bottle, surprised that he'd thought to buy it when she hadn't mentioned it.

Ignoring her outstretched hand, he opened the bottle. "This may sting."

She gasped as the cool peroxide poured onto the cut, bubbling and stinging.

"Sorry," he offered. Liquid ran down her shin. He cupped his hand at her ankle to catch it, then ran his palm upward. Tingles exploded from his touch, racing up her legs to the juncture of her thighs.

Her panicked brain tried to remember if she'd shaved that day. Yes, thank you God and the hotel for providing a razor. That offered only a small consolation when his touch, his scent, his nearness were turning her on. If he figured that out, she'd die. She'd just die.

He bent closer. And blew on her knee.

She let out a startled yelp.

"Sorry," he said again, and laid his hand on her thigh to hold her still as he continued to dab at the cut.

Trying not to move or even breathe, she stared at his profile. She was struck again by how much darker his eyelashes and brows were than his hair. They were nearly black, while his hair fell in golden brown waves to his shoulders. Looking closer, though, she noticed something very odd. His hair didn't thin next to his face the way most people's did. She squinted. Was he wearing a wig?

She nearly laughed at the notion of virile Lance Beaufort going prematurely bald and being vain enough to hide it. Silly man. With his physique and face, he'd probably look just as sexy bald—which some men considered so cool they shaved their heads.

His gaze shifted suddenly, colliding with hers.

With her leaning forward, he was close enough to kiss. What would that be like? Heat flooded her whole body at the thought.

He straightened abruptly and stepped back. "It does not look too bad."

"It isn't," she insisted, trying desperately not to blush.

He narrowed his eyes. "Then why didn't we stop for your clothes?"

"I'll go by myself and get them tomorrow."

"With a hurt knee?" He pointed at it accusingly. Strangely, his accent became less pronounced when he was angry.

"I'm sure it will be fine by morning," she said.

"And what will you wear until then?"

"I'm fine," she insisted, ignoring the grimy feel of her damp clothes. "Really."

He studied her a long time as the muscles in his jaw worked. Finally he turned and started for the door to the dining hall, tossing an order over his shoulder for her to stay where she was.

The minute the door swung closed, she stuck her tongue out. She didn't need him hovering over her as if she couldn't take care of herself. And with him gone, she didn't have to pretend to be hurt more than she was. She hopped down, and caught her breath as pain shot outward from her knee. Okay, so maybe it wasn't all pretend. The pain was only a minor annoyance, though, compared to her clothes.

What she wouldn't give for something clean and dry to put on. She didn't have anything, though, so she'd just have to live in what she had until nightfall when she could wash everything and hang it up to dry overnight. That would mean sleeping in the nude in a strange place, she realized. Again, though, what choice did she have? Dwelling on it now did no good, especially when she had work to do.

She hobbled over to the refrigerator to organize the bags he'd stuffed in there. Finding the butter in the freezer made her eyes roll. Once she had the dairy and meat in order, she started on the canned goods.

"What are you doing?" Lance's angry voice demanded. She turned to find him standing in the doorway, holding a wad of black and gray fabric. Accusation blazed in his eyes.

"Putting away the groceries," she said, thinking it was obvious.

"So, I see." He stalked forward.

"Then why did you ask?"

"Did I not say to stay where you were?" He looked pointedly at her knee.

"I didn't go anywhere," she said calmly.

"I will put the groceries away." He thrust the fabric at her. "You go and change."

"What is this?" She held the items up and discovered a long-sleeved black dress shirt and a pair of gray sweatpants that had been cut into shorts.

"I thought you might want something dry to wear."

Her eyes widened. "Oh, my God. Did you get these from Mr. Gaspar?"

"Who else would I get them from?" he tossed back as he took over putting cans away in a totally random order.

"What did you tell him?" With Lance so angry, she imagined him telling her new employer that he'd hired a complete ditz who couldn't even get around a town the size of Gustavia without getting lost. One who happened to be a klutz, to boot, and didn't have enough sense to get in out of the rain. "I think I want to die."

He looked at her as if her embarrassment made no sense. "Why?"

"Because . . . Never mind." If he couldn't understand something this simple, how could she explain? Then she looked down at the clothes, and humiliation swerved toward gratitude so deep, tears prickled her eyes. "Just . . . thank you. And thank Mr. Gaspar."

The anger seemed to drain out of him, which oddly seemed to make him angry at himself. "I will finish here. You change and lie down with the knee up."

"I need to get supper going."

"Amy . . ." he growled, then sighed. "Go lie down."

"All right," she said and limped for the door. She didn't need to lie down like some whiny weakling who went to bed over the least little thing. A shower, however, would be nice. Exhaustion swamped her unexpectedly, making her emotions rise. Even in his prickly mood, Lance had been very kind. And he'd gotten her something to wear. She turned at the door. "Lance . . . ?"

"*Oui?*"

"I'm sorry to be so much trouble. I'll do better tomorrow." She slipped into her room before he could respond.

The minute the door closed, Byron stared at the ceiling. What had he gotten himself into? The woman was a liar. About what, he had no idea, but she was definitely lying.

And yet . . . He looked back at the door, picturing the look on her face just then, the genuine gratitude. The sweetness. That hadn't been faked. Had it?

In the bathroom, Amy dug through her beach bag for the tiny bottles of shampoo and conditioner from the hotel room where she'd stayed the night before. She'd found towels along with extra bed linens in the cabinet under the sink.

Other than those basic necessities, the room was empty. She mourned the lack of scented lotions, face creams, candles, and pretty knickknacks that cluttered her bathroom back home. Maybe she would splurge on a few things if she could find a drugstore tomorrow.

Stepping into the tiled shower with its frosted glass door, she let the hot water wash over her. A good scalp massage helped ease some of her tension as the floral scent of the shampoo perfumed the steamy air. By the time she stepped out, her emotions had steadied.

She finger combed her waist-length hair and left it loose to dry. The shorts and dress shirt Lance had provided were both freshly laundered, so they smelled of detergent and scented dryer sheets, giving away nothing of their owner's scent. They gave away other clues, though. The shirt was designed by Ermenegildo Zegna and quite possibly the finest cotton she'd ever felt.

The label surprised her since Zegna appealed to young jet-setters. That didn't fit her image of a re-

cluse at all. The color fit, though. Black. How very
appropriate for a beast.

She slipped it on her naked body since she didn't
have any underwear and needed to wash her swimsuit. The shirt engulfed her—something she didn't
mind in the least. To her, loose clothes were the best
kind. Mr. Gaspar had to be a big man, she decided.
The sleeves hung well past her fingertips, so she
rolled them up but left the shirttails hanging halfway
down her thighs.

Next came the shorts. In contrast to the shirt, these
had seen a great deal of wear. Did Mr. Gaspar work
out? Or was he a total couch potato who lay around
in sweats all day? When he wasn't wearing Zegna.

A knock on the door startled her.

"Amy?" Lance called through the closed panel.
"Do not get up. I only want to know if you need
anything."

"No, I'm fine," she called back, hoping he couldn't
tell her voice came from the bathroom, not the bed.

"I will be in the entryway plastering walls."

"Okay."

She gave him a minute to leave the kitchen, then
carried her clothes to the laundry room and started
the ridiculously small load. There wasn't anything
else to add, though, which left her to wonder if Mr.
Gaspar did his own laundry or if he had Lance do
it for him. She nearly laughed at the notion of a man
who couldn't even put groceries away properly trying to tackle laundry. As for the workings of the
house, she supposed she'd learn as she went along.

Sticking her head into the kitchen, she saw no sign
of Lance, so she padded in barefoot and set to work.

Before long, she had chicken simmering in a stockpot and bread rising in a bowl.

Moving to the sink, she set to work on a fruit salad to go with dinner. One of the monkeys from the courtyard hopped onto the windowsill, startling her. A second one quickly joined it.

"Goodness." She laughed, then offered the pair a smile. "Well, hello. Are you friendly?"

They held out their hands for a piece of mango. Since mangoes were far too much work to cut, she offered them each a banana instead. They snatched the fruit from her hand and dashed away, leaping onto the rail of the gallery, then into the trees where the thick vegetation swallowed them up. She leaned out to see where they had gone, wishing they'd stayed to keep her company.

Resigned to working alone, she let daydreams play through her head as afternoon gave way to evening.

"You are up," Lance said behind her. "I hope the rest helped."

She turned from the stove to find him standing in the doorway. "Yes," she said, feeling guilty since she hadn't lain down. "I'm feeling much better."

"*Bon*." He nodded. His gaze dropped to the big shirt and her bare feet before he looked away as if uncomfortable about something. "I come to let you know I leave for the day. I will return in the morning."

"Oh. All right."

He sniffed the air. "Something smells delicious. Is that supper?"

"Not yet. I'm just making stock to have on hand." Plus, the lean chicken meat would make several low-fat meals for her. If she ate the sort of food she had planned for Mr. Gaspar, she'd gain back every pound she'd lost and then some. "I thought I'd do the beef medallion with savory sauce for tonight, and serve it with artichoke hearts, grilled tomatoes topped with Parmesan and bits of toasted garlic, and some sautéed mushrooms. Do you—" She started to invite him to stay out of habit. Southern manners dictated as much. She wasn't sure how comfortable she'd be having Lance plop down on one of the bar stools and fill the kitchen with his disturbing presence while she cooked, but in the end habit and hospitality won. "Do you want to stay? I can easily make enough."

He shook his head. "No, lunch is the only meal you need to fix for me. Unless . . ." He frowned. "Are you nervous to have me leave you here alone? I will stay a little while if you wish."

"No, don't be silly. I'm fine."

"*Très bien*. I promise you have nothing to fear from Monsieur Gaspar. He will not bother you as long as you return to this wing after you take his supper."

"I'll be fine," she assured him again.

"Well then," he said, "until tomorrow, I wish you *bonne nuit*. Good night."

"Yes. Good night." She frowned when he went back into the dining room rather than head for the carport. Of course, she'd only seen the one car, Mr. Gaspar's Alfa Romeo. Apparently Lance walked to work.

That made her wonder about where he lived. What sort of life did he have here on the island? A man as affable as Lance Beaufort would likely have lots of friends. And women chasing after him. Did he have a girlfriend? One who lived with him perhaps? Not that his personal life concerned her, but curiosity and an active imagination seemed to go hand in hand—and she'd always had too much of both.

That curiosity soon turned to thoughts of *La Bête* in the tower and ghosts roaming about until she spooked herself silly. Having another storm blow over the island at nightfall certainly didn't help. She raced to the window over the sink to close the shutters against the wind-driven rain.

As she leaned out to grab them, lights appeared in the third-story windows of the tower. Through the louvered shutters, she saw a silhouette move by. Her heart skipped as a shiver went down her spine.

She was alone in this strange place with a beast in the tower.

Chapter 6

Byron stood at the window watching the storm. His muscles held the good ache that comes from physical labor, but the work had done little to settle his mind.

Fingers of wind reached through the shutters, chilling his skin beneath the black silk robe. He welcomed the kiss of air against his bare face and short dark hair while the sound of the storm fill the room. The sweet scent of wet flowers and fertile earth contrasted with the sight of the wildly bobbing boats down in the bay. Nature, like life, could be nurturing and destructive all in the same breath.

The combination suited his mood.

Not for the first time since coming to St. Barts he felt like the beast he claimed to be, with conflicting emotions warring inside him.

Nurturing and destructive. Gift and curse. Were those not the two sides of the Midas touch? He had the power to make people's dreams come true. Ironically, dreams and nightmares often came hand in hand.

Lightning streaked across the sky, followed by a clap of thunder, and he snorted at his own melodramatic thoughts. He gave himself too much credit. Yes, he'd given Chad a break, but that didn't make him responsible for the destruction of Chad's marriage.

What might make him partially responsible though, was his lack of caring. Or of acting.

He'd spent his life watching others from a safe distance, never allowing anyone or anything to really touch him beyond the surface. Was that what had sucked him so thoroughly into the world of Hollywood?

He'd turned that question, along with so many other, over in his mind enough during the past six months to know his attraction to the movie industry wasn't simply that he'd grown up around it. Being bounced back and forth between his parents, he could just as easily have wound up doing something on the European fashion front.

Ironically, the two worlds had one thing in common: they both dealt in illusion. Fashion created visual illusion. Movies, though, transported you into a whole different world. They allowed you to be someone else for a little while.

He remembered his conversation with Amy in the car about how escaping into fiction made life bearable. For him, it was more than that. He actually preferred the imaginary world to the real one. Standing in the tower, protected from the storm that surrounded him, he realized why. The only times in his life he let himself feel, really feel the full height and

depth of any human emotion, was through stories—
when the things that were at stake weren't real.

Was that also what had attracted him to Gillian?
The perky ingenue she pretended to be wasn't real,
so he didn't have to worry about hurting her. They'd
played the roles of the perfect couple in public and in
private. Unfortunately, illusions wear thin with time,
until they no longer hide the truth that lies beneath.

He remembered clearly the day that had happened. He'd taken Gillian to Spago to celebrate an
audition she'd landed. She'd spent their entire lunch
obsessing over whether or not she'd get the role and
what it would mean for her career. He sat across
from her listening in growing disgust as every sen-
tence that came out of her mouth contained the word
"me" or "I." That was natural under the circum-
stances, but for some reason that day her self absorp-
tion emphasized her shallowness and vanity in a way
he could no longer ignore. It made him stop and ask
himself for the first time what it said about him that
he'd be drawn to her because of it, not in spite of it.

Once that question popped into his head, it grew
at a frightening pace. Until, as they were leaving,
something in him had snapped. He'd turned to her
on the sidewalk outside Spago and made some cutting remark he didn't even remember now. He'd always been good at cutting remarks.

She'd gone into a tirade, drawing the attention of
everyone within earshot, claiming that of course he
didn't understand how much she wanted the part
because he didn't care about anything. He had no
emotions.

"You never feel anything unless you're having sex. But that's just physical," she'd yelled right before she'd delivered the slap that wound up on every tabloid cover. "Well, how about *that*, Byron? Did you feel that?"

Yes, he thought now, as he had then. He'd felt that. On so many levels he was still feeling the sting of that slap and those words. Because he'd deserved both.

After that, the paparazzi gauntlet had become unbearable with Gillian feeding the tabloids sob stories about what a cold, heartless bastard he was. He'd hated the rags since the days when his parents had filled them. So he hardly found it surprising that his mind had turned to his mother's solution: run off to St. Barts until things die down.

With that thought came memories of the "haunted" fort that had always fascinated him. He'd wondered: *What would it be like to be a ghost? To be the reverse of what I am: dead in body rather than dead in soul. To be invisible rather than constantly in the public eye.*

So Byron Parks became invisible.

Ironically, in living like a ghost, with endless hours to think, to consider, to question, he felt as if the dead places inside of him had been slowly, cautiously stirring to life. The process came with the same pain he imagined burn victims feel as their damaged nerve endings start to heal. He just hadn't realized until escaping how badly he'd been burned inside.

Turning from the window, he crossed to the wet bar to pour a glass of wine. Amy should be bringing his supper soon. Perhaps then he could settle enough to read or watch one of the hundreds of movies he had on DVD.

Amy Baker. The likely culprit for his current restless mood. He realized the rejuvenated part of him wanted to believe she had a simple, logical, innocent reason for not wanting him to help her move her things.

For which the cynical Byron called him a fool.

His gaze flickered toward the monitors. The one for the kitchen was still off, but he didn't need it to picture her standing there barefoot, wearing his shirt. Black definitely was not her color, but she'd looked incredibly appealing with that mass of curly brown hair spilling down her back.

Was it his imagination, or did the woman get prettier every time he looked at her? When he'd opened the door that morning—had it really only been that morning?—all he'd seen was a slightly plump, not unattractive woman applying for a job as his housekeeper. Any desire to kiss her came from his desperation for a cook, not because he wanted to taste that adorably puckered mouth of hers.

His groin twitched at the thought and he scowled. *Stop that*, he scolded his body. *She's your housekeeper.*

He wondered briefly if six months of abstinence had his libido going haywire, but he dismissed that thought. Being on St. Barts, he'd seen beautiful, sexy women every time he'd ventured into town. None of them had stirred any physical interest. He'd wondered a bit fearfully if Gillian's inference that he couldn't feel anything unless he was having sex had somehow killed his sex drive entirely.

Yet here came a woman who didn't fit his normal type at all, and he felt an unexpected zing of desire every time he looked at her.

She appeared as if conjured on the monitor that showed the dining room, and, yep, there was that zing. He shook his head in amusement as he watched her cross the room carrying a dinner tray. As he remembered the meal she had described, his stomach growled in anticipation.

Then his eyes narrowed when he realized she wasn't limping. At all.

Cynical Byron flared to life. Goddamn it. So much for honest and forthright. The arousal died a quick death. Anger replaced it as he watched her move from monitor to monitor through the dark house. Lightning flickered through the gallery doors, distorting her features like a strobe light. The boom of thunder made her jolt.

When she reached the office downstairs, she peeked inside as if expecting some monster to leap out at her. She entered hesitantly and managed to get the light switch with her elbow. He'd been so distracted, he'd forgotten to leave the light on for her.

The floor lamp in the corner sprang to life but left much of the room shrouded in shadows. She crossed to the dumbwaiter and set the tray inside. Or so he assumed. The camera didn't allow him to see that part of the room.

He waited for her to send the tray up and leave.

She stepped back into view without working the dumbwaiter, then stood there glancing about.

"Come on, Amy," some still-hopeful part of him whispered. "Don't do this."

Fury shot through him when she headed straight
for the table and started rummaging through the
books and blueprints. He raced to the desk and
slapped on the intercom system. In his haste, he'd
opened all the speakers throughout the fort as he
demanded, "What are you doing!"

Amy screamed as the booming voice echoed
through the whole fortress. Whirling about, she fell
against the table behind her. No one was there. After
that explosion of sound, silence descended inside
while out in the courtyard the monkeys and birds
screeched in terror.

She stood frozen, clutching the table for dear life
as her heart tried to pump out of her chest.

The voice came again, this time at normal volume
but filled with anger. "I asked what you were
doing."

"I—I—I—" She sucked in a breath. "Wh-where
are you?"

"Watching you on a monitor. Now what the hell
were you doing?"

She glanced frantically about and saw the lens of
a camera in a niche over the door to the tower and
an intercom next to the door. That calmed her some
as she realized he wasn't some invisible phantom
standing in the room with her. "I w-was looking for
a piece of paper."

"You don't have paper in the kitchen?"

"I do, it's just . . ." She swallowed the lump of
fear in her throat. She'd expected him to be French
like Lance, but he sounded American. "I didn't think
of it until I was here."

"Think of what?"

"Of thanking you. For the clothes." She fisted her hands in the shirt, holding it toward him. "I wanted to give you a thank-you note."

"Lance Beaufort has no more wish for you to snoop through his things than I would have for you to snoop through mine."

"I wasn't snooping. At least, I didn't mean to. I'm sorry."

"Pardon me if I find that hard to believe, since I already know you're a liar."

"What?" Her eyes bulged. No one had ever called her that before.

"Your knee has made a remarkable recovery."

"Oh." Guilt exploded over her face.

"So what is the real reason you didn't want to move your things today? What are you hiding?"

"Nothing!"

"Ms. Baker, you have two seconds to come up with a believable reason why you didn't want Lance Beaufort to see where you've been staying or you're fired."

"Oh, no, please!"

"One."

"I don't have any things!" she blurted out.

"Excuse me?"

Tears blurred her vision. "I don't have any things and I haven't been staying anywhere. Please don't fire me. This job is my only hope."

"I think you better explain yourself."

"I'm stranded here." The admission brought on more tears and a renewal of fear. "I was traveling on a cruise ship and I got left behind. I don't have anything but what I was carrying when I arrived here today." After that, the whole humiliating story spilled out in a jumbled rush.

Standing in the tower, Byron watched her cry as she told him about taking the trip as part of some challenge with two friends, about getting fired, about how she couldn't go home early or she'd be a failure. If she was acting, she deserved an Oscar. Not even Gillian had been this convincing, and she certainly knew how to cry on command. Gillian's downfall, though, was that she cried too pretty. She couldn't stand looking less than her best, so she'd taught herself to cry without her eyes and nose turning red.

Amy didn't come close to mastering that trick. She was a mess, sniffling loudly and wiping her face with the back of her hands like a child whose world had come to an end. Watching her, Byron felt another of those long-dead nerve endings come to life followed by self-loathing for reducing her to tears.

"Please don't fire me." Her eyes beseeched him. "I really need this job. It's my only hope for completing my challenge."

He closed his eyes and fought a painful urge to go downstairs and hold her. Why did feeling have to hurt? Not just him, but everyone apparently. And knowing that, why did people let themselves feel?

Because, he realized, the alternative was to move through life like a hollowed-out shell.

"I'm not sure I understand·the challenge," he said. "Why can't you go home early?"

"Because Jane Redding called me a coward in her book, *How to Have a Perfect Life*."

"Jane Redding? The news anchor from the *Morning Show*?"

"Yes." A shuddering breath helped her regain some of her composure. "We were roommates in college. My friends Maddy and Christine were our suite mates. After we graduated, Jane moved to New York, so we lost touch. But the rest of us have stayed very close.

"So when we heard Jane was having a book signing in Austin, we decided to go together. I was baffled at first when Jane seemed uncomfortable to see us. It wasn't too noticeable, just a sense I got that something wasn't quite right." Her brow wrinkled unexpectedly with anger. "I certainly found out the why behind that quickly enough. She used us, all three of us, in her book!"

"I thought people were usually flattered to be put in a book, if they even manage to recognize themselves."

"But she used us as examples of how women let fear keep them from pursuing their dreams. She happened to be wrong about Maddy's fear. And I think she's wrong about my fear too."

"What did she say was your fear?"

"She said I was afraid of taking a risk." She made a face. "According to Jane, I'm so afraid of trying anything new and failing, I'd rather stay in my safe routine than take a risk that might bring me a more satisfying life. And while that's true to an extent, she completely missed my biggest fear."

"What is that?" He saw her hesitate. "Please, I'd like to know." Actually, he needed to know—not just what she feared, but how she was conquering it.

She tipped her head, as if sensing his need in his voice. Something passed between them that defied the stone walls and locked door that separated them, and he realized she understood his questions weren't mere curiosity.

"Traveling," she finally answered. "Jane knows I've always wanted to travel, so when I moved home after college, she thought it was because I was afraid of striking out on my own. And, yes, that does make me nervous, but not enough to make me phobic about leaving the house the way I've become."

"Have you?"

"Sadly, yes." Color stained her cheeks. "I have this fear that something bad will happen while I'm gone. Whenever I get lost, which I do a lot, that fear escalates a thousand times. So now, here I am." She lifted her arms and let them drop with a self-mocking smile. "Lost in the Caribbean halfway through a two-week vacation. Everything in me wants to rush home a week early, but I have to stay the full time, to prove that I can. Only I couldn't afford a hotel on St. Barts for a week, so I answered the ad to be your housekeeper."

"Why didn't you explain any of this to Lance earlier?"

"Because it's embarrassing. And . . ." She bit her lip.

"And?"

"He makes me nervous!" she blurted. "I can barely think straight around him."

"Why?"

"I'm always nervous around attractive men. And he's beyond attractive. Good heavens, he's *stunning*!"

Her eyes went so wide he laughed as much at her

expression as her words. Other than that, he took no satisfaction in her claim. How he looked was a result of genes and being raised in a world that taught him how to make the most of what nature had given him. Although if the slightly sloppy Beaufort frightened her, how would she react if she ever came face-to-face with the real him?

He'd learned the art of being lethally attractive and intimidating as hell from a master: his mother.

Amy's shoulders sagged. "I'm sorry I wasn't honest with Lance. I just get really tongue-tied around attractive men. I always feel so dumpy and stupid."

"That's understandable."

"I know. I'm so dang *fat*!"

"That is not what I meant." He felt a stab of self-directed anger that she'd taken his words wrong. "Outward appearance can be as much a weapon as a shield, and some people know how to wield it well. I assure you, though, Lance Beaufort does not think of you as either fat or stupid."

"I didn't say I *was* stupid. I just feel that way sometimes."

"Well, that's a pity." He cocked his head, studying her, seeing so much potential. That clear skin. The long hair. And good God in heaven—those eyes! The body was a bit of a question mark, but he knew after lifting her today that she wasn't as big as that awful T-shirt made her look. Besides, every woman had the potential for beauty. Tapping that potential was simply a matter of finding the right clothes. The right look.

An idea began to take form.

He might not have much to offer women in general, but he did have one thing he could give this woman.

"So, let me see if I understand your situation correctly. You're stranded on St. Barts and you can't go home early, or you will have failed in your challenge with your friends."

"Yes." She nodded.

"Can I ask what your plan was? Did you intend to buy a plane ticket with your first paycheck and leave me once again without a housekeeper?"

"No!" she insisted, clearly distressed. "I was going to work two weeks, then give two weeks' notice so you'd have a chance to hire someone else."

"An admirable plan—except that no one on the island will work here."

She bit her lip. "I'm sorry, but that's all the time I have. My friends are getting married the second weekend in April in a double wedding. I have to be there a couple of weeks before that because I'm throwing a bridal shower."

"Any chance you would return after the wedding if I buy you a round-trip ticket?"

"I can't do that," she gasped, but he could tell the idea intrigued her. "I have a business to run back home. I own a franchise called Traveling Nannies. That's how I came to be on the cruise ship."

"I've heard of them," he said. Chad and Carolyn had used the main office in LA a time or two. "Heaven forbid couples take care of their own kids while traveling."

"It's a good service," Amy defended staunchly. "Good for the kids as well as the parents."

"Then you shouldn't have any trouble selling your

franchise. I'll make returning financially worth your while."

"To move to the Caribbean?" She shook her head. "Really, I can't."

"Why not?"

"Vacations are one thing. Moving is simply not an option."

"I don't think you understand the situation here," he persisted. "The women on the island are too afraid of this place to work here. I can't even get the catering companies to deliver meals after dark. I thought I might starve until you took the job."

"Well, maybe if you didn't scare people half to death with that loud, angry voice, they wouldn't be afraid of you." The spark of fire that came into her eyes intrigued him. So Beaufort scared her, but Gaspar didn't. Very interesting. She moved to the dumbwaiter and worked the ropes to send up his supper.

His stomach leapt with gratitude at the thought. Food! "Actually, it's a little more complicated than that," he said as he went to the opening on his level and retrieved the plate. The aroma of succulent steak, sautéed mushrooms, tomatoes, and garlic would have seduced him on their own, but her presentation made him marvel. He'd had meals in five-star restaurants that couldn't compare to this.

He dipped his finger into the sauce to taste it. His eyes rolled back in ecstasy. There had to be a way to get this woman to stay on as his housekeeper. And no thoughts of anything else allowed, he warned himself. "Okay, here's what I'm willing to do," he said as he moved back to the desk, which doubled as a dining table. "If you agree to stay for the full four weeks and return after the wedding, I'll buy you a new wardrobe as incentive and I'll pay for your plane ticket on top of your salary."

"I just told you, I can't move to St. Barts."

"Or I could fire you now."

The fear that flashed in her eyes told him she believed him—but only for a second. Then her eyes narrowed in speculation. "How about you advance me some money for clothes, I stay for the full four weeks, and buy my own ticket home?"

"No way." He tried the grilled tomato with Parmesan and garlic bits, which sent his taste buds into delirium. "Not if what you had on earlier is an indication of what you plan to buy. I'll pay for the clothes, but you don't get to pick them out."

"What do you mean?" Her brows snapped together.

"Lance Beaufort will pick out your new clothes."

"Lance?" The idea clearly horrified her.

"Trust me. The man knows more about how to dress a woman than most women know."

Skepticism lined her face, but she didn't voice it.

"What?" he prodded her. "You're free to say what you think."

"Well, then, in my experience, men only know how to dress skinny women and usually want them to look like hoochie mamas."

He choked at hearing that term come out of Amy's mouth. "To look like what?"

"Hoochie mamas," she repeated in that cute Texas accent of hers. "Or in Lance's case, he'll probably try to put me in a French maid's outfit."

He suppressed a laugh. "A completely unfair assumption. And politically incorrect stereotyping."

"I refuse to wear anything that makes me look ridiculous, and even fatter than I am."

He resisted the impulse to point out that she'd just described the T-shirt she'd had on earlier. "First, I promise, Lance will make you look gorgeous. And second, you do want to stay on St. Barts long enough to fulfill your challenge, right?"

Her bravery wavered. "You'd really fire me?"

No, he thought as he took another bite of steak. He wouldn't fire her, but he wasn't above lying to keep her. Then he looked at the monitor and realized that the food alone wasn't what drove this idea. Here was real beauty. Inner beauty that was hidden away. She didn't know how to showcase it, but he did. "I'm afraid I have to insist. Do we have a deal?"

"Do I have a choice?"

"None whatsoever." He grinned, knowing he had her.

She made a face at the camera but sighed in defeat. "Well, in that case, I supposed we have a bargain. I'll leave you to enjoy your supper."

"I assure you I will." As he hadn't enjoyed anything in a long time. If ever.

Chapter 7

Challenge yourself to stretch and grow a little every day.
—How to Have a Perfect Life

Byron watched Amy fidget from the corner of his eye as he drove the narrow streets looking for a place to park. She'd started to fret the moment he went to the kitchen that morning, dressed as Lance, and told her he was ready to take her shopping as per "Gaspar's" orders.

"I can't believe I agreed to this," she said for at least the tenth time.

"I do not understand." He found a parking place in the shade of a tree amid a herd of scooters. With the top down, the breeze blew over them, rustling the leaves overhead. He did a quick scan of the pedestrian traffic for anyone who might recognize him in spite of his disguise. St. Barts attracted quite a few Hollywood types—something he'd failed to consider when he picked it as his hideaway. More than once he'd had to turn his head or duck into a shop. The coast appeared to be clear, so he turned back to Amy. "You have the chance to do something most women only dream of. To spend the whole day shopping at the expense of a very wealthy man."

"Whole day?" Her brows went up. "I can't spend the whole day doing this. I need to get back to the fort to fix Mr. Gaspar's lunch."

"Do not worry about Gaspar." He dismissed her concern, eager to begin their shopping excursion. He couldn't wait to see Amy dressed in something that flattered her figure and gave her confidence a boost. "Today is for you. This morning we shop, then I take you to a fabulous lunch. This afternoon, the salon."

"As in a hair salon?" She covered her head. "I am *not* cutting my hair."

"We will see what the stylist says." He considered the way she wore her hair scraped down, covering her ears and the sides of her face. Even combing it back and French braiding it would help. "Perhaps merely a trim and a conditioning treatment. I also schedule a facial, massage, and pedicure at the day spa in the salon."

"Really?" The idea clearly intrigued her. "A day spa?" She laughed as if the whole idea were silly. "I've never been to one."

"Non?" He frowned. Most of the women he knew went to the spa nearly every week. "You will feel very pampered."

"I'm sure I will." She looked torn between excitement and doubt. "But it can't take too long. I need to get to the Internet café this afternoon so I can check with the woman who's taking care of my grandmother. Plus, my friends and I e-mail each other every day about four o'clock Texas time. If I miss it, they'll worry."

"You plan to walk to town every day to e-mail your friends?"

"Since I don't have my laptop, I have to."

"I thought coming to town frightened you."

She tipped her head. "How did you know that?"

Great, Byron, give yourself away. "Um, Gaspar, he mentioned it. He told me of your challenge and that you have a fear of getting lost. I am to help you learn your way around the island."

"Oh, would you?" Gratitude filled her eyes.

"I would be most happy to." He realized he meant it. After months of relishing his solitude, the thought of having to come to town and mix with people didn't irritate him the way he thought it would. He reached for his door handle. "Now, are you ready to buy your new wardrobe?"

"Oh, goodness." She covered her face with both hands. "I think I should warn you, I hate clothes shopping. Really, truly hate it with a passion."

He settled back in his seat, stunned. "Most women adore to shop."

"Women with perfect figures who look good in everything." She made a face. "For me it is an ego-deflating necessary evil of life. Today, I think, will be even worse than usual."

"Why worse?"

"Shopping with a man?" She shuddered. "You're not going to make me model everything, are you?"

"How else will I know what works and what does not?"

"You could trust me to tell you," she suggested hopefully.

He looked pointedly at the striped T-shirt. *"Pardonnez moi* if I do not have faith in your judgment. So we go?"

"Wait."

He settled back and waited.

She bit her lip. "The problem is, I need more than just outer clothes."

"Lingerie?" He lifted a brow at the thought of helping her pick out underwear. "We make that the first stop."

"And you will wait outside," she insisted with a stern look that was more adorable than intimidating. "I am not going to let you see what sort of underwear I buy."

"Too sexy for my eyes?" He wiggled his brows.

"Hardly." She scoffed. "They don't make sexy lingerie in my size."

"You jest." An image of Amy lounging seductively on a bed with nothing but red lace covering voluptuous curves and lots of smooth, silky skin begging to be touched sprang to mind. *Whoa! Strike that*, he ordered his brain, which did no good. The image was there to stay. He shifted his legs to hide his body's reaction. "*Ma chère*, they make sexy lingerie in all sizes."

"And I would look ridiculous wearing it. Oh, this is all so unfair," she complained. "I just went through this a couple of weeks ago. Christine took me shopping right before the trip and helped me pick out appropriate clothes for a cruise. I got through the day because she was there and helped me laugh my way through it even as we argued over every purchase."

"Why did you argue?"

"She and Maddy are always trying to get me to

wear more fitted clothes." Her nose wrinkled. "But I like loose clothes. They make me feel thinner."

"Hmm, how to say politely. They do not make you look thinner." He scowled at the offending T-shirt. "That shirt you wear would fit two of you. In the right clothes, all women, they are beautiful."

"Spoken like a true Frenchman." She sent him a shy smile.

The answering flutter in his chest startled him. When was the last time something as innocent as a shy smile did that to him? Never, actually. She seemed more comfortable with him today, though, and that emboldened him to tease her back a bit. "I think you will be very sexy, if you do not hide yourself."

She rolled her eyes. "Reasonably attractive, maybe, but I'm a long way from sexy. And I don't need to be. It's not like I'm trying to attract attention."

Something in her voice made him study her more closely and remember things she'd done and said yesterday, the way she'd panicked when he flirted with her. Realization struck him. "You are afraid to be pretty."

"What a thing to say." A nervous laugh escaped her. "I'm not 'afraid' to be pretty."

He noticed how she wrapped her arms about the beach bag she carried in lieu of a purse, hiding behind it. "You wear clothes that are very much too big. I think that you do not even know what size you are."

"You sound like my friends." She frowned. "They say I keep picturing myself the way I used to look,

not the way I am. Maybe they're right. I've lost a lot
of weight over the last two years."

"How much?"

"A lot," she insisted.

He studied the parts of her he could see, her face
and neck, her arms and legs. Whatever weight she'd
been, she'd worked hard to get down to a healthier
size. From watching other women struggle with diets
over the years, he knew that was no small feat. "I
think it is time to show off your new body. Come.
We shop."

"Do I have to?" she whined, which amused him
since she didn't strike him as the whining type.

"I promised Gaspar to spend his money well." He
raised a brow, giving her a menacing look worthy of
who he really was. Or had been. Or whatever. "You
do not want him angry with me, do you?"

"No." She gave in with a sigh and he realized he'd
found the key to nudging Amy in the right direction:
tell her she would be helping someone else.

He nearly laughed in amazement as he climbed
from the car. Normally he fed people's greed to get
what he wanted. With Amy, generosity was the
soft spot.

Amy would never understand how a day could be
fun and scary at the same time. Actually, it didn't
start out fun at all. It started out with all the same
battles she'd had when Christine had taken her shopping. After leaving the lingerie store, where Lance
had thankfully let her shop on her own, he started
in on her.

"That top is entirely too big for you," he said. "Try this size."

"I told you, I like loose clothes," she countered. "I hate things that bind and squeeze and cut me in half."

People who didn't have to struggle with their weight didn't seem to understand how huge a part of life it was every single day. Having her stomach roll over the top of her waistband served as a reminder every time she sat down that she was fat.

Rather than give in, as Christine had, he held firm. He more than held firm. He thrust some hangers into her hands and bullied her into trying on an outfit that included a tank top. A tank top? Was he insane? Expose her flabby arms to the world?

The rest of the outfit wasn't so bad. In the dressing room, she discovered wheat-colored capri pants to match the loose tank, and a large pullover top with a wide neck, which would have been great, except it was see-through. How would that hide her numerous bulges? At least it was pretty, she thought, admiring the tiny shells covering the creamy gauze like beadwork.

She slipped it on, surprised to find everything very comfortable, but couldn't bring herself to look in the dressing room mirror.

She nearly balked at stepping out, but the only way to prove to Lance that she knew more about what looked good on her body type than he did was to let him see for himself. Tugging at the wide neck to the gauzy top, which kept trying to slip off her shoulders, she stepped from the dressing room ready to tell him, "See? I told you I'd look awful in this."

But when he turned and saw her, the expression on his face stopped her. He stared. Goggled, actually. Then a smile spread over his handsome face.

Her stomach went strangely tight.

"*Exactement*," he said, coming toward her. "This is the look for you."

"You're joking, right?"

"Come see." His warm hand slipped about hers, and he pulled her toward the three-way mirror.

The simple contact of skin to skin made her pulse jump. She turned her head away, knowing her cheeks had gone pink.

"Look," he said.

"Do I have to?"

"*Oui*." He tugged on one of the sleeves and the wide neck slipped off her shoulder. Everything inside her went haywire when he placed both his hands on her shoulders, one of which was now bare, and she turned her to face the mirror. "See?"

She opened her eyes, prepared to point out everything wrong with the outfit. The image in the mirror jolted her into silence. She looked . . . elegant. The see-through top obscured her shape enough to keep every figure flaw from showing, but revealed that she did at least have a figure.

When had her waist started dipping in like that? Had all those hours of Pilates finally started paying off? But when? She realized in a daze how rarely she looked at herself in the mirror until she had clothes on. Baggy clothes. Maddy and Christine were right; she had been picturing herself much heavier.

"We need something more," Lance said, tipping his head as he studied her. The movement drew her attention to his reflection. He stood behind her, all tall and broad shouldered in another tropical shirt—buttoned, thank goodness. She still looked short in comparison, but not so dumpy.

Turning to the salesclerk who hovered nearby, he said something in French. The woman went to a case and gathered several pieces of costume jewelry.

That snapped Amy out of her trance. "Jewelry?" She shook her head. "Lance, no, you need to remember I'm not paying for this. Mr. Gaspar is. We need to keep things simple."

"Hush," he said as he selected a clunky necklace made of white shells and light brown beads and draped it into place. The feel of his fingers working the hook sent a little shiver down her spine. A matching bracelet followed. Since she'd never worn any jewelry other than a few dainty pieces, she shook her wrist at the unfamiliar feel. The weight and rattle of it felt fun. It distracted her enough that she didn't notice Lance reaching for the rubber band holding her hair until he pulled it off.

"No, don't!" she gasped. "What are you doing?"

His quick fingers destroyed her neat braid before she could stop him. To her horror, he plowed his fingers into her hair and rumpled it into a mass of curls. Even as she tried to duck, she felt his hands all over her scalp, rubbing back and forth. Tingles exploded all through her body, flustering her even more than the fact that he was turning her hair into a disaster.

So many women dreamed of having long curly

locks, but they didn't have to live with the reality of brittle frizz that couldn't even be brushed without it turning into a big scary Afro.

"Be still," he said as he started twisting her hair. The salesclerk handed him a clip, which he used to secure the mass of curls into a messy bun high on the back of her head. Then he tugged a few strands free around her face. *"Voilà!"*

She peeked at the mirror, fearing what she'd see. Then stared. Was that her? She remembered the evening of the art show, months ago, when she'd let Christine and Maddy do her hair. They'd left most of it down in long corkscrew curls, with the sides pulled up and back. She'd loved it but hadn't considered wearing it like that on a daily basis. When she was little, her grandmother had always braided her hair. Since that was fast, easy, and kept it out of her way, Amy had worn it like that all her life.

Now she wondered why.

This style changed the whole appearance of her face. Her eyes looked exotic, her cheeks hollowed, and her lips inviting. How could something so simple as pulling her hair up make such a big change? The volume of it also balanced her body, making her look taller and slimmer.

The strangest feeling shimmered in her belly, part wonder, part panic. The person staring back at her was genuinely pretty. A woman men would notice.

You are afraid to be pretty, Lance's voice echoed in her mind. The idea seemed absurd. All women long to be pretty, don't they?

Yet her heart raced painfully fast.

Lance nodded in approval. "We need more outfits like this, but with color. Something bright, *non*?"

"Not too bright," she insisted quickly.

"You do not like color?"

"I love color, but not on me," she said. "As my grandmother always says, 'A woman whose face is her best asset shouldn't draw attention away from that.'"

He pulled his head back as if she'd socked him. "Your *grand-mère* would insult you like this?"

"You'd have to know Meme." She laughed at his expression. "That's actually her way of saying I have a pretty face."

"*Mon Dieu.*" He rolled his eyes. "With compliments like that, I am shocked you are not unbearably vain."

"She's only offering advice because she cares."

"Let me ask, is she the one who tells you that baggy clothes make you look thinner?"

"Not in so many words." Amy frowned. "She just doesn't harp on me about my weight if I wear loose clothes. Ironically, the more she harps, the more I eat, which is partly why I moved out of the house two years ago and finally started losing some pounds instead of constantly gaining."

Her face scrunched as she turned toward him. "What I don't understand is why I'm the only fat person in my family. All my cousins are knockouts, yet there I was my whole life, Fat Amy, the Cabbage Patch kid. But Meme's the one who was always stuffing me full of sweets. I swear to you"—she held up a hand—"no exaggeration, when I was growing up, she'd actually say things like, 'Amy, honey, you need to go on a diet. Here, have a cookie.' So if wearing baggy clothes spares me from that, I'll do it gladly."

He studied her a moment, then put his hands back on her shoulders and turned her to face the mirror. He bent so his lips were near her ear and whispered, "Amy, your *grand-mère* is not here. You can dress any way you wish."

Her heart raced even faster.

You are afraid to be pretty.

Maybe she was. But wasn't that the purpose of the challenge? To face the things that frightened her? The things that held her back?

Remembering that helped push the panic back and let excitement pour in. It bubbled up and spilled out as laughter. "Okay, okay." She pressed her hands together, prayerlike, to keep them from trembling. Her eyes met Lance's in the mirror. "Perhaps a little more color."

The smile that moved over his face held a wealth of approval. He knew somehow, he knew what a huge step this was. And he admired her for taking it.

For the rest of the day, Amy bounced between apprehension and excitement as Lance created her wardrobe. They bought breezy sundresses, fabulous silk shirts that fluttered with every movement, capri pants in several colors with just as many tank tops to mix and match. And jewelry. They bought so much fun and funky jewelry, Amy tried to protest. "Please, Lance. No more. This isn't my money we're spending."

"No, it is not," he countered. "So you have no say."

"I don't want to take advantage of Mr. Gaspar's generosity."

"You do not take advantage. Most women, they would spend many times this much if given carte blanche the way he give to you." He looked at her oddly. "Why do you not?"

"Because it's not right," she insisted. "And because look at everything we've bought today. Good heavens! It's too much."

"A woman can never have too much jewelry," he proclaimed.

After lunch, where the conversation flowed with remarkable ease, he dropped her at the salon and day spa. What an experience that was! She felt like Dorothy in the *Wizard of Oz*. The flamboyantly gay stylist gasped at the thought of cutting her hair more than "just a smidge to banish the dry ends."

He also lectured her about overshampooing and explained the correct way to care for extremely curly hair. According to him, she should shampoo only once a week and use conditioner to clean her hair the rest of the time. Amy had her doubts but promised to give his advice a try. He insisted the results would be "glorious, sim-ply g-lor-ious!"

The way he said it made Amy laugh. She had a fondness for gay men. They were the best of both worlds—and completely nonthreatening.

Next came a massage, by a woman, thank goodness, but even that was disconcerting to have someone touching her body. Then a pedicure with bright pink polish, which she adored, and finally a makeup lesson that she listened to very diligently. So diligently, in fact, that she didn't really notice the overall effect until Lance walked in. And stopped dead.

"Do I look okay?" she asked nervously, suddenly feeling a little too buffed and polished. "Is it too much?"

"No. It is . . ." He shook his head as if speechless. "You are stunning."

Blushing, she turned back to the mirror and felt the same thrill she'd been feeling all day. Was that really her in the mirror? Nathan had piled her hair up in back, much the way Lance had earlier, only now it had a few dramatic blond streaks and a lot more moisture and shine.

Lance cast several disconcerting glances her way as they went to pay. He seemed mesmerized by her transformation. In truth, she found it boggling as well. She kept staring at herself in every reflective surface, then blushing because that was so vain. Even so, she couldn't seem to stop.

She caught another glimpse of her reflection as Lance settled the bill. This time, though, her gaze went past the glass surface to the display of ankle bracelets behind it. They dangled from a rotating rack on the countertop, the silver chains sparkling in the salon track lighting. She zeroed in on one with a butterfly charm and smiled.

It reminded her of her one big secret, the thing about her very few people knew: she had a tattoo of a butterfly on her bottom.

"Do you want one?" Lance asked, pointing to the anklets.

Did she? Oh, yes! "That depends," she said, suppressing her excitement. "How much are they?"

"Does it matter?" He opened the glass door and spun the rack, making the anklets swing.

"Yes, it matters," she told him. "We've spent enough of Mr. Gaspar's money today. This I want to buy for myself."

"There is no need. Which one do you want?"

"The butterfly." She plucked it off the display and checked the price, relieved to see it wasn't too much. "I'm definitely buying this."

"But—"

"Don't even think of arguing with me over this." She silenced him with her most formidable look. "I've let you have your way all day, but I'm buying this for myself." She laid it on the counter and told the woman to ring it up separately from the pile of hair and face products Nathan had selected.

The instant the anklet was hers, she cradled it in her palm and smiled. For the first time since college, she felt as if the cocoon that bound her was starting to open.

Chapter 8

We see more clearly when we're looking at others.
                          —*How to Have a Perfect Life*

That evening, as Amy carried the supper tray to the tower, the balancing act between excitement and apprehension her nerves had played tipped decidedly back toward apprehension. Lance had left shortly before sunset. Had he told Mr. Gaspar how much money they'd spent? She'd gone through the shopping bags to put everything away and nearly hyperventilated looking at the price tags.

Well, if Lance hadn't told Mr. Gaspar, she would.

"Hello?" she called as she ventured tentatively into the office. Lance had left the floor lamp on, so she didn't have to wrestle with the wall switch. She felt self-conscious, though, knowing that somewhere overhead a man was watching and listening. "Mr. Gaspar?"

"Good evening, Amy."

"Oh, good, you're there." Relief came at hearing his voice. He sounded relaxed this evening, and happy to see her. She hurried forward, put the tray in the dumbwaiter and pulled the ropes to send it up. "Well, of course you're there. I meant, I'm glad you have the speaker on. I wanted to thank you for all the wonderful new clothes."

"Did you enjoy your shopping day? Lance wasn't too sure."

"I did enjoy it, but, heavens . . ." She backed up so she could address the camera. "We bought way too much. I left the tags on most of it, though, so I can return what I don't need."

"You don't like your new clothes?" He sounded disappointed.

"Are you kidding? I love them!" she assured. "They're all so beautiful. You were right about Lance. He has fabulous taste."

"Then why would you want to return them?"

"It's just too much. I don't need so many clothes."

"Amy." She heard him chuckle. "Trust me when I say I can afford it. And if it gives me pleasure, why not indulge?"

"Why would it give you pleasure? I'm the one with the incredible new wardrobe."

"I don't often make women happy. In fact, I frequently do the opposite. Speaking of incredible, is this chicken fricassee? It smells fantastic."

"Yes. I don't know how spicy you like your food, so I tried to go easy on the pepper."

"Don't hold back on my account. I like spices. And, oh, mmm, this is *so* good!"

"I'm glad you like it." She beamed with pride.

"See? That gives you pleasure, doesn't it? The fact that I enjoy your cooking. So why not give me the pleasure of watching you enjoy my gift?"

"Oh, goodness." All the conflicting emotions bubbled up inside her again. "I want to, it's just . . ."

"Just what?" Byron asked. Settling in his desk chair, he looked at Amy's image on the monitor. She wore crop pants and a tank top that captured the deepest blue of the Caribbean Sea with a long, sheer overshirt with a parrot motif that blended elegance and whimsy. Her hair was piled up, showing off the dainty shell of her ears and the smooth column of her neck. Her face, though, truly held him spellbound: the expressive eyes, the quick blushes, the coquettish looks that were so sweet, he doubted she knew how alluring they were. "Seeing the beauty you were trying so hard to hide shine brings me a great deal of pleasure."

"It does?" The notion seemed to baffle her.

"I have known a lot of physically beautiful women, but few who are truly beautiful inside and out. You are one of that rare breed." He marveled at the words coming out of his mouth, at the freedom anonymity gave him to feel something, then simply voice it without hesitation. Or maybe it was something, about Amy that gave him that freedom. "That makes you a treasure."

"A treasure?" She laughed, and he savored the bright, musical sound. "I don't know about that. But if giving me the clothes makes you happy, then I will accept them and say thank you. I have to confess, though, I feel a little uncomfortable dressed in a way that draws so much attention. People stared at me today. Not just Lance, but other people too. I'm used to being invisible, so it felt strange to be noticed."

"Strange how?"

"I don't know. It's the same excited but scared

feeling I get when I'm faced with going someplace I've never been before."

"Really?" He pondered that a moment. "Is that the real reason you want to return the clothes? You don't like being noticed?"

She dipped her head and gave him a sideways look he would have called teasing on any other woman. "You're full of questions tonight."

"I have found this is a good place for asking questions. And it's not just the hours of solitude, although that helps. I think removing yourself from everything familiar changes your perspective."

"That sounds like something from my friend Jane's book, *How to Have a Perfect Life*. She says a little distance can bring things into focus."

"Too bad distance doesn't make the answers more attractive when find them."

"Is that what you've been doing here? Searching for answers?"

"Either that or hiding from them." He probed his mind for something that kept eluding him. "I think, at times, that I'm gathering pieces to a puzzle. That maybe when I have all the pieces, the picture as a whole will make sense. Maybe you can use the next four weeks to find the missing pieces to your own puzzle. Then you'll understand why you're afraid. And when you understand the why behind the fear, the fear might go away."

"I already understand why I'm afraid to travel."

"I meant why you're afraid to be pretty."

"I'm not sure I'm afraid, exactly." Her brow dimpled. "I'm just not entirely comfortable. I'll work on it, though, so that I can enjoy your gift."

"I hope so." In time, he thought, maybe she would grow comfortable with her own beauty, and that would be a greater gift than the clothes themselves.

"Okay, then." She gestured toward the door, seeming as reluctant to leave as he was to watch her go. "I'll be going. Good night."

"Good night, Amy. Sleep well."

"You too." Turning off the floor lamp, she disappeared into the darkness of the library. He watched her on the monitors as she made her way to her side of the fort. When she was in her own room and out of his sight, he glanced about the tower at the comfortably furnished haven he'd created for himself. For the first time the space felt more empty than safe.

Then a smile settled over his face as he thought about the other gift he'd bought for Amy that day, the one he'd give her tomorrow.

Amy woke to the sound of male voices out in the courtyard. Wearing the white silk night gown she'd purchased yesterday at the lingerie store, she padded over to the louvered doors and peeked outside. The sun was just rising and its light played through the tops of the palm trees, turning the fronds a bright green against a vivid blue sky.

Down in the shadowy garden, she heard Lance talking to the landscape crew. She saw only glimpses of him as he moved through the tangled growth, explaining in French what he wanted done. She could hardly wait to see the garden transformed into the spectacular space she knew it could be.

For now, though, she had breakfast to cook.

Stretching her arms over her head, she turned on the balls of her feet like a dancer and headed for the shower.

Remembering Nathan's instructions about her hair, she used conditioner with no shampoo, and had to admit it did get her hair clean and left it more manageable. She pampered herself with scented body lotion and face cream, then slipped into a floral sundress in the cheerful yellows, oranges, and reds of a bird-of-paradise flower. She'd argued over the idea of a dress that left her arms bare and stopped above the knees, but looking in the mirror, she realized her Pilates classes really had paid off. Her arms weren't skinny by any means, but they had a nice shape, and she'd managed to get a bit of a tan during the cruise in spite of all the sunblock she'd slathered on. A fun, clunky necklace and dangly earrings completed the outfit.

Makeup posed more of a challenge, but she managed to duplicate what the facial specialist had taught her. That brought her back to the issue of her hair. Nathan had shown her several quick and easy ways to fix it. She finger-combed the sides up and secured it with a clip so the ringlets spiraled down her back. Then she pulled three long curls free, one at each ear, and one at the temple.

Finished, she turned to the full-length mirror on the bathroom door—and stared. The person looking back at her was more than pretty. She looked confident, outgoing, and . . . well, sexy. Her stomach turned jittery at that thought, and she had to fight an urge to take off the jewelry, scrub her face, and braid her hair her usual way. With a deep breath, she reminded herself of the things Mr. Gaspar had said last night.

The fact that he enjoyed, rather than resented, beauty in others gave her courage—even though seeing this person in the mirror would take getting used to. If nothing else, Maddy and Christine were going to be ecstatic; they'd been trying to treat her to a makeover for years.

She'd stopped at the Internet café the day before to check in with Elda—who said Meme was fine— and tell her friends about her day. Unfortunately, she'd wound up with a keyboard even worse than the one before. She'd had to settle for simply telling everyone she was okay and would be in touch later. When she went to town today, she was determined to find one keyboard in that darned café that worked.

With that at the forefront of her thoughts, she stopped in surprise as she entered the kitchen. A laptop computer sat on the center island, open and running. Colors swirled on the screen in a mesmerizing pattern.

Could Lance have left it there on his way out to the courtyard? Excitement tingled along her skin as temptation drew her to it. Did the fort have wireless Internet access? Would he let her use his laptop to contact her friends? She bit her lip against the urge to bring it out of sleep mode. Did she dare?

No, she couldn't. Really. Not without permission.

Oh, but she wanted to.

"Do you like it?"

She whirled to find Lance leaning in the window over the sink, his arms crossed on the sill. His daz-

zling smile jolted her as much as his sudden appearance. Heart racing, she snatched her hands up
against her chest. "I'm sorry. I was just—"

"Go ahead." He nodded toward the computer, but
his gaze remained on her, her hair, her face, her outfit. He didn't say anything, but she saw approval in
his eyes and discovered that being noticed by men
was like staying on St. Barts—scary and thrilling at
the same time. "Try it," he said.

"You don't mind?"

"Why would I? It is yours."

"Mine?"

"A gift from Gaspar."

"Are you serious?" She gasped in delight. "Where
did it come from?"

"I buy it yesterday while you are at the salon.
When I tell Gaspar you need to e-mail your friends
every day, he insist."

"Oh, my goodness." Happiness fluttered through
her as she brought the computer to life. In the middle
of the screen was a message, like a card on a gift box.

For Amy,
A small thank you for the gift of your culinary art.
With High Regards,
Guy Gaspar

She turned to speak to Lance, but found him gone.
He appeared a moment later, coming through the
door that led from the kitchen to the gallery.

"Here, I show you all the software," he said, join-
ing her at the island. "I would have given it to you
yesterday, but Gaspar, he want to set it up for you."

"He set it up himself?"

"He enjoys high-tech toys."

"Does he?" Everything she learned about Guy Gaspar made him seem more like an ordinary man to her, which made her ache for his self-imposed imprisonment.

"Here is the Internet browser," Lance said, using the tap pad to move the curser. "So you can stay in touch with your friends."

"Oh, heavens." She pressed her hands to her cheeks. "This is just the best gift ever!"

He smiled broadly, clearly pleased with her reaction, then frowned warily. "You do not hear the price."

"Price?" She blinked.

"Since your cooking is *magnifique*, I tell the landscape crew we feed them lunch. This might help them stay until the job is done, *non*? I will even go to the market for you if you tell me what to purchase."

"You call that a price?" she asked laughing. "I would love to cook for everyone. Cooking for crowds is one of my favorite things to do. Especially if you do the shopping!" Her mind spun with plans. "In fact, I'm in the mood to do some baking. Do you think the men would like cinnamon buns as a midmorning snack?"

"I think they will swoon with pleasure." He gave her a wicked look.

She shook her head, since he made the words sound just a little bit naughty. "Well then, you shoo." She waved her hands at him. "Out of my way so I can get started."

"Très bien." He inclined his head in a salute. "I will leave you to your cooking, *mademoiselle.*"

"Oh, and Lance," she called as he reached the door. "Please, tell Mr. Gaspar thank you for the laptop. I really am just thrilled beyond words."

He gave her one of his slow smiles. "He will be pleased to know."

When he left, she realized she didn't need to relay messages through Lance. She could tell Mr. Gaspar herself when she delivered his breakfast. She hurried through making eggs Florentine with crisp bacon and a side of fresh berries.

She sank with disappointment, though, when she delivered the meal. Lance sat in his office, rather than overseeing the work in the courtyard. She couldn't very well talk to Mr. Gaspar with Lance in the room. That would feel too awkward.

She did ask if Lance had delivered her message. He assured her he had and said that Gaspar was glad to hear the gift pleased her.

Well, she decided, if nothing else, maybe Mr. Gaspar had listened in, which was sort of like hearing her thanks personally. Maybe that evening, she could tell him how much the gift meant to her. The thought of talking to him again, even through the camera, gave her spirits a lift.

Maybe the camera was why she found talking to him so easy when talking to men normally left her tongue-tied.

Back in the kitchen, she checked the clock. With Christine in Colorado visiting her fiancé, she and Maddy were both on Mountain time, so the chances of finding them online this early were slim. Even so, she opened the computer to familiarize herself with the software. She was in the middle of composing a message to her friends, to fill them in on all the exciting things that had happened in a mere three days, when the laptop chimed. She jumped in surprise and watched a window appear in the upper left corner.

It was a message sent simply from "Guy," no long e-mail address. It read: *Good morning. I was hoping you would sign online.*

Smiling in delight, she typed her reply: *Good morning to you. I didn't realize I was online.*

Guy: *You're set up to be on all the time, but I also have a direct link between our two computers. Much more private than talking through the Internet.*

Amy: *Thank you again for the laptop.*

Guy: *Thank you for last night's dinner. It was excellent. As is breakfast.*

Amy: *I'm glad you enjoy my cooking.*

Guy: *I enjoy your company even more. And I don't want you to take this the wrong way, it's a strictly platonic invitation, but, will you have dinner with me this evening?*

She blinked at the invitation. Here she'd just been thinking that the camera made talking to him easier. What was he like in person? Was he really as hideous as Lance claimed?

She heard her own thoughts and frowned. Lance might be perfectly nice, but he was also somewhat shallow. What did he know about physical imperfection? The man was so vain, he wore a wig, for heaven's sake. And some of the things he'd said—especially in light of the fact that he'd said them in the office where Gaspar could hear—had not been the most sensitive things in the world. *Some days I can barely bring myself to look at him.*

She'd always believed external appearance didn't matter. Yet here she was, afraid to look upon ugliness? Shame on her. As for the other Meme-esque sort of fears suddenly springing to life—like, what if he's an ax murderer or rapist?—she dismissed them as silly. The man she'd talked to last night was kind, intelligent, sensitive. And probably very lonely.

Taking a deep breath, she typed her reply: *If you're willing to let me join you, yes, I would love to.*

Guy: *I see you had to think about that one for a while. And to put your fears to rest, I thought you could sit in Beaufort's office, and we could simply visit while we eat.*

Oddly, she felt disappointment rather than relief, so she typed: *I would rather we sit together.*

Guy: *Someday, maybe. For now I would be more comfortable with this arrangement.*

Amy scrunched her face in frustration: *All right. For now. But I have to warn you, I can be very persistent.*

Guy: *I look forward to sharing your company this evening. Enjoy your day. PS: You look beautiful.*

She stared at the screen a long time after he'd disconnected. How very unexpected. Had she just agreed to a dinner date with the man in the tower? No, she quickly assured herself. Not a date. He'd specified that himself. He was simply a lonely man who wanted company while he ate.

Still, she found herself looking toward the sun repeatedly throughout the day, willing it to sink faster.

Chapter 9

Amy paused in the doorway of Lance's office when she saw that the makeshift desk had been completely cleared. Had Mr. Gaspar told Lance she'd be eating dinner in here? What would Lance think? Or maybe Mr. Gaspar had come down and cleared the table himself and would put everything back after she left.

"Mr. Gaspar?" she called.

"This is going to be a very dull evening if you insist on being so formal." His answer over the speaker came so quickly she wondered if he'd been watching for her.

"Well, I didn't want to be presumptuous."

"Please, call me Guy."

"That is much friendlier." She moved to the table and set her place with the things she'd loaded onto the tray: a place mat, linen napkin, silverware.

"So, what are we having this evening?" he asked.

"For you, pan-fried snapper with an almond crust and the hollandaise I had leftover from breakfast, plus some side dishes I hope you'll like. I'm having grilled fish, no sauce, and a salad."

"Mine sounds better, and I'm salivating already. How about some wine?"

"Oh." She drew up short. "I didn't think of that."

"I have some up here. Send up the dumbwaiter, and I'll send down a glass. Since we're having fish, I assume Pinot Grigio will do?"

"Yes, thank you. That sounds nice." She set the tray on the dumbwaiter, making sure the stem of white orchids in the bud vase faced forward. "Here you go."

She worked the ropes, then waited, staring up into the dark shaft. What did the rooms above look like? Were they dark and dreary, befitting a beast? Or had Lance finished them out nicely, like her part of the fort.

When the dumbwaiter came back down, the bud vase sat next to a glass of pale white wine.

"You didn't like the flowers?" she asked, a little hurt.

"I believe the head gardener gave them to you as thanks for the cinnamon buns."

"How did you know that?"

"I can see the courtyard from my window."

"Of course." She frowned at the image that came to mind of a solitary figure standing at the window high up in the tower, staring out at the world beyond. He'd be able to see a lot from that vantage, not just the courtyard but the town and the bay. Did he spend his days watching the ships come and go?

Taking the flowers and wine, she settled in Lance's

chair. "They're making good progress in the garden. Do you know, I didn't even realize there was a swimming pool out there until they cleared away the undergrowth."

"It's going to take a lot of work to get it working again." His voice grew stronger, as if he were walking toward the microphone. She heard what sounded like someone taking a seat in a swivel desk chair followed by the clink of silverware on china. "Oh, this is good. Are you sure you don't want any of this sauce on your fish?"

"I'm sure. I had a taste of it while I was cooking, enough to be sure I had it right, but not enough to bust my diet."

"For the record, I think you look fine exactly how you are."

"Thank you. But, also for the record, I'm doing this diet for me, which might be why I'm finally succeeding."

"What do you mean?"

"It's kind of a long story, but I'm doing a lot of things for me these days. Sort of like a makeover on the inside that's been under way for two years now."

"Isn't that what dinners are for? To share stories over food and drink?"

"I suppose." She took a bite of fish and nodded in satisfaction over the tasted. Not as good as what Guy was eating, but still tasty. "Let's see, where to begin?"

"At the beginning," he suggested. "Tell me everything about you."

"Everything? Oh, my." She smiled at the humorous note in his voice, then tried to think. Normally, she had no problem telling stories, a gift she'd inherited from her mother. But spinning imaginary tales was not the same as talking about oneself. "I guess I should start with the biggest thing that shaped my life, and that would be my mother. She was quadriplegic. She died when I was ten."

A beat of silence followed. "I'm sorry. That must have been rough."

"Yes," Amy sighed. "Losing her was very rough, but before that everything was wonderful. She was such an amazingly brave and upbeat person. So much fun to be around. When she was alive, living at my grandparents' house was . . ." She gazed off into space, searching for the right words. "Magical."

"How did your mother become paralyzed?" Sitting at his desk, Byron watched her on the monitor, fascinated by the play of emotions over her face. Her smile, her eyes, everything about her fascinated him.

"She and some of her college friends were out at Lake Travis diving off the cliffs into the water. She slipped right as she dove and hit the shore. The impact broke her neck. They rushed her to the hospital, which was when she found out she was pregnant. Until then, she hadn't had a clue. She could have terminated the pregnancy since it was early term, and some of the blood pressure medication they wanted to give her would have killed me. But she begged them to do everything they could to keep me safe. She always told me that during that horrible time when she realized she'd never walk or even use her arms again, I became her reason for living."

"It's amazing she didn't lose you."

"It really is," Amy agreed. "She carried me nearly

full term and we made the news when the doctors delivered me by C-section. So that's why I grew up in my grandparents' house."

"With the grandmother who stuffed you with sweets."

"Exactly." Amy nodded, cutting off a bite of fish with her fork. She had dainty hands, he noted, and a grace to her confined movements. "Daphne Baker, or Meme, makes the best homemade candies, cookies, and cakes you've ever eaten."

"I can believe it," he said, enjoying his own meal. "If it's not too personal, can I ask where your father was during all of this?"

"There is no father." Her smile faded. "Well, technically, there is somewhere, or I wouldn't exist, but I don't know who he is."

"I'm sorry, I shouldn't have pried."

"No, it's okay," she assured him. "I worry, though, that people will judge my mother harshly when I reveal that she had to put 'unknown' for the name of the father on my birth certificate. In her defense, I'd like to point out that she was young and in college and going through a bit of a wild phase. She wasn't *that* wild, though. It's not like she couldn't name him because she slept around so much it could have been any number of boys. Instead, she met someone at a disco one night. Sparks flew. They went back to his hotel room, since he was from out of town. She gave him her phone number before she left, but he never called." She wrinkled her nose as if to say, *Isn't that typical?* "So, whoever he is, he has no idea I exist."

"His loss," Byron said, meaning it. "So tell me about this magical childhood at your grandparents' house."

"Mom and I became their whole world," she said with feeling. "As you can imagine, taking care of a quadriplegic and an unexpected grandbaby is a lot of work. Going anywhere was always a major production. Partly because of the logistics, but also because my grandmother, Meme, is the consummate worrier. If Papa wanted to take us someplace, Meme could come up with a whole list of catastrophes that were sure to happen. So they worked together to make staying home fun."

"Did they succeed?"

"Oh, definitely." She brightened. "It wasn't hard since they knew everybody in town. I grew up in a little speck on the map that used to be outside Austin but has been swallowed up in recent years. The Bakers are quite the bigwigs, and owned half the businesses in town at one time. Papa sold off everything after Mom's accident so he could stay home and help. As for the house itself, it's a real traffic-stopper."

He noticed her accent thickened when she spoke of home, and her gestures gradually became more animated. He found both utterly charming.

"Picture Tara from *Gone with the Wind*," she said, "only scaled down to simply big rather than huge. It's been in the family for generations. Papa always liked to putter in the garden, so when he retired he joined the men's garden club and turned the grounds into a prize-winning showplace. We have meandering footpaths connecting grassy areas and secluded sitting spots, each surrounded by flower beds that bloom year round.

"With Daphne as the reigning queen of her social circle, we had parties all the time. Or people just dropping by. Most of the time, though, Momma and I would sit out in the garden, in one of the special places Papa created for us. While he worked, we'd make up stories. Maybe we couldn't go anywhere for real, but we traveled all over the world in our magic flying ship that could take us to any time and any place we wanted to go."

"That does sound fun." He wondered how it would feel to have that much love and attention.

"It was." She sighed, her expression turning wistful. "I had a very special childhood."

He studied her. "Why does that make you sad?"

She shrugged and picked at her salad. "I guess because I really miss how things were. Everything changed after my mom died."

"May I ask what happened?"

"Are you sure you want to hear this? It's not very happy from here on out."

"A lot of stories aren't." He thought of his own childhood, filled with traveling in the real world rather than her imaginary one. Hers sounded better. "And yes I want to hear."

"Okay, well, as I got older, my mom worried that I didn't have a 'normal' childhood because I didn't have any playmates. None of our neighbors had children my age, and most of the people who came to visit were my grandparents' friends. So my mom decided I should go to summer camp.

"I loved the idea," she said brightly. "I think I was expecting it to be like the imaginary trips Mom and I took. Meme, of course, nearly had a stroke at the very thought of sending a ten-year-old off on her own. Mom insisted, though, so off I went to summer camp.

"It was not at all what I expected." She wrinkled her nose. "At first I was miserable. Kids can be so cruel to anyone who isn't perfect."

"Yes they can," he agreed.

She tipped her head, staring into the camera as if she could see him. "Did you have problems fitting in as a child?"

No, he thought. He'd never had a problem fitting in to the unique world of children of celebrities. But he'd witnessed the kind of cruelty she talked about and had never spoken out against it because that wasn't "cool." And Byron Parks had always been extremely cool.

"I'd rather talk about you." He stabbed at his meal. "Tell me about summer camp. Why were you miserable?"

"I missed my mom and I didn't know how to interact with other children. It was like school, only worse!" She emphasized the words with an eye roll. "I was always the oddball because I was short and chunky and I acted like a miniature adult. I had really old-fashioned, ultrapolite manners that the other kids made fun of.

"At first, I just wanted to go home. But my mom always said, there's a bright side to everything. You just have to find it. I realized she was right." Amy nodded. "I liked the camp itself, with all its hiking trails and the woods, and I'd never had any trouble entertaining myself. So I'd take my Big Chief tablet and wander off on my own until I found a spot where I could sit and write stories to mail home to my mom." She laughed. "I'm sure you can see the problem with this scenario."

"You'd get lost," he guessed.

"Every time." She nodded. "Back then, getting lost didn't bother me. I had the kind of trust only a child can have that everything will turn out fine. All that changed that summer."

She took a deep breath as if whatever came next would be hard to tell. "Whenever I got lost, the counselors would form a search party until they found me, then scold me for wandering off alone. One of those times, halfway through camp, that's exactly what happened. Only, instead of taking me back to my lodge, they took me to the office. The counselors looked so somber, I thought, boy, I'm really in trouble this time. When I got to the office, though, Papa was there."

Tears sprang to her eyes, and her voice wavered. "The last thing in the world I expected was to have him break down right before my eyes and tell me my mother had died."

Dear God, Byron thought, but didn't know what to say.

"I'm sorry." She wiped her eyes. "I still get emotional when I talk about it."

"I'm sorry too." He marveled at the range of emotions she expressed so freely once she opened up. "How did she die?"

"Her heart gave out." With a deep breath, Amy

pulled herself together. "Paralysis is very hard on the body. My mom and my grandparents always knew she wouldn't have a long life, but it never occurred to me that I'd lose her. It hit all of us really hard. Meme's grief"—she shook her head—"oh, heavens, it was beyond measure. I think losing a child is the hardest thing any woman suffers."

"I can't even imagine feeling that much pain. I'm so very sorry." The words seemed paltry, but what else could he say?

"Papa was devastated too," she went on. "They both just withdrew inside themselves. Papa would work in the garden for hours every day, but it wasn't like before. The joy had gone out of it. I worked with him, trying to cheer him. And I think it helped. He and I were really close."

"What was he like?"

She gazed off into space, smiling. "He was a tall, gangly stork of a man who always seemed mystified that he'd landed a wife as pretty as Meme. He used to thank the good Lord that their two children, my mom and my uncle, took after her, not him. Meme adored him, though. We all did. He always called me his little okra blossom." She laughed at the memory. "That was his nickname for me. Okra."

"Okra?" Byron frowned. "Like the vegetable?"

"Yep." She laughed. "He claimed people came in two varieties. The showy kind that are a feast for the senses and the nourishing kind that are a feast for the belly. He considered the okra plant the best of both because it's a vegetable, but it has such beautiful flowers. It's a type of hibiscus, you know, with great big blossoms that look like the sun right at sunrise."

"No, I didn't know that."

Her smile faded with a sigh. "Anyway, while Papa grieved out in his garden, Meme's health went. She seemed to be ill all the time. And she became obsessed with the idea that she'd lose me too. It frightened me sometimes, knowing that if anything ever happened to me, Meme wouldn't be able to handle it. So I stuck really close to home, taking care of Meme and helping Papa in the garden. That was when I really started to gain weight, and I realize now that a lot of it was angry eating."

"Why angry?" he asked.

She sighed. "I don't mean to be disloyal, but it bothered me that Meme complained so much over every little ache. My mother lived the last eleven years of her life totally paralyzed from the neck down, and she never complained. Never." Amy stabbed sharply at the fish on her plate. "Yet here was Meme, practically swooning on the sofa because her head hurt, so 'Oh, dear, I must have a brain tumor. I need to go to the hospital.' Of course she didn't. Half the ailments she suffered were completely in her mind. Not all of them, but enough to make me mad." She attacked her salad next. "So many times, I wanted to fuss at her about that."

"Did you?"

"No." She sighed heavily. "I didn't want to be a complainer, like her. So I swallowed the words—and a whole lot of food along with them. I ate and ate and ate, as if the act of chewing and swallowing would make the anger go away. It didn't, though. It just made me fat. By the time I went to college, I was desperate for escape."

"I don't blame you. There's a difference, though, in speaking up and being a whiner. I think you should have told her off a time or two."

"You sound like my friends." She sent him a thoughtful look.

"What happened to your grandfather?" he asked to keep the conversation off of him. "I take it he isn't alive anymore."

"No." She sighed. "Losing him was nearly as hard for me as losing my mom. Basically, he was my dad. The only dad I ever had. He died while I was away at college, so I wasn't there when that happened either. That's when I started associating my being away from home with something bad happening. What makes it worse, though, is that I was close, so close, to escaping that house for good, and I think I feel guilty and disloyal for seeing it as escape."

"What do you mean?" Finished with his dinner, he settled back with his glass of wine, thinking he could listen to her all night.

"College was a real blast for me," she said, still working on her meal. "Mostly because I was lucky enough my freshman year to get paired up with Jane as my roommate, and we had Maddy and Christine as our suite mates. Being away from home, I started dropping weight like crazy. I even dated a little." She made a face as if the last were distasteful. "I was a disaster at dating, but I did discover something I was good at. And that's kids. One of the big ironies of my life is that I was terrible around kids when I was one, but now I'm really great with them.

"I worked at a day care center all through college—which a lot of people would find a hectic nightmare, but I really enjoyed it. I used to tell the kids some of the stories my mom and I made up. There's nothing like watching a child's face when they're enraptured by a story you're telling."

"Have you ever written any of these stories down? Other than when you were ten?"

"Quite a few, but just for my own enjoyment." She waved the accomplishment away as if it were nothing. "Anyway, as graduation approached, my roommates and I talked about what we wanted to do with our lives. Remember, this was before I started thinking travel equals death, so the two things I wanted most were the chance to see the world and to have children. Since I have no sense of direction, I decided the perfect life for me would be to marry a man who did know north from south so we could travel whenever we weren't having babies. Finding the guy to marry was the only part of that plan that scared me, because dating truly is horrendously awkward for me, but I was hopeful.

"Jane, on the other hand, had bigger dreams. She was headed for New York, determined to succeed in broadcasting, come hell or high water. Christine was going to med school to follow in her father's footsteps, and Maddy hoped to get her artwork in a gallery.

"Since Maddy and Christine were so close, they decided to get an apartment somewhere near campus. I was so flattered when they asked me to room with them." Her eyes lit. "I said yes, of course, and to celebrate I—" She stopped abruptly and bit her lip as mischief danced in her eyes.

"What?" he asked, riveted.

"I can't believe I'm going to tell you this." She pressed her hands to her blushing cheeks.

"What?"

"I got a tattoo!"

"You did *what*?" The idea floored him. "You have a tattoo?"

"I do." She giggled. "Christine took me to the tattoo parlor, mostly for moral support and so I wouldn't get lost, but she wound up getting one too. A little devil girl right on her behind."

"What did you get?"

"A butterfly." She grinned. "I thought it was a fitting symbol for breaking free from my grandparents' house, since I had been planning to move back there before Christine and Maddy made their offer."

"Where'd you get it?"

"I'm not going to answer that." She looked scandalized.

"Come on, Amy. You can't leave me in suspense here."

"Okay," she said primly as she neatened the napkin in her lap. "Let's just say that Christine and I are tattoo twins, in a manner of speaking."

Amy Baker had a tattoo on her butt? The idea boggled his mind. And turned him on.

"Unfortunately"—her brow creased—"I was premature in thinking I'd broken free. Papa died of a heart attack days before graduation and Meme fell apart. My uncle begged me to move back home 'just for a little while.' We were all that worried about her. So I canceled my plans to live with Maddy and Christine. At first I didn't mind, because the grief hit me so hard I needed to be home. But as the years passed, the anger returned and built into resentment, which I'm ashamed to admit."

"Maybe you have a right to be resentful."

"No." She sighed as if physically exhausted. "Not all of Meme's complaints are drama. Some are quite real. Her arthritis, for instance, has become so advanced, she has to have help around the house. After the first couple of years, my uncle and I talked about hiring a nurse so that I could move out on my own, but every time we brought it up, Meme's health would take a turn for the worse and I couldn't bring myself to leave her. I started worrying about what would happen if I wasn't there. I got so bad, even leaving the house to go to the grocery store would make me panic.

"Then, one day, about two years ago, I realized what I was doing. I'd let fear turn me into a prisoner in my own house. I'd let it cost me everything I once dreamed of having.

"There was no traveling. No babies. No husband. I'd settled for running Traveling Nannies as a poor substitute and I'd gotten so fat, I had little chance of attracting a man.

"The weight gain was partly from living with so much anger and worry every day. Plus Meme has a way of sending me into binge mode. She's always saying that if I'd only lose weight, I could catch a nice young man. But she doesn't want me to do that at all. A husband isn't going to want to move into Meme's house so I can continue taking care of her."

"Then why does she say it?"

"I don't know." Amy rubbed her stomach as if it hurt. "She makes no sense. It's like the cookie thing.

'Amy, dear, you need to lose weight. Here, have a cookie.' The more she harps on me about overeating, the more I overeat."

"Do you think she knows that?"

"What?" She frowned. "No, of course not. That's a terrible thing to suggest. That's saying she intentionally made me fat."

"Maybe she did." He sipped his wine thoughtfully, as anger on her behalf began to simmer inside him. "It's one way to keep you from leaving her. And she started it when you were really young. As if right from the beginning she feared you'd meet a man, get pregnant, have an accident, and wind up in an early grave like your mother."

"Oh, my God." She sat back. Emotions played over her face as she digested that, then shook it off. "No. I refuse to believe that. That's terrible. She would never consciously do that to me."

"Maybe she didn't do it consciously."

"Still . . . no, that's a terrible thing to do to your grandchild. I will admit she's a bit of a hypochondriac and definitely a drama queen who likes everyone's attention on her, but I refuse to believe she'd intentionally make me fat to keep me from ever leaving home."

"Did it work?"

"We're getting off the subject." She scowled at him. "I was about to get to the whole point of this story."

"Sorry." He smiled, finding her adorable when she got mad. "Go ahead."

"When I had my big epiphany, I realized something else. Meme wasn't the only one who didn't want me to get married. I didn't want that either. I'm that awkward around men. The decision was a huge relief," she sighed. "And it solved the problem of us trying to talk Meme into letting us hire a nurse. If I'm not hoping to get married, there really isn't any reason for me to move out.

"So, I sat down with Meme and made her a promise. I would make living with her permanent, rather than the 'just for a little while' that had stretched into years, but I couldn't live 'with her.' I desperately needed my own space, so with her permission, I converted the carriage house out back into a combination office and apartment.

"It's been the ideal arrangement. I'm there to take care of her, which calms both our fears, but I have my own quarters. That, combined with the permission slip I gave myself about not dating, has finally let me go on a diet and stick to it."

"Do you ever worry about gaining it back?" he asked.

"Actually, not this time." Confidence shone in her smile. "Because this time I'm doing it for me—not with the hope that if I lose weight I'll get a date. My only regret about my decision not to marry is not having children."

"You could always adopt," he suggested.

"I've actually been toying with that idea. But first, I have something else I've decided to do for me. And that's learn to travel on my own. I've made a commitment to Meme that I will live at home and take care of her, but she has to let me go on vacations." Her eyes widened as if in terror, but she laughed.

"A frightening thought, I know, but I want to see the world, and I'm determined to do it. In spite of my lousy sense of direction, in spite of my panic when I get lost, in spite of worrying myself sick over something happening to Meme while I'm gone, I'm determined to conquer this."

He lifted his glass toward her. "And I think that makes you one of the bravest women I've ever known."

She laughed, fully and freely. "You wouldn't say that if you knew how terrified I get sometimes."

"I'm saying it because of that."

"Thank you." She smiled straight into the camera. "That may be the best compliment anyone has ever given me." She went to take another bit of salad and realized it was all gone. "Goodness, I've talked through the whole meal."

"I don't mind. I love listening to you talk. You have a wonderful knack for conversation."

"Not normally." She tipped her head, considering. "You're very easy to talk to. I think because you remind me a bit of my grandfather. He was very patient and a good listener."

Byron nearly choked. "I remind you of your grandfather?" The tall, gangly stork? "Uh, hmm, considering that you loved him, I'll take that as a compliment, but trust me, I'm nothing like your grandfather. And just so we're straight here, I'm not old."

"Oh." She blinked and looked suddenly disconcerted. "I'm sorry. I didn't mean— It's—it's hard to tell a person's age just from their voice."

He could see her wondering, somewhat fearfully,

how old he was. She wasn't going to ask, though. So he volunteered, "Lance Beaufort and I are the same age."

"I see." The look in her eyes told him she never would have opened up so much if she'd known he was in the "dateable" age range.

"Amy," he said, "I promise, you have nothing to fear from me. I will admit, I find you very desirable, but conversation over supper is as far as this will go." The thought filled him with more regret than he'd expected. "Does that make you feel better?"

"It does." She visibly relaxed at the reassurance. "But please don't take that personally. I was serious about hating the whole dating thing."

He thought about pursuing that subject a bit but suspected she'd be nervous now that she knew his age. Lord, if she knew the rest, she would probably bolt. He decided to lighten the mood instead. "How's your wine?"

"Very good." She took a hasty sip. "Thank you."

"Is this key lime pie?" He studied the slice of pie that she'd garnished with a flower from the courtyard.

"Yes it is. I hope you like it."

He took a bite and let the tangy sweetness melt on his tongue. "Oh, mmm, it's delicious. I take it you aren't having any."

"No."

"Well, I'll be good and not tempt you."

"Thank you." She sent him a smile that was so alluring with her dark curls spiraling about her, he could only stare. He knew she didn't mean it to be flirtatious, but how had someone so naturally sexy reached her age without some man blasting through her inhibitions about dating?

And beneath those inhibitions, he suspected she had a wellspring of passion longing to be tapped. Otherwise, she never would have gotten a butterfly tattooed on her bottom. Now there was something to think about. No, best to *not* think about that, he told himself.

What would it be like, though, to be the man who helped her release that inner spirit?

Chapter 10

A good place to ask questions. Amy remembered Guy saying that over the following days as she watched—and helped—the garden take shape. He'd told Lance about her grandfather being a master gardener, so Lance asked her opinion regularly. She'd promptly taken up a hand spade and clipper to pitch right in.

She adored working in the garden. The curious monkeys watched from the treetops as she and the crew cleared and cleaned the beds and repaired the flagstone patio while a separate crew worked on the swimming pool.

It seemed appropriate to dig and weed and plant while turning questions over in her mind. Could Meme really have sabotaged her all her life on purpose? She didn't want that to be true, but now that the seed had been planted, she had trouble keeping it from growing.

She finally accepted that maybe it was true, but whatever harm Meme had done hadn't been done consciously. People didn't intentionally hurt those they loved, and Meme did love her. Sometimes, though, people hurt others unintentionally.

Sitting back on her heels, with the sun beating down on her back, she looked toward the tower. What questions did Guy wrestle with while he watched the garden's transformation? She knew so little about him and felt a growing need every evening to draw him out during their conversations over supper.

All she'd managed to learn was that his parents had divorced when he was very young and both had married more than once since. He seemed to harbor quite a bit of resentment and disgust over that. He'd had every material thing a kid could want, but almost no love or even attention. That made her ache inside just thinking about it.

The most surprising thing she'd learned, though, was that he'd traveled all over Europe and could pass on firsthand stories about the places she longed to visit. She had trouble imagining the recluse in the tower going anywhere, but she loved his descriptions of foreign places, especially southern France, which he clearly favored.

They were so different, she thought at times. He had a confidence she hadn't expected and a dry wit that could make her laugh at the most unexpected things. The only thing they seemed to have in common was their love of stories. He was a self-professed movie junkie as opposed to her bookaholic tendencies, but they could talk about stories endlessly.

That gave her an idea. A smile settled over her

face as she turned her attention back to the garden. One way or another, she was determined to get him to open up to her.

"What's your favorite movie?" she asked him that evening as she sat in Lance's office.

"Old or new?"

"Old first."

"*Casablanca*," he answered without hesitation.

"Agreed," she said. "But why?"

"What do you mean, why? There is no why. It's the best movie ever made."

"Yes, but why does it appeal to you? I find people always have different reasons for liking certain movies."

"Okay, give me a minute. Got it. Humphrey Bogart," he finally said. "He's the center of a constant party, yet he's completely alone. The gaiety in the midst of human suffering disgusts him, yet he's still part of it. And that disgusts him too."

Well, now that surprised her. "Have you ever felt like that?"

He took his time before answering. "Let's just say, I know what it's like to feel isolated in a crowd. So why is *Casablanca* your favorite old movie?"

"Ingrid Bergman," she answered with a sigh. "I cry every time she has to choose between what she wants to do and what she should do. That is so sad."

"And very telling," he observed.

"What do you mean?"

"You had to give up living with your friends after college to take care of your grandmother."

"True," she allowed. "So what's your favorite new movie?"

"*The Incredibles*," he answered again without hesitation.

"Really? A cartoon?" She blinked over that. "Why *The Incredibles*?"

"Are you kidding?" He laughed, something he did more often and more freely each evening. "Elastigirl is hot! She's gotta be fun in bed."

She released a startled laugh and had to press her napkin to her mouth. "I can't believe you said that! She's a cartoon character."

"So?" he said. "She's still hot."

She sent him a scolding look, but feared her amusement ruined the effect. "What's the real reason it's your favorite new movie?"

"You know, I hadn't really thought about that before. I think because you have a married couple who are both superheroes. They have demands and expectations on them that are far higher than if they were normal people, yet they still manage to put their marriage and their kids first. I know a lot of parents, mine included, who could learn a lesson or two from that. So what's your favorite new movie?"

"*Shakespeare in Love*." She sighed.

"Why?"

"Are you kidding? Joseph Fiennes is hot!"

"Smartaleck. Okay, real reason."

"Oh, there are so many. I think, though, it's that I connected with Viola, when she's standing at the window and says if she could dream herself into a company of players, she would stay asleep forever."

"And in the end, she chose a daughter's duty over what she wanted," Guy pointed out. "I sense a common thread here."

"To think I started this game to learn more about you." She laughed.

"What did you learn?"

"Nothing I didn't already know," she answered. The only thing she'd learned was that she liked Guy Gaspar, she feared far more than he liked himself.

As she climbed in bed that night, she realized part of why that made her ache for him. Every day, he was making her feel good about her outward appearance, helping her see herself as attractive. She wanted to do the same for him.

Opening her laptop, she sat up against the headboard, the mosquito netting closing her in a small private world, while she typed out all her thoughts in an e-mail to her friends. Outside, the moon made its trek over the island as night slipped into the wee hours of morning. She sent the post, not expecting any answers until the next day. Christine, though, was back in Austin and had just come off a long shift in the ER.

She answered with: *Amy, are you falling in love with this man?*

That startled her so much, she stared at the words for several minutes. Her fingers shook as she typed her reply: *No, not at all. I admit, I find him fascinating. He's intelligent and funny but so sad it breaks my heart. So much of me wants to reach out to him, but it's just compassion, not love.*

Christine: *I'm sure some of it is compassion, because that's how you are. And if anyone can draw this man out and help heal whatever has him hurting inside, you can. But this sounds like more than compassion to me. Let me ask, are you physically drawn to him?*

Amy: *Christine, I've never even seen him. And we're not dating, we're just talking. Which is why I'm so comfortable with him. When we have supper together, I don't have to spend the whole time wondering if he's going to want to kiss me good night, or maybe want more than a kiss. We're friends. Period.*

Christine: *So? Do you find yourself wondering what he looks like and imagining what it would be like if he did want to kiss you?*

Amy blushed at the question. Like any woman, she had her fantasies, but they'd always been about some nameless, faceless man, not anyone in particular. Had Guy become that faceless man in her dreams? A tingle stirred inside her as she typed: *I admit, I do wonder. Maybe that's why I haven't encouraged meeting him face to face.*

Christine: *Maybe you should.*

The tingle settled low in her belly, leaving her with that antsy feeling she always found uncomfortable. Shifting lower against the headboard, she typed: *I may, but only as his friend, not for anything romantic.*

Christine: *Why not? Because he might be ugly?*

Amy: *No. If I were interested in being more than his friend, how he looks truly wouldn't matter. Besides, what's the worst that it can be? That he's disfigured? That he's scarred? That he has some birthmark covering half his face?*

When I was growing up, I knew a girl who had that, a really big red birthmark and her mouth was deformed so that she talked funny. In first grade, a lot the kids seemed almost afraid of her. They were even meaner to her than they were to me. But she had this fun, outgoing personality, and pretty soon she was friends with everybody.

Then we went to middle school, and I watched it start over again. I realized that when people first meet her, the birthmark and lip are all they see. But once you get used to it, you don't even notice it. I think that's how it would be with Guy. Whatever's wrong with his face, I'd notice at first, but then I'd get used to it.

Christine: *Okay, so why don't you want to meet him?*

Amy: *I guess because I like things the way they are now. He's the first man I've ever been truly comfortable around and I don't want to spoil that.*

Christine: *And how much better would that be if you could be with him in person?*

Amy chewed her lip, debating how to answer. What if she could meet Guy in person without spoiling the connection she felt between them? Maybe Christine was right, and it would be even better. Before she could decide what to say, her computer chimed. A message from Guy appeared on her screen: *What are you doing still awake at this hour?*

She felt the unexpected rush of pleasure she always felt when he sent her a message, which happened frequently during the day but never so late at night.

She hit reply: *Chatting with a friend. What's your excuse?*

Guy: *Trouble sleeping. I was hoping you'd distract me, but if you're online with a friend, I'll let you go.*

Amy: *No, hang on. I'll be right back.*

Amy went back to Christine: *Would you mind if we continue this tomorrow? I need to go.*

Christine: *Let me guess, Guy just signed on, didn't he?*

Amy: *How'd you know?*

Christine: *It wasn't hard. Hey, if you don't want to meet him in person, ask him if he wants to have cybersex.*

Amy: *Christine! You are so bad!*

Christine: *It was just a thought. And no, I don't mind letting you go. I need to go to bed, even if it's really hard to work up much enthusiasm over that when Alec is two thousand miles away. Sometimes I think our wedding day will never get here.*

Amy: *Only a few more weeks to go, then both you and Maddy will be married. I'm so excited about the idea of a double wedding and being the maid of honor for both of you at the same time. I just hate that you'll both be living so far away and I'll be in Austin all alone.*

Christine: *That's the only thing I hate about it too. But we'll find ways to still get together. After all these years, I refuse to let distance wreck our friendship.*

Amy: *I agree. I'll talk to you tomorrow.*

After signing off with Christine, Amy hit reply to Guy's message: *I'm back. Why can't you sleep?*

Guy: *It's all your fault, actually. Talking about why we like certain movies got me thinking about too many things. So now I'm sitting here wondering why I like all the stories I like. Not just movies, but books too.*

Amy: *Have you come up with an answer?*

Guy: *Try a lot of answers. And don't ask me to share, because I won't. I just want to know how to shut it off. I thought stories were supposed to help us escape from our lives, not examine them closer.*

Amy: *They can do both, I suppose.*

Guy: *At the moment, I would prefer a little escapism so that I can unwind enough to go to sleep. But I can't watch a movie or read a book because what would my choice say about me?*

Amy: *Oh, goodness, I did get you going. I'm sorry. If you want to know the best way to escape into a story, though, you should try making one up. It's really fun and the best distraction in the world. Your mind can wander when you're reading, but it's hard for it to wander when you're typing the story out yourself.*

Guy: *I've never tried that. I'm not sure I know how.*

Amy: *I'll help you. We can make up a story together. The way I did with my mom.*

Guy: *You mean take a trip on your magic flying ship? How does that work?*

Amy: *First we pick a time and place.*

Guy: *Okay, you pick.*

Amy: *Medieval England.*

Guy: *Why there? Not that I object. I happen to like the period, I'm just curious.*

Amy: *Well, we're in a fort that looks like a castle, and—don't laugh because I play make-believe in my head a lot, but the first day I was here and Lance told me your first name was Guy, I thought it sounded like a good name for a Norman knight. Sir Guy.*

Guy: *Really? I'm flattered. Do I get to fight fire-breathing dragons and rescue damsels in distress?*

Amy: *I was thinking the damsel could rescue you. After all, you're the one trapped in the tower.*

Guy: *Not trapped, really. Here of my own choosing.*

Amy: *Same thing.*

Guy: *Maybe. So how will you rescue me?*

Amy: *Well, you've been locked up by an evil sorceress who's angry because you spurned her affections. Lady Amelia—that's me—steals the key when the sorceress isn't looking. She sneaks up the tower steps, tiptoeing quietly, glancing over her shoulder to be sure no one is following. Does she make it undetected?*

Guy: *Why Lady Amelia? Why not Lady Amy?*

Amy: *Because Amy is such a plain name, and too modern. Whoever heard of a Lady Amy? Plus, Lady Amelia is tall and blond and gorgeous. Now, does she make it undetected?*

Guy: *Why can't she be short, lushly figured, and have sexy brown curls?*

Amy: *Because this is fantasy. And in fantasy, we can be anything we want to be.*

Guy: *Well, in this case, I like reality over your fantasy.*

He was right, she realized. The best story of all would be for the short "lushly figured" girl to have the adventure and win the hero. So she typed: *Okay, Lady Amelia is short, a little chunky, and has exasperatingly curly brown hair.*

Guy: *In other words, she's gorgeous. And yes, she makes it up the stairs undetected. What happens next?*

Amy: *She knocks quietly on the door and whispers, "Sir Knight, can you hear me?"*

Guy: *What does he do?*

Amy: *I don't know. What does he do?*

Guy: *He moves cautiously to the door and whispers back, "Who is there?"*

Amy: *" 'Tis Lady Amelia. I have come to release you."*

Guy: *"Do I know you?"*

Amy: *"Nay. I am a prisoner here too, and have been looking for a way to escape. Mayhap together we can find a way to free ourselves. If I let you out, will you help me?"*

Guy: *"I will pledge myself as your champion if you will release me from my prison."* Is that what he would say?

Amy: *That's exactly what a valiant knight would say. So she opens the door and sees her knight for the first time. He is tall and broad shouldered and looks very fierce standing there with his red tunic flowing over his chain mail. He wears the scars of many battles well on his rugged face.*

Guy: Why does he have to be scarred?

Amy: Because woman love scarred heroes. It brings out their nurturing side.

Guy: Is Lady Amelia frightened at what she sees?

Amy: *Not at all. She is excited to see that he looks capable of handling himself in a fight. "Quickly,"* she tells him. *"We must hurry, while the witch's black knights are sleeping off too much ale in the great hall."*

Guy: *"I will need a weapon."*

Amy: *"I brought you a sword."*

Guy: Oh, I do love a woman who plans ahead.

Amy: *Lady Amelia is very smart and brave. "Follow me,"* she tells him. *"I will show you the way out."* They move quietly down the stone steps. When they reach the bottom, Amelia peeks out to be sure the drunken knights are still sleeping. She sees them lying on their pallets snoring, and motions Sir Guy to follow her. They make their way around the edge of the room, stepping over the sleeping men, moving toward the door to the bailey. Are they going to make it?

Guy: *Alas, no. Lady Amelia steps on a bone that was tossed on the floor. It snaps beneath her foot, and the sound is like a loud crack in the quiet hall. How many knights does it wake?*

Amy: *None. Lady Amelia is so graceful, her dainty slipper wouldn't break a bone. It was Sir Guy's armor-clad foot. She holds her breath waiting for the great hall to erupt into action, but none of the knights even stir. Looking back she silently cautions Sir Guy to be careful.*

Guy: *The noise didn't wake a single knight for him to battle with his sword? How is he going to impress Lady Amelia like that?*

Amy: *Okay, the witch's beast of a dog, who is sleeping at the base of the steps to her tower, lifts his head and looks right at them. He growls ominously, his glowing yellow eyes narrowing to slits. And then he charges straight toward them, teeth gleaming as he bounds over the slumbering knights. What will they do?*

Guy: *"Get behind me!" Sir Guy shouts and takes a stance with feet braced and sword held in both hands, prepared to protect his lady. Please tell me Amelia obeys.*

Amy: *Of course not. Thinking quickly, Lady Amelia scoops up the meaty bone Guy stepped on. She waves the bone at the dog, then tosses it toward the far wall. Does the dog go after it?*

Guy: *Yes, but now the knights are all sitting up, looking about. They spot their two prisoners about to escape. Now does Sir Guy get to do something heroic?*

Amy: *Yes. "Run for the door," he shouts at Amelia as the black knights take up their swords. He follows her, fending off the knight. The sound of steel meeting steel fills the hall. Amelia is awed by her knight's skill and bravery as he fights them off one after the other, sometimes two or three at once. Finally they are out the door. They slam it shut. She turns to him, her heart racing. "What will we do? They'll be out the other door and after us in a thrice."*

Guy: *"We must get to the stables," he tells her. "Which way is it?"*

Amy: *"This way." Grabbing up her skirt, she races across the bailey with Sir Guy right beside her. Will they make it?*

Guy: *They do. Nice legs, by the way.*

Amy: *Sir Guy! I'm shocked. A knight wouldn't look at a lady's legs.*

Guy: *Wanna bet? A knight is a man, and a man is going to look. Inside, they find Sir Guy's great white steed. He saddles him quickly. "Get on," he tells her and takes her by the waist to toss her into the saddle. "Can milady ride?"*

Amy: *"Of course I can ride."*

Guy: *He swings up behind her. "Hold on. If we make it across the drawbridge, we are free." Trusting him completely, she puts her arms about him and holds on tight as they gallop out of the stables to find the bailey filled with black knights. "Do not be afraid," he tells her. "I will protect you."*

Amy: *"I am not afraid," she says and pulls a jeweled dagger from her belt. She knows it will do little good against trained warriors, but she would rather die than go back to being a prisoner. Sir Guy fights valiantly, but is his skill enough against so many?*

Guy: *Yes. They make it through the men and are charging toward the drawbridge. Will they make it across?*

Amy: *They fly under the portcullis with Amelia held safely against Guy's powerful chest, his strong arms about her. When suddenly he pulls up, making his great white steed rear and paw at the air. Amelia turns her head to see what has stopped them. The evil sorceress is standing*

*in the middle of the drawbridge, moonlight shining down
on her long black hair, her face too beautiful to be real.*

*"I will not let you escape me," she says in her frighten-
ing voice. She lifts her arms out to the side, then up
toward the moon. The sleeves of her black gown slip down
her white arms. A strange wind swirls around her, lifting
her hair. Summoning her powers, she turns from human
form into a dragon. How will Guy keep Amelia safe while
battling a giant winged beast such as this?*

Guy: *He draws back his sword and throws it at the
dragon's heart. Does it kill the beast?*

Amy: *Yes. It hits the dragon right in the heart. The
beast screams in agony, clutching at the sword hilt. Then
it tumbles sideways into the moat with a hiss of steam.
Guy cradles Amelia against him as they canter off across
the moonlit countryside toward the kingdom where he
lives. And they live happily ever after.*

Guy: *That's the end of the story?*

Amy thought for a minute. She didn't want to end
the story, but didn't know where else to take it.
Christine's suggestion about cybersex popped into
her mind and made her blush. She would never have
the guts to even suggest something like that, much
less do it, but she did feel comfortable enough with
Guy to at least joke about it: *Well, that depends on if
we're writing a children's fairy tale or a romance novel.
I'm afraid I have no experience with the latter.*

Guy: *Have you ever tried?*

Amy: *I have, but I guess I'm as hopeless at dating in
fiction as I am in real life. I always freeze up when it
comes to the "you know" scenes.*

Several seconds passed before Guy responded: *Is
that why you don't like dating?*

Amy: I was talking about writing.

Guy: Are you sure? I'm not asking you to get specific or anything, but I've been very baffled by your decision not to marry. You seem like someone who would enjoy having a family and you've talked about how much you'd like children.

Amy debated what to say. How much could she open up to him? Biting her lip, she typed: *Okay, I'll confess, I don't enjoy the "you know" scenes in real life either. I find it all embarrassing and awkward.*

The instant she hit send, she regretted what she'd said and sent off another message as fast as she could: *I'm sorry, that was a completely inappropriate thing to confess. Please forget it. Please.*

Guy: After this past week, I like to think we've become friends. If you can't discuss something like this with a friend, who can you talk to?

Amy: I don't think sex is an appropriate thing at all for us to discuss.

Guy: Ah, but that's the beauty of cyberspace. People can talk about a lot of things here they'd never discuss in person.

Amy: If I can't even talk to Maddy and Christine about how I feel on the subject, how on earth can I discuss this with a man?

Guy: Maybe that's exactly who you need to discuss it with. I'm not trying to pry. I guess it's like the clothes—you have so much to offer, I hate to see you hiding yourself away from the world. Away from life. So, if you want to talk about this, I'll be happy to listen.

Amy wondered if she could do that, then realized how badly she needed to talk to someone: *The prob-*

lem is, I'm not sure how to talk about it without completely embarrassing myself.

Guy: *Okay, let me ask, are the two related? Do you dislike dating for the same reason you wore baggy clothes?*

Amy: *Yes, exactly. Whenever a man is touching me, I'm so aware of every bulge on my body, it's all I can think about.*

Guy: *And that right here is why I'd like to go out and burn every "beauty" magazine ever published. I grew up in that world, and I hate it more than I can say. I've spent my life watching beautiful women starve themselves because that's what they had to do to stay employed. On top of that, the photos of those emaciated models are airbrushed, which presents an unrealistic ideal to women, telling them what they have to look like to be beautiful.*

If there was one thing I could tell the women of the world it's that men don't care about skinny. When we're in bed with a woman, we're not thinking, "She has a little extra bulge here." Nor are we thinking, "I do believe her thighs are larger than a supermodel's. Let me go get the latest issue of Cosmo and compare." Women are the most incredible, beautiful, sexy things in the world, in all your fabulous sizes and shapes. And I wish more than anything I could convince you of that.

Amy: *I would like to believe it, but it's hard when we're constantly bombarded with images of what we should look like.*

Guy: *I know. But after getting to know you, I think you're smart enough to reject that nonsense and brave enough to take a more objective look at your body and accept it as something to be proud of. Something to enjoy. I'm not saying it will be easy after a lifetime of being self-*

conscious, but look at everything else you've conquered. I think you can do anything you set your mind to.

Amy sat back against the headboard after reading Guy's message. He'd just obliterated all her hesitancy to meet him face-to-face. She realized just how much her distaste of dating in general, but meeting him in particular, was fear. Not because of what *he* looked like. But because of what *she* looked like.

She placed her trembling fingers on the keyboard: *Thank you for that. You've helped me a lot these last days to feel differently about myself, but that helps most of all. I would like to return the favor and I don't think we can do that by talking like this. I want to meet you. In person.*

Guy: *No.*

Amy: *Yes. I know you're uncomfortable with letting people see you, but it'll be all right. Tomorrow night, I want to have dinner with you. Face-to-face.*

Guy: *Absolutely not!*

Amy: *If I can be brave enough to go clothes shopping with a man and discuss how I feel about sex, you can be brave enough to have dinner with me. I'll see you tomorrow evening.*

She snapped her laptop closed before he could answer. Excitment tugged at her lips even as nerves danced in her belly.

Chapter 11

Nothing is ever as easy as we hope it will be.
—How to Have a Perfect Life

Amy wanted to meet him. The thought had Byron in a panic as he paced before the monitors wondering what to do. The screen for the kitchen remained off, but he knew she'd be appearing on the others soon, bringing his breakfast.

What was he going to say to her?

He couldn't meet her. She'd freak.

She thought he was a lonely, scarred recluse hiding in a tower, ashamed of how he looked. How would she react when she discovered he was Byron Parks, the bored billionaire, hiding from his meaningless life?

He realized suddenly he'd give up all his looks if he could be the man Amy thought he was. If he could step out of the tower that evening and have her smile and assure him his appearance didn't matter. If he could take her into his arms and kiss her, the way he'd wanted to for days. If he could take her upstairs and make love to her all night.

That fantasy brought him up short.

What was he thinking?

Amy wanting to "meet" him didn't mean she wanted to become physically involved with him. Just because they'd been discussing sex right before she'd dropped her bomb didn't necessarily mean she wanted to meet him *that* way. Kind, compassionate Amy simply wanted to draw out the lonely man living in the tower.

Okay, that settled his swirling thoughts some. Nothing to panic over. When she brought his breakfast, he'd simply tell her no. She couldn't make him reveal himself. And while he didn't mean to hide his identity forever, he could certainly keep up the game for the three weeks she'd be around.

"Good morning," she said brightly. He whirled toward the monitors and realized she'd snuck up on him. She was already in the office below, carrying his tray to the dumbwaiter. From the color staining her cheeks, he knew the cheer in her voice was hiding a lot of nervousness. "Did you manage to get some sleep last night?"

Not a bit, he wanted to tell her.

"Are you there?" she asked when he didn't respond.

"I'm here." He saw the tray arrive on his level but made no move to retrieve it. Instead, he stayed before the monitor, riveted by her image.

"I'm glad," she said. Wearing one of her sundresses, she stepped back to smile at the camera. The dress emphasized the fullness of her breasts, the dip of her waist, the roundness of her hips. His hands ached to explore those curves. "I want to thank you again for talking to me last night. As I'm sure you noticed, that is not a comfortable subject for me, but

I'm glad you encouraged me to share how I feel. You can be very determined when you set your mind to helping me with my hang-ups.

"So I've decided to give you fair warning that I mean to be just as determined to help you. I realize you're nervous about tonight, but don't be. I truly don't care what you look like. And once you've let me see you, I think you'll be glad you did. Facing your fears, and winning, really is one of the best feelings in the world."

"Amy . . ." He sighed. "I cannot let you see me."

"Yes you can." She beamed at him. "I promise, it will be all right."

"You don't know me, Amy. I promise, you wouldn't like me if you did."

"But I already do," she insisted in earnest. "Just because I've never seen you, doesn't mean I don't know you. I know you're honest, and caring, and passionate about a lot of things. I feel comfortable with you in a way I've never been with another man. You said yourself that we're friends. So as your friend, I'm asking you to trust me, to be brave enough to do this."

He felt his earlier panic return. He had to talk her out of this, convince her it was a bad idea. "What if I told you that if we meet, I might want to be more than friends?" *There*, he thought. That ought to scare her out of this notion of meeting him. "I'm attracted to you, Amy," he added for good measure. "Very attracted."

He expected her to blanche at those words. Instead, her cheeks went crimson and she ducked her face to hide a smile. "I know."

What? He stared at her, knocked speechless.

She sent the camera a shy look that did nothing to hide the strength of her will. "I'm not promising anything. We haven't even met, really, so who knows how we'll react to each other in person. All I'm saying is you make me feel different about myself. And I think, with you, I can be different. But neither of us will ever know if you don't unlock that door and step through it. Let me meet you, Guy. Please."

He looked at her and wished with all his heart that he could be the man she thought he was. A gangly stork or hulking beast. Anyone but who he was: lethally attractive on the outside, ugly on the inside. "I can't. Amy, I would terrify you."

"You won't." Her chin went up, and he realized his mistake. Amy was always bravest when fighting for others. Trying to scare her off would only make her more determined. "I'm braver than you think. And a little bit insulted that you doubt that. I won't push you right now, though, because I know you're frightened. I'll give you today to build up your courage. Then, tonight, we will have dinner together."

"No."

Her face took on a mutinous frown. "We will," she said and, turning on her heels, marched out of the room.

He stood there, completely dumbfounded. So much for thinking she didn't want to meet him *that* way. He thought of what she'd confessed last night. And what she'd said just now. *I think, with you, I can be different.*

He couldn't even imagine the courage she'd needed to voice that. To basically offer herself to a man she thought was hideous. Although maybe it wasn't courage alone. Maybe she simply felt that comfortable with Guy.

If only he was the man she thought he was. Then he could welcome her into his bed and introduce her to physical pleasure. He knew he could. As more than one woman had pointed out, he was good in bed. It was out of bed where he disappointed woman time after time.

What would making love be like with Amy?

His whole body came alive at the thought, not just with physical lust but with a rush of longing, an overwhelming need like nothing he'd ever felt before.

He tried to push it aside, but the rejuvenated part of him latched on to the idea of making love to Amy and refused to let go. And with that idea came another. What if he could be the man she thought he was? He wasn't physically ugly, and he wasn't a recluse—well, not normally—but what if the man he was during all those suppers together was the real him?

He realized then how little desire he had to go back to playing the bored, cynical Byron Parks. Did he have the courage, though, to let the world see that he did care about things? That, in fact, he cared a great deal about a lot of things? He remembered Chad's reaction. If he went back to Hollywood and acted the way he was around Amy, quite a few people would laugh their asses off. After all the years of Byron Parks sneering at the bleeding hearts of the world, he suddenly becomes one?

What if he didn't go back to Hollywood?

He nixed that idea. He couldn't hide out on St. Barts forever. Sooner or later the world would figure out his hiding place. Besides, he wasn't going to spend the rest of his life disguising himself as Beaufort. The plan had always been a temporary one. He just hadn't decided yet how temporary.

Maybe it was time to come out of hiding.

That thought sent another streak of terror through him. Was he ready? And how would Amy react?

He turned those two questions over in his mind as he donned Beaufort's disguise. Reaching a decision by nightfall seemed far-fetched, but he'd have today to think about it.

Dressed, he took the spiral steps down to the door in the outer wall, then followed the path to the courtyard so if Amy happened to be standing at the sink, she'd see Lance Beaufort arriving as if from town.

He marveled at how much the landscape crew had accomplished. Standing in the courtyard, he could see most of the ground floor, with dozens of doors leading into the old storerooms, the stables, the prison in the base of the tower. He remembered Amy's comment about how well suited the place was for parties.

She was right. If he finished out all three floors, the fort would house lots of overnight guests. When he did come out of hiding, he could invite the people he actually liked to come stay, not for any of the lavish, free-for-all type parties he'd thrown at his house in Hollywood Hills, but quieter, more relaxed dinners and days of sitting by the pool. He imagined Amy cooking and being by his side as they entertained together.

He stopped, jolted by his own thoughts. What the hell was he doing? He was planning a future—a radically different one from his past—with Amy smack dab in the middle of it. Without any clue how to tell her who he was. Or how she'd react to the fact that he'd lied to her. That he wasn't who she thought. And even if he made St. Barts his new main residence, he'd still have to go back to Hollywood on fairly regular basis. His life came with a whole circle of celebrities attached and the paparazzi never far behind. If Byron Parks married Amy Baker, the tabloids would eat her alive.

Married? Where had that word come from?

Was he insane? He wasn't remotely good enough for her. Besides, the only thing his parents had taught him about marriage was: be sure you hire a good divorce lawyer. Well, that and do it on a lark. His eighty-six-year-old father was on wife number five and had a toddler, for Christ's sake. And his mother had recently ditched husband number three, who was connected to the Saudi royal family in some obscure way Byron had never quite figured out. Not that he'd had time to figure it out.

He had half siblings who ranged from twenty-five years older to thirty-two years younger. The only one he got along with was Mia, his father's daughter from wife number two. Oh, yeah, Christmas at the Parks' house in Beverly Hills was always loads of fun. Amy would fit right in and feel perfectly at home. He snorted aloud at the thought.

"Lance?"

He looked up to see Amy standing on the gallery outside the kitchen, waving at him. The morning sun shone off her long, tumbling hair. Good God, she took his breath away.

"Good morning," she said with a cheerful smile. "Are you going back to town for anything today?"

His dazed brain took a moment to process the question. "I can. Do you need something?"

"Just a few things from the market, if you don't mind."

He reminded himself to speak as Beaufort, something he was finding more difficult every day. This morning, in particular, he wanted to stop pretending and simply talk to her as himself. "I am most happy to."

"Great." She beamed. "I'll make a list. You can pick it up before you go."

He checked his watch and decided to go immediately. He needed to be back before she delivered his two lunches. His presence as Beaufort was the only thing that kept her from talking to Gaspar. If she did that when he wasn't there to answer back, Lord only knew what she'd think.

After picking up the list—which meant being in the same room with Amy, acting as if everything inside him wasn't going haywire—he headed into town, his mind still whirling with thousands of questions.

There had to be a way to test the waters before he dove in and revealed who he was. He needed some clue as to how she'd react.

The answer, ironically, came to him in one of his least favorite places on earth: the grocery story checkout line.

There on the stands were a few remaining issues

of last week's *Globe*, with his picture on the cover and the claim that he'd been spotted in Paris. Perfect. The grainy photo showed only part of his face, so—despite his paranoia the day she'd arrived—he didn't think she'd be able to look at it, then him, and notice too many similarities. It would, however, give him an opening to discuss what she'd be in for if they became involved.

He dropped the tabloid into his basket and headed back to the fort.

Amy jumped when she heard Lance enter the back hall from the carport. Heat flooded her cheeks at having him walk in while she fantasized about what might happen with Guy. She couldn't believe how bold she'd been with him that morning. For tonight, all she wanted was for them to get past the hurdle of him letting her see his face. How things progressed from there . . . ? The possibilities had her struggling between impish grins and fits of nervousness.

"That was fast," she said as Lance entered the kitchen.

"I did not want to miss lunch." He looked tanned, windblown, and sexy, the way he always did. She realized that at some point during the last week, she'd stopped noticing how gorgeous he was. Or at least quit letting it fluster her as much. Maybe birthmarks and deformities weren't the only things people got used to with time.

He set the bags on the counter. "I find everything you ask for."

"Did they have any mangoes that looked ripe?"

"How is this?" He held the ruby-and-amber-skinned fruit out to her.

She took it from him and tested it for softness. "Just right."

"I, uhm, I also get you this." He reached into one of the bags and pulled out a tabloid. "I notice you showed interest your first day, so I thought to get one for you."

"Oh, I was only mildly curious." She laughed as she took the mango to the sink. Her interest had only been over why a man like Lance would read a scandal rag. "I never read those things."

"You do not?"

"No." As she peeled the fruit, she gazed out the window toward the tower. Would Guy find the courage to let her see him? And if so, what would happen between them? The thought had another of those grins sneaking up on her.

"Why not?"

"Hmm?" She glanced over her shoulder to find Lance still standing by the counter, looking oddly tense.

"The tabloids." He nodded to where he'd lain it beside the grocery bags. "Why do you not read them?"

She shrugged as she cut up the slippery orange fruit into a bowl. "I've never had much interest in the lives of celebrities. Maybe that's odd, since I've actually met quite a few through my Traveling Nannies work. Although I think the celebrities who choose to live in Austin are probably a little different than the ones who live in Hollywood."

"Why do you say that?"

"Well, Austin is very laid-back, even if it is being touted as the 'New Hollywood.' And we've always had a ton of musicians living there. But it's still different from LA. Those celebrities seem so over the top to me. The extravagant lifestyles, the obsession with beauty and money, the outrageous behavior. It's amusing sometimes, but mostly it's disturbing."

"Disturbing?"

"The affairs. The overindulgence." She sucked the sweet, sticky juice from her fingers before washing her hands. "On the other end of that, I feel uncomfortable invading people's privacy. Especially after knowing a few celebrities. How do people put up with having their picture taken every time they go someplace?" Carrying the bowl of mango to the center island, she arranged the pieces to top a green salad with coconut-battered shrimp. "If there's one thing I hate more than clothes shopping, it's having my picture taken. Of course, I don't look like a movie star. Maybe I'd feel differently if I did."

"*Oui*. A lot of them, the movie stars, they court the press. To stay in the public eye is good for their careers."

"Well, for me it would be like living in one of those nightmares we all have—where you realize you're naked in public. Only without any hope of waking up. Totally horrifying." She shuddered.

Lance stared at her with an oddly blank expression, then looked back at the tabloid. "Not everyone courts it. I think there must be ways to avoid it if you try."

"Oh, yes, like this guy." Laughing, she leaned toward him to see the picture on the cover. It was the shot of Byron Parks, King Midas of the Movies, ducking away from a camera. "He's doing a great job of avoiding the press, isn't he?"

"Actually, he is. This is the only picture I see of him in a long time."

"Only because he's been driven into hiding by the paparazzi." Retrieving the green onions and a bundle of cilantro from the bag, she set to work making the mango-and-lime vinaigrette dressing. "A few months ago, you couldn't go to the grocery store without seeing another picture of him and that new star who's so popular, Gillian Moore. I admit, I feel sorry for him, though. All those awful photos of her slapping his face. How embarrassing must that be? But there's part of me that thinks he probably deserved it."

"Why do you say that?"

"I don't know." She shrugged. "Maybe because she came off as really sweet in the TV interview I saw."

"She may not be that way in real life," Lance said, his expression growing dark.

"Maybe not." She whisked oil into the dressing. "Mostly, though, there's just something about him that bother's me."

"What is that?"

"He's an excellent example of that extravagant lifestyle I mentioned, the son of one of the wealthiest, most powerful men in Hollywood. He's gorgeous. He's rich. He's always jetting all over the world, dating beautiful women, hanging out with celebrities, attending fabulous parties, but he doesn't look like he appreciates any of it." She tasted the dressing,

found it too bland and added more cilantro. "So
when someone as happy and fresh looking as Gillian
Moore started hanging off his arm, I thought,
'Honey, you are just asking to get hurt.'"

"Why do you think this? As you say, he has
money and connections in Hollywood. This is what
she want. Maybe he is the one who is hurt."

"Are you saying you think he actually loved her?"

"*Non*. I only say, maybe she get what she want
from being with him."

"Ah." Amy smiled. "But that's the difference between her and me. She wants fame, and I don't. I
shudder at the thought of that much public attention."

"So, you are saying you would not date him?"

"Date Byron Parks?" She laughed at the mere idea
of it. "Not for all the money in the world! And not
just because he seems shallow and jaded, but because
I would hate that whole lifestyle."

"I see," Lance said in a clipped voice. He stood
staring at the tabloid a long time, then carried it over
to the trash can and threw it away.

"Why did you do that?" she asked in surprise.

"You do not like them."

"Well, that doesn't mean you can't read it."

"It has no interest to me."

She puzzled over his odd mood, wondering if
something had happened in town to upset him. Not
wanting to pry, she turned her thoughts back to the
coming night, wondering if Guy would find the courage to let her see him. He let Lance see him; why
not her? Of course she hoped to do more than "see"
him. Eventually. She blushed at her own thoughts

but assured herself they'd take things as slowly as they needed to, for both their comfort's sake. Seeing him, though, was the first step.

"Lance?" she said hesitantly as she arranged the two lunches on the tray. "May I ask you something?"

"*Oui.*" He remained by the trash can, facing away from her.

"It's about Guy—I mean, Mr. Gaspar." A tingle moved through her just saying his name.

He sent her a wary look. "What do you wish to know?"

She debated what to say since she didn't want Lance to suspect there was anything going on between her and their employer. Actually, there wasn't. Yet. "When you first hired me, you said that, in time, Mr. Gaspar might feel comfortable enough to let me see him. I hate that he feels he has to hide from me, that my presence makes him a prisoner of the tower when he doesn't need to be. I've tried to assure him I don't care what he looks like, but I'm afraid he doesn't believe me. So I was wondering, can you give me any advice on how I can convince him?"

"No."

"No? That's it?" She scowled at him. "You can't tell me anything?"

"I can tell you only that you should not try."

"Why not?"

"Amy . . ." Byron's jaw worked as he considered what to say, but the disappointment crushing his chest made breathing difficult, much less thinking. He looked at her standing there in the sun-filled kitchen. What had she called Gillian? Happy and

fresh? With Gillian that had been an illusion. With
Amy it described her very essence. He took a painful
breath and closed his eyes. *Speak as Lance*, he reminded himself. "I suspect these last days that you
have developed the tender feelings for Guy Gaspar.
Do not. He is not the man for you."

"Why not?" Her voice turned as fierce as a mother
bear. "Because *you* find him repulsive?"

"I am not the only one," he said as ominously as
he could. "I promise, if he reveal himself to you, you
would not like what you see. Do not pressure him
to show his face. He will not."

"But you said he would eventually. When he became comfortable around me."

"He has changed his mind."

"When?" Her hands went to her hips.

"This morning."

"He told you that?"

"He did."

"Well, I like that!" She grabbed a dishcloth and
began wiping down the counter in angry swipes.

He felt the hurt coming off of her in waves and
fought the urge to go to her. To hold her. But he
couldn't even if she would let him. He didn't dare
touch her. "Amy . . ." He turned to lean the small
of his back against the counter, struggled for the right
words, to make her understand even as he struggled
to accept. *Date Byron Parks? Not for all the money in
the world!* He gripped the counter to either side of
his hips. "You must leave Gaspar alone. I tell you
this not only for you, but for him. I do not think . . ."
Jesus, how could he explain this? The pain of it tore

him in two. "I do not think he could stop himself from falling in love with you. Has he not suffered enough for one life?"

That thought clearly hadn't occurred to her. Her shoulders sagged. "I don't want to do anything to hurt him."

He studied her noting the concern that lined her face. "I fear you have already hurt him some. Do not make it worse."

She remained still a long time. "Will you tell me, at least, why?" she asked. "Why does he hide his face? Is he scarred? Disfigured? What does he look like?"

"You do not want to know." He looked at the tray, desperate to escape. "If this is ready, I will take it."

"Yes. Fine. Take it." She waved a hand.

"Now you are angry."

"I don't know what I am." Crossing her arms she refused to look at him.

Resigned, he took the tray and left the room, aching with regret.

Chapter 12

The surest way to lose is to stop trying.
—*How to Have a Perfect Life*

That evening, Amy stomped into the office and slammed the food tray into the dumbwaiter.

"I have something to say to you," she announced as she worked the ropes. When the dumbwaiter reached the top, she stepped back and faced the camera. "I have shared things with you that I've never shared with anyone. I've talked to you about my weight, about my grandmother, how I feel about men—and you don't even have the courage to let me see your face? In my book, that makes you a coward. And I don't have supper with cowards. So until you're ready to open that door and let us sit in the same room while we eat, I won't be having supper with you. I'll be your housekeeper, but not your friend."

With that she turned and strode from the room, head high, expecting him to call her back. He didn't. How disappointing. After gearing herself up for a confrontation, she felt a bit deflated to have it over and done with so quickly.

With anger and hurt still simmering inside her, she

returned to the kitchen and cleaned with a vengeance, enjoying the loud bang of pots and pans. Eventually every surface sparkled and gleamed. She looked about the cheerful kitchen she'd grown to love and realized she had nothing more to do but go to bed.

She poured herself a large glass of wine, hoping it would help her sleep. Climbing into bed, she closed the netting about her and stared at her laptop. Christine was frequently up at this late hour and would provide a good venting buddy, but what if she opened the computer and Guy sent a message?

Well, then, she'd be able to rail at him more. As angry as she was, her stomach still clenched at the thought. She hated confrontation and would usually do anything to smooth things over so everyone was happy.

Taking a sip of wine, she realized anger wasn't the only thing pumping through her system. All day she'd been thinking about his admission that he desired her, and where that might lead. She hadn't expected him to open the door and them to throw themselves at each other in instant passion, but she had hoped that tonight they might take a tentative step or two in that direction, moving at a pace that was comfortable for both of them.

After her confession, he knew she wasn't technically a virgin, but that she found sex embarrassing. With him, though, she really did think maybe it could be different. He hadn't seemed the least bit shy about it. In fact, he'd seemed to possess a kind of confidence and knowledge she found baffling for a man who hid himself from the world.

Although talking about sex and having it were two different things. Like reading about it in a romance novel, where it was always hot and wild and fulfilling.

Why couldn't sex in real life be the way it was in novels? Where women saw fireworks every time. Frankly, she thought female orgasms were a myth invented by bragging men. Since women didn't want to admit they were the only ones missing out, they faked a climax even to themselves. All she wanted was the kind of sex where two people were totally comfortable together. Maybe that only existed in books too.

She sipped more wine, considering. She remembered Guy asking if she'd ever written anything like that, and she'd confessed that she hadn't. Good grief, she really did feel as awkward about sex in the imaginary world as she did in the real one. Well, she might not be dispelling any of that awkwardness in real life tonight, but maybe she could find the courage to overcome her shyness in the imaginary one. A little thrill went through her at the thought. In stories, she could be anything she wanted—not just physically, but in personality too. So why not a bold temptress?

Just tipsy enough to give it a try, she opened the laptop—and found a message from Guy: *Amy, I'm sorry if my decision upsets you, but I think you're right. Keeping our relationship on a strictly impersonal basis is for the best. I want you to know though, that I will miss your company in the evenings.*

Amy made a face at the screen and typed: *Fine.*

Closing the window, she opened the word processing software. Staring at the blank page, she considered how to begin. Just how wild and explicit did she want to get?

A message from Guy popped up: *I was beginning to think you wouldn't respond. I'm glad you did. Even if we won't be sharing meals anymore, I don't want things to be uncomfortable between us.*

Amy: *Too late.*

Guy: *I hope after you've had time to calm down, you'll feel differently.*

Amy: *Go away. I'm not online to talk to you.*

Guy: *Very well. Good night, then.*

With an irritated punch, she closed the message window. Now for her story. She thought of the story she and Guy had made up last night and how it had ended so chastely. A wicked grin pulled at her lips. Oh, wouldn't that be just deserts to write a very different end. One where she could have her way with Sir Guy. She might not be able to control anything in real life, but here in the fantasy world she could have people do anything she wanted.

Sipping more wine, she began to type. The words flowed with surprising ease. After riding away from the castle of the evil witch, they entered an enchanted wood. Sir Guy reined to a halt beside a lake where moonlight glimmered on the dark waters.

He slid from the horse and held his arms up to assist Lady Amelia. His strong hands slipped around her waist and he lifted her from the saddle with surprising ease. Her body slid down the full length of his as he lowered her to the ground.

Few words were exchanged before they were kissing, their hands exploring freely as their mouths mated in a ravenous dance. Amy's own body responded to the embrace she described. She imagined Guy, the Guy she had begun to picture in her mind, holding the real her.

He was a big man, as tall and broad shouldered as Lance, but not as trim through the stomach and hips. Few men were that fit. He had strong hands that touched her without hesitation, stirring responses she'd never felt before. Rather than shrinking from his touch, she offered herself to him, touching him back.

Their clothes dissolved magically and she ran her hands over his body, her touch making him shudder with need. When he lowered her to the cape he'd spread there by moonlit lake, she opened her arms to him, inviting. He came down beside her, hovering over her. Shadows made his face vague, but with her fingertips she traced his strong features, felt his lips move in a smile. "I would have you, milady," he said in a voice gone rough with need.

"Yes," she answered back and welcomed his weight as he covered her.

Amy stopped to pluck at her silk nightie, her body flushed with heat. Oh, heavens, imaginary sex was a lot better than the real thing. She reached for her wineglass and found it empty. Deciding to indulge in a second glass, she hurried to the kitchen, then, on impulse, grabbed the whole bottle. Scrambling back onto the bed, she considered what she had written so far. Would a knight really be so aggressive with a lady? And would a lady respond so boldly, especially her first time? Lady Amelia was, of course, a virgin, being trapped all those years in the evil castle.

Amy laughed and decided, *To heck with realism and political correctness!* She needed a bit more wine, though, to actually write what would come next. The scene quickly drew her back in. She felt the weight of a hard male body as Sir Guy settled over her, pressing her into the bed of grass beneath the cape. She cupped his strong face, caressing it with fingertips as his thighs moved hers apart.

Her breath caught when his manhood pressed against her, begging entrance. "Do not be afraid."

"I am not." She lifted her hips in invitation. He answered it with a smooth, sure thrust that drove him to the hilt inside her. She cried out when he pierced her maidenhead. He held still, cradling her against his chest until her body adjusted to his. And when it did—

Amy's computer chimed, startling her so badly, she spilled wine down the front of her nightgown.

Wiping at it, she glared at the message from Guy that appeared on the screen: *Amy, please, if you're upset enough to still be up at this hour, talk to me.*

She glanced at the clock on her nightstand and realized quite a bit of time had passed. Writing about sex apparently took longer than having it. In a pique, she typed her response: *I'm not upset. Now go away.*

Guy: *If you're not upset, why are you still up?*

Amy: *If you must know, I'm having hot sex with Sir Guy. Just because I can't have a real love life I don't see any reason why Lady Amelia can't.*

Guy: *You're doing WHAT?*

Amy: *You heard me. What are you going to do? Tell me that because he has your name, I can't see him either?*

Guy: *I didn't say that. I'm just—I don't know what I am.*

Amy: *You're a coward and a jerk.*

Ignoring Guy, she went back to the scene. Sir Guy thrust hard and deep, and she responded with wild abandon. Their passion sent them rolling across the cape until she was straddling his hips. Smiling down at him, she told him how beautiful she found him. Caressing her full breasts with his battle-scarred hands, he told her the same.

Feeling glorious and free, she tossed back her head and let the moonlight bathe over her as she brought them both to a bright bursting pinnacle of pleasure that felt like flying out of her own body. When it passed, she floated down over his chest, where he wrapped his arms about her and cradled her to him.

There, she thought in satisfaction. She'd written her first fictional love scene—and done a darn good job. That's how passion should be in books and in real life. Her breath had actually turned shallow, and a light sheen of sweat covered her body. Goaded by the devil that had been driving her all night, she opened an e-mail document and addressed it to Guy.

Subject: *From Lady Amelia.*

Message: *Care to read what you missed out on tonight?*

She attached the scene she'd just written, hit send—then gasped.

Horror struck fast.

Frantically, she tried to unsend the message. Nothing worked. Oh, God. Oh, God, what had she done? Hands shaking, she fired off a second e-mail begging him not to read the attachment. Covering her mouth with both hands, she stared at the screen wondering if she stood a chance of him honoring that.

About the same chance that a snowball had of surviving in hell.

With a moan, she snapped the laptop closed and covered her eyes. If ever there was a good moment for the floor to open up and her to fall though, this was definitely it. What had she done? And how on earth would she ever face Guy after this?

How on earth would Byron ever face Amy? He paced before the monitors the following morning, waiting for her to bring his breakfast. Should he lie and say he hadn't read the scene she'd sent?

He'd tried to resist. He really had. But after lying awake for an hour wondering what was in the file, curiosity got the better of him. What he'd read had completely stunned him. And aroused him beyond belief. Over the past few days, he'd imagined many times making love to Amy, but it had always been sweet and slow. Or fun and filled with laughter. He'd certainly never imagined anything that hot, desperate, and just a little bit rough.

Good God, hours had passed, the sun was up, and he was still hard with need. How was he supposed to resist her now? He wasn't sure he could be in the same room with her without breaking into a sweat. As Gaspar, he had the safety of a locked door to hide behind, and all he had to deal with was any awkwardness Amy felt. As if that would be a small feat, considering that things were already strained between them.

As Beaufort, though, he'd have to pretend he knew nothing about last night. He'd have to talk to her. Be around her. Act casual, when he wanted to jerk her into his arms and kiss her hard and long as they ripped each other's clothes off.

His groin tightened even more at the thought. Jesus, what a mess.

Sitting down with his head in his hands, he racked his brain for what to say as he waited for her to arrive with breakfast. And waited. And waited.

What if she felt so awkward that she refused to bring his breakfast?

That thought had him grabbing the remote control. He clicked on the monitor for the kitchen. She wasn't there. And the room showed no sign that she'd even started breakfast.

Panic seized him. What if she'd left? She could be at the airport even now trying to book a flight off the island. He donned his Beaufort disguise as quickly as possible and hurried to the kitchen.

"Amy?" he called. No answer came. He went to the door of her room and knocked. "Amy?"

He thought he heard a moan, then silence. "Amy?" He knocked again, then pressed an ear to the panel. "Are you all right?"

He heard another moan, then something fell. Terrified she was hurt he tried the knob and found it locked. To hell with it. He stepped back and kicked in the door.

The sound of Amy's scream drew his attention to the bed. Through the netting, he saw her sit bolt upright, then drop back to the pillows with both hands pressed to her forehead.

"Jesus, what's wrong?" He rushed over and whipped the netting aside, so worried he forgot to speak with an accent. "Are you sick? Are you hurt?"

"Please don't talk so loud," she whimpered.

Understanding dawned. She was hungover! He spotted an empty wine bottle that had fallen on the floor—which explained the thud he'd heard—and returned it to the nightstand where a tall glass sat next to a wineglass. He sniffed the melted ice and realized that at some point last night she'd switched to the rum punch she'd been learning how to make. Huge mistake. Rum hangovers were bad enough, but a rum-on-top-of-wine hangover? *Oh, Amy.* His heart melted on her behalf as he eased his weight onto the mattress. "Looks like you had a wild night."

"You have no idea," she moaned. "I was hoping I'd wake up dead."

"I am afraid you are only halfway dead."

"Are you sure?"

"Very." His gaze ran over her. The sheet had slipped to her waist, gifting him with the sight of her lying in bed in nightgown that looked like a white silk slip. Virginal and sexy. Just what he needed: one more visual to add to the images already in his head. "Do you have aspirin?"

"No."

"Lie still. I will return."

He went back to the tower and retrieved a bottle of aspirin, then stopped in the kitchen for a large glass of water and an ice pack. When he returned, he found Amy gingerly crossing from the bathroom back to the bed. The silk nightgown barely came to the tops of her thighs. He stopped in his tracks, staring at her legs.

"Lance," she complained, drawing his name out to two syllables with her Texas drawl. "Do you mind? I'm half naked."

Not in my head, you're not, he thought, picturing her completely naked. Dismissing her modesty with a snort, he went to help her back into bed. "Some of your sundresses cover only a little more."

"I don't care. It's still different." Climbing onto the mattress, she pulled the sheet nearly to her chin. "I'm dealing with enough embarrassment as it is right now."

"Here. Take these." He handed her the aspirin. She downed them and the water in big gulps, draining the glass, then closed her eyes with a heavy sigh. "Better?" he asked.

"I'm not sure I'll ever be better."

Carefully, he brushed a curl off her forehead and tucked it into the mass of other curls. "The headache is this bad?"

"It's not just that." Tears leaked out as she squeezed her eyes tighter. "I did something really stupid last night. I'll never be able to face Guy again."

"Can you tell me?" He pressed the cloth-wrapped ice to her forehead. "Maybe it is not so bad."

"No, I can't tell you." She took over holding the ice pack. "And don't you dare ask him. Please. Promise me you won't ask him."

"I promise."

"And that you won't tell him about this." She

looked over at the door. "I can't believe you did that."

"I will fix it and no one but you and me will know."

She burst unexpectedly into tears. "Oh, God, I want to go home! I know I promised I'd stay until my friends' bridal shower, but I can't. I just can't! *I want to go home!*"

"Shh, shh." Unable to stop himself, he pulled her into his arms and gave thanks when she let him. He held her close as she cried against his chest. "Whatever happened, it cannot be so bad."

"You have no idea." She relaxed against him, their bodies melding together.

He closed his eyes to revel in the chance to hold her, to touch her. His palms made circles on her back as he breathed in her scent. "When you feel better, maybe it is even a little funny."

A choked laugh escaped her. "Trust me, this will never be funny. My only hope of living past the embarrassment is to get as far away from St. Barts as I can." She sat back and wiped her cheeks. "And the minute I'm home, I'm going to visit a hypnotist and have last night erased from my brain."

"Nothing can be so bad. Nothing." His arms felt empty, but he let her lean back against the headboard. "Talk to Gaspar about whatever happened. I am sure he will say for you to feel no embarrassment."

"I can't. I just want to go home."

"You would break your word and leave early?"

"I can't stay here." She reached for his hand and squeezed it. "Will you take me to the airport?"

He hesitated, not sure what to do. Finally he took a deep breath. "I will make with you a bargain."

"Not another bargain," she moaned, pressing the ice back to her forehead.

"Do not make a decision today. Take today off and sleep to help you feel better." He tucked another curl behind her ear. "I will take care of Gaspar. Tomorrow, if you still wish to run away, we will talk."

"Did you have to say it that way?"

"You do not strike me as the coward."

She made a sour face.

"You will wait until tomorrow to decide?"

"Yes, I'll wait."

"*Bon*. Then I will leave you to rest." He rose and went toward the door. It hung by one hinge, and the jam had splintered.

"Lance," she called as he struggled with the door.

"*Oui?*" He looked at her.

"Thank you." Tears welled in her eyes, making him want to go back and hold her again.

Instead he nodded and propped the door closed. His heart sank at the thought of Amy leaving—but maybe it was for the best. Every day he fell a little more in love with her, yet she'd made it clear she didn't want anything to do with the real him. If watching her go now was this hard, how much harder would it be in three weeks?

Yes, letting her go now would be best for both of them. He only hoped he could find a way to lessen her embarrassment first. He wanted her to remember her time with him fondly, not cringe every time she looked back.

*   *   *

By late afternoon Amy felt human again. She'd slept all morning, then ate the soup Lance heated up her for lunch. It was the perfect meal for an uneasy stomach. After that, she'd pampered herself with a long shower and a mini facial with the creams from the salon. Ending the routine by painting her toenails reminded her of her friends and the "girlfriend days" they'd shared, sometimes just for fun, other times to soften the punches life could throw.

Noticing the time, she debated e-mailing her friends. This was the hour they always set aside for each other. But what if Gaspar tried to send her a message? She really wasn't ready to face him. She needed her friends, though, more than she feared running into him.

Opening the laptop, she found both Maddy and Christine already online and discussing plans for the wedding. Or rather their fiancés' plans for the wedding. A few months ago, Maddy's fiancé, Joe, had become impatient with her lack of progress and had taken over everything. When Christine became engaged, Joe was the one to suggest a double wedding. So now he and Alec were planning it together. Apparently the men were doing a great job and were becoming good friends through the process.

They'd decided on an outdoor wedding at the Wildflower Center in Austin, ordered the invitations, hired a decorator and a caterer, even settled on birdseed instead of rice at the end. The women had been told to stay out of it. All they had to do was buy their dresses and show up for the ceremony. Maddy and Christine found the whole thing vastly amusing.

Somehow Amy built up the courage to interrupt their happy chatter and tell them what she'd done.

Christine was the first to respond: *Oh, Amy, please don't hit me for laughing, but that is kind of funny. Ouch, though, honey. You have my complete sympathy.*

Maddy: *I agree with C. Funny, but painful. What are you going to say to Guy?*

Amy: *Nothing, I hope. I just want to go home. I've been here long enough to fulfill my challenge, so I don't have to stay.*

Maddy: *Wait a second. Back up. Are you saying you're going to run out on Guy without even talking to him? What about the deal you made with him to stay the full four weeks?*

Amy: *I know it's cowardly, but I just can't face him. And I met my challenge.*

Maddy: *Yes, you did. However, let me remind you that when I had to gut it up and talk to Joe, neither of you let me off the hook that easily. You made me face him. I think you owe it to yourself to face Guy. Well, in a manner of speaking, since he won't let you see his face.*

Amy: *But this is different. You were in love with Joe.*

Maddy: *Are you saying you're not a little bit in love with Guy? What happened to all the gushing about how wonderful he is? Amy, when it comes to things you think are worth fighting for, you're one of the strongest women I know. Are you really going to give up on Guy just because you're embarrassed about last night?*

Amy: *Try mortified!*

Christine: *I hate to gang up on you, but I agree with Mad. This man could be The One. If you turn tail and run, you'll always wonder. Don't let feeling foolish hold you back from something that could change the rest of your life. Although, just for argument's sake, are you sure you don't want to reconsider Lance Beaufort? A gorgeous guy who kicks down doors to be sure you're okay, then brings you aspirin and water for your hangover? And fixes you lunch? This is my kind of guy!*

Amy: *Actually, he is very sweet, and I'd be lying if I said I don't find him attractive, but he doesn't tug at my heart the way Guy does.*

Christine: *Okay then, I have to go with Maddy all the way. I know I'm usually the cynical one, but I can honestly say there is nothing more powerful than finding the man who's right for you. Love really is the greatest thing in the world.*

Amy: *I think both of you are letting the prewedding bliss go to your head. Did you not read the part of my message that said Guy has made his not-seeing-him rule indefinite?*

Christine: *I don't know, after last night, he might have changed his mind! Just how hot was that scene you wrote?*

Amy: *It was so hot, I deleted it from my computer for fear the case would melt.*

Maddy: *Oh, yeah, he could definitely be changing his mind. I know it's hard, Amy, but my advice is that until you're sure he's not The One, fight harder. Don't give up, and don't give in.*

Amy: *Lord, you sound like Jane.*

Maddy: *Well, she did get some things right in her book. I still don't believe anyone can have a perfect life, but sometimes you can get pretty dang close. So, good luck. And report back.*

Amy made a face, thinking friends could be the

most wonderful thing in the world. But sometimes they could be a real pain in the behind.

They were right, though, dang it. This evening, she would find the courage to talk to Guy.

Chapter 13

Life is full of unexpected surprises that should be welcomed, not feared.

—*How to Have a Perfect Life*

Byron drew up short as he entered the kitchen that evening. He expected to find it empty. He expected to pass straight through to Amy's room and find her packing. Instead he found her standing at the sink chopping vegetables. She'd dressed in one of her short, sexy sundresses that showed off the deepening tan on her legs. The silver anklet with the butterfly charm drew his attention to her dainty bare feet with pink polish on her toes.

He snapped his attention away from the anklet, which always made him think about her tattoo. Or rather the location of her tattoo.

"What are you doing?" he asked a little too harshly.

She turned and smiled. The fading sunlight streaming through the window bathed her face and kissed her hair with touches of gold. "I'm fixing Guy's supper."

"There is no need." He approached her, keeping his gaze on what she was doing, rather than looking at her, afraid something in his eyes would give him away. "I tell you I take care of him."

"Yes, but it's time for you to leave for the day." She scooped carrots into a bowl. "Someone has to take his supper to him."

"I'll take something up before I leave." The thought of spending the evening alone in the tower, knowing this was Amy's last night on St. Barts, promised hours of agony. He'd get through it, though, and in the morning he'd take her to the airport and he'd watched her get on a plane and fly out of his life. "Here." He held out the envelope he'd brought with him. "Gaspar ask me to give you this."

"What is it?" A frown dimpled her brow as she wiped her hands on a dish towel.

"A letter."

"Oh, my God." Her eyes went huge. "Is he firing me?"

"No!" He jolted at that assumption. The letter was meant to make her feel better. Not frighten her. "I believe it is to tell you *au revoir*."

"Oh, thank goodness." She sagged with relief.

He watched her take it, praying he'd managed to word everything right. She stared at it but made no move to open it. "You do not read it?"

She bit her lip, debating, then shook her head. "I'll open it later." Her eyes filled with uncertainty. "Did he say anything about . . . last night?"

"No," he assured her, unable to stand the thought of her thinking two men had spent the day having a good chuckle over her getting drunk and e-mailing one of them a sex scene. A really erotic and intense sex scene that still had him aching with arousal.

Or maybe the heat coursing through him came from simply being in the same room with her, from seeing the way her long brown hair spiraled from the clip at the crown of her head down to her waist. He yearned to touch it, to bury his face in it as he had earlier that day. The memory of that would surely haunt him forever.

Looking away, he cleared his throat. "I tell him of your wish to go home. He is sad to hear this, but says he understands. Tomorrow I am to take you to the airport and buy you a ticket home."

"Well"—she took a deep, fortifying breath—"I appreciate the offer, but . . . I'm not going."

"*Pardon?*" He blinked.

"I changed my mind." She set the letter aside. "I'm not going."

He stared at her in disbelief. What did she mean, she'd changed her mind? She couldn't change her mind. He'd just spent a miserable day reconciling himself to letting her go when everything in him wanted to beg her to stay. He'd finally managed to harden his resolve—and she changes her mind?

No, no, no. She couldn't stay. He'd go insane.

When he just stood there, staring at her, her chin went up a notch. "I know you disapprove, but I am determined to draw Guy out. So, even though I told him I wouldn't, I'm going to have supper with him tonight, and every night, until he finally agrees to open that door and come out of the tower."

"He will not," he told her, and himself, firmly. "He will not let you see him. Ever."

"We'll just see about that." She gave a curt little nod and crossed to the refrigerator.

Byron stood there staring at her back while she gathered butter, eggs, and cream. He wanted to argue but couldn't find the words. He finally told her good night, that he'd see her in the morning, and left the kitchen in a daze.

What did he do now? He couldn't let her stay. He had a terrifying certainty that if she did, she'd succeed. She'd wear him down with that gentle determination of hers until he finally told her the truth. Then she'd hate him for deceiving her and reject him for who he was.

Far better to rip his heart out now and find a way to make her go. Even though . . . dear God, he wanted her to stay. He really, quite desperately wanted her to stay.

If Amy hadn't already changed her mind, the letter would have done it. Guy had written it by hand in a bold, slashing script that she found somehow elegant and aggressive at the same time. In it, he told her how much their dinner conversations had meant to him, how he would always remember her fondly, and how he wished that things could have been different. He seemed convinced, though, that letting her see him was a mistake.

As for last night, he begged her not to be embarrassed. Yes, he'd read the scene even though she'd asked him not to, but he refused to apologize. Instead he commended her on her talent with words. Then he said if he had but one wish, it would be the chance to live the scene out with her—but that was not to be. He ended by wishing her every happiness in life because he couldn't think of anyone more deserving.

She held the letter to her breast and blinked back

tears. Maddy and Christine were right. She needed to fight harder.

When she finished cooking, she dressed carefully in one of the longer dresses, a romantic floral print that flowed over her curves and draped nearly to her ankles. She willed the sun to set faster as she did her makeup and piled her hair up in back. When darkness fell over the world outside, she took up the tray with two dinners and a bottle of wine. Thank goodness she'd recovered enough to consider indulging again—albeit moderately.

Her stomach began to flutter as she walked through the dark rooms, her way lit only by the moonlight slanting in through the louvers. Lance had managed to finish the rooms during the last few days, armed with how-to books and a tool belt. She always found the beach bum carpenter an amusing contradiction.

Now the rooms stood empty, waiting to be filled with furniture. She wondered briefly if Guy would bother. Did he leave the tower at night while she slept and wander these empty rooms. Would he enjoy them when they were furnished? But enjoy them alone?

How sad, she thought, that he wouldn't fill the rooms with people, and laughter, and life. The thought strengthened her resolve.

Crossing the library, she found the door to Lance's office open only a crack. Darkness filled the room beyond. That hardly surprised her. Lance normally left the lamp on, but today he hadn't expected her to be bringing Guy's supper. She transferred the tray to one hand, balancing it as she entered and flipped the light switch. Nothing happened.

That was when she noticed the door to the tower. It stood wide open. Gaping black lay on the other side.

She went very still.

A finger of awareness brushed the back of her neck, raising the hairs on her arms. Someone else was in the room. She took a slow shuddering breath. "Guy?"

"I'm here." The smooth, masculine voice came from the depths of the room.

Tremors assailed her and she clutched the tray with both hands, afraid she'd drop it. As her eyes adjusted, she made out the shape of a man standing between the two windows, in the darkest part of the room. Her breath caught, in joy and in fear. She fought a sudden urge to run, even though she'd hoped and fought for this very moment. Now that it was here, she didn't know what to do.

"Don't come any closer," he said. "Please."

She managed a nod, knowing he could see her with the faint light from the library behind her. "All right."

"Lance told me that you've changed your mind about leaving."

"I have. I want to stay. I realized that running in embarrassment would make me a coward. I'm no coward, Guy."

"But as you pointed out last night, I am." She heard him take a deep breath, as if gathering courage. "I want you to go, Amy. I thought maybe if I told you in person, you'd believe me. We cannot have anything more than what we've already shared. Ever. When I invited you to eat with me, I never meant for things to go this way. I never meant for you to develop any kind of romantic notions about me. I don't even understand how that happened. Why would you think for even a moment that you would want to be with me?"

Her heart melted at the painful confusion she heard in his voice. "I already told you why. Because you are intelligent and caring, and I've never enjoyed talking to any man as much as I enjoy talking with you. You make me feel good about myself. And I want to do the same for you."

"I'm not the man you think I am."

"I know you're frightened. I'm frightened too. It's okay to be afraid." In saying it, she found the courage to move forward, to set the tray on the table. "But it's not okay to let fear hold us back."

"Amy, don't," he said when she started around the table toward him. "Stop!"

"No." Even with her heart racing, she continued until she stood a few feet in front of him. The pale light from the windows showed her nothing more than his outline. "It's dark enough in here that I can't see your face, but I want to touch you if you'll let me, just to be sure that you're real."

"I'm not."

"Let me . . ." She raised her hand and he shrank back against the wall, disappearing into darkness. "Please." She moved her hand closer and her fingertips met his palm. She gasped and nearly pulled back—but didn't. Bracing herself, she flattened her hand against his so they stood palms together for a moment. A smile blossomed inside her. "You are real."

"No."

"I was afraid I'd dreamed you up. A man who would find me beautiful. Who would make me feel beautiful." She let her fingers explore his. They were long and masculine and roughened by a callus or two. She hadn't expected that. Her touch moved to his palm, learning the contours. "A man who would make me feel sexy. And bold."

"Amy." His voice sounded strained. "Do you have any idea what you're doing to me?"

"Tell me." She struggled to see him and could make out the glint of his eyes.

The hand she touched closed about hers, clinging tightly. "I want you more than I have ever wanted anything in my life."

"Then let me turn on the light. Let me see you."

"No."

"All right. No light then. Only this." She raised her other hand until her fingertips found more skin. His cheek. He didn't pull away. He stood flattened against the wall, breathing shallowly as she learned his face.

With each touch, confusion grew. Where she expected to find scars or deformity, she found smooth skin, even cheeks and jaw, arched brows, a straight nose. Then her fingertips came to his lips and trembled against them as she felt his warm breath fan over her skin.

"Oh, Guy, you feel . . . beautiful."

"I'm not." His voice cracked, and she realized he was on the verge of tears. "I'm not, Amy."

"I don't care." Moving on instinct, she stepped forward and slipped her arms about his shoulders. He was as tall as she'd imagined, and solid. Laying her head on his chest she held him tightly. With their bodies pressed together, she absorbed more details. He wore a short-sleeved shirt but long trousers. He felt trimmer than she'd expected, and well-muscled. "I don't care what you look like."

His arms came around her in a fierce embrace. "I'm not good enough for you. You deserve so much better."

Lifting her head, she stared up into the glimmering eyes. Her heart beat so wildly, she could barely draw breath to speak. "But *you* are who I want."

"Then heaven help you." His mouth came down on hers in a hungry kiss that first startled, then excited her with its intensity. No shy, clumsy boy here, making her feel awkward, but a man who seemed desperate for her. She wound her arms about his neck and welcomed his greedy lips and demanding tongue. Her bones dissolved, making her cling to him for strength.

Her senses were reeling by the time he tore his mouth away and pressed his forehead to hers. "Oh, Amy, Amy, I want you so much I'm shaking."

"I want you too," she whispered and realized she meant it. Excitement coursed through her, making her yearn for things she'd always feared. "For the first time in my life, I actually want this."

"Listen to me, though." He cupped her face in

both his hand, and she knew enough of the moonlight hit her face to let him see the desire in her eyes.
"This is all I can give you. Pleasure in the dark. There
can never be more between us than this. But I promise you, I can give you pleasure."

She bit her lip, knowing she should say no. For his
sake, she should refuse him until he showed his face.
Letting him have her in the dark wouldn't help him
accept himself as he was. He wanted her, though. As
no man had ever wanted her. And he filled her with
heat and desire rather than embarrassed uncertainty.

Lifting a hand, she traced his lips. "Yes. I
understand."

"Then come." He stepped away from the wall.
Keeping one of her hands in his, he led her toward
the forbidden door into the tower.

That surprised her. What had she expected,
though? For him to make love to her in Lance's office? Trepidation fluttered through her as she wondered what she'd find in his private lair.

She could make out the shape of him as he crossed
the room. His clothes and hair appeared solid black.
He glanced back briefly over his shoulder, and the
moonlight teased her with a hint of a face that looked
as perfectly formed as it had felt. But light and
shadow could play tricks.

Then he drew her through the door and darkness
swallowed them.

"Be careful of the steps," he whispered.

She felt along the floor with her sandal until she
found the edge of the first stone step. He guided her
up the spiral staircase.

They passed an archway, and she glimpsed a room

beyond. Soft lights from an entertainment center revealed just enough for her to see it was a well-
furnished living room. So this was where he spent
his days. What little she saw looked both masculine
and elegant.

They continued up, through nearly pitch black. If
not for his hand on hers, she would have frozen in
fear. Finally they reached another archway and
passed through it. She reached out with her senses.
The space felt large and mostly open. Faint moonlight pressed through windows on three walls, giving
her hints of a dresser, a chair.

A bed.

The massive four-poster had the same sleek lines
as hers, but with larger proportions. The white netting gave off a bluish glow.

She stood staring at it, emotions warring inside
her.

Guy turned and cupped her face with his hands.
His thumbs stroked the corners of her mouth. "I have
dreamed of you here so many nights, I'm afraid I'll
wake and you'll be gone."

"I'm here." She tipped her face upward, almost
able to make him out. "And I'm really frightened."

He went very still. She felt him withdraw—not
physically—but somehow he pulled inside himself.
"We don't have to do this—"

"No." She grabbed his wrists before he could pull
his hands away. "I meant, I'm afraid I'll disappoint
you. I told you I'm no good at this. With you, I want
to be different, but I'm very nervous."

He laid his lips against her forehead and she felt
him smile. "I'm nervous too, but I think I can make

it different for you, if you let me. I can't give you what you deserve, but I can give you this."

"I don't know what to do."

"Then I'll tell you." He teased her mouth with his thumbs. "You admitted you haven't enjoyed this in the past because your mind was too busy thinking negative thoughts about your body for you to relax and enjoy. So I'm going to keep your mind so busy, you won't have time for thoughts of your own."

Before she could respond, his mouth came down over hers. He kissed her feverishly, but briefly, then moved his lips to her ear where he whispered, "Are you brave enough to let me pleasure you, my bold Lady Amelia?"

She trembled with apprehension and excitement. "I don't know. I want to be."

"Will you let me touch you however I want?"

She thought about his hands on her fat stomach, her big behind, her lumpy thighs and froze up inside.

"Already thinking, aren't you?" He nibbled along her jaw. "Then let me give you something else to think about."

To her complete shock, he took her hand and placed it directly on the front of his pants where a very noticeable bulge pressed against his zipper. Too stunned to react, she didn't even try to snatch her hand away. He encouraged her fingers to close about his erection as much as they could with the restriction of clothing.

"Do you feel that?" He moved her hand up and down the length of him. Her eyes widened at his size. "I want you to think about that. Picture it in your mind. Imagine it inside of you."

The moment he said the words, her brain did exactly what he told her. Other words followed. Delicious, explicit, tantalizing words that had her trembling. His shirt disappeared and he laid her other hand on his chest, telling her where to touch him, kiss him, lick him. His breath hissed in through his teeth when she obeyed. Her fingers and lips delighted in the feel of crisp chest hair, hot skin, and hard male nipples. Only barely did she register that he was undressing her, until his hands were on her bare breasts with her dress pooled at her feet.

Before she had time to cover herself or shrink away, he dipped his head and suckled at her. Heat coursed through her at the feel of his mouth pulling at her breast. Her breath turned ragged with wonder.

When he straightened, she realized she stood before him in nothing but her panties and sandals. Soon even those were gone. The brush of air on her skin brought her out of her daze for only a moment. He whispered in her ear that he wanted to touch her, to pleasure her, to make her shiver as he led her to the bed. Lifting her, he laid her on the dark silk comforter. It felt cool against her back as the netting closed about them.

He was there with her, as naked as she. He guided her hand back to the evidence of his desire for her, only this time nothing kept her from touching, flesh to flesh.

He touched her as well, all the while whispering to her, telling her how she excited him, how he loved her body. Something in her began to unfold. Some secret, wild part of her that grew and grew, pushing aside shyness. She caressed him freely and returned each ravenous kiss with increasing demand. When his hand moved between her legs, she opened up to him, eager and willing.

He whispered in her ear how good she felt, how her response excited him, how he couldn't wait to be inside her.

"Yes, yes," she panted, dizzy with need. "Now, please, I want you now."

"Not yet. Not until you come for me."

That frightened her. There wasn't any such thing. If she didn't fake it, she'd never know the feel of him inside her. That was enough, to give him pleasure and experience the joy of that. She tried to protest, to urge him on top of her.

But then he was touching her deeper, harder. His thumb moved over her just so. And an arrow of sensation shot through her and exploded.

She gasped from the shock of it as her body arched and held. When the waves subsided to ripples, she let out a huff of air and lay panting.

"Oh, my God," she managed between breaths. Then laughed. As her senses cleared, she found him propped up on his elbow beside her. The hand that had brought her such startling discovery rested on her belly as if to calm the spasms. She didn't even care that he was touching a part of her body she normally worked very hard to hide. That realization made her laugh again and the heat in her cheeks grew to match the heat elsewhere. "Goodness," she giggled. "So that's what all the fuss is about."

"Goodness indeed," he purred.

Dipping his head, he nuzzled her neck as he shifted on top of her, parting her thighs with his own. She welcomed his weight, wrapping her arms around his solid chest and kissing him deeply. He'd already sheathed himself. When, she had no idea.

He slid smoothly, easily into her, as if he should always have been there and always would be. The wonder of it filled her heart as fully, as beautifully as he filled her body. When he moved, he brought every tingling nerve ending back to life. This time, when the pleasure came, it felt even sweeter with him wrapped around her as she was wrapped around him, each of them clinging tightly to the other.

When it passed, she turned her head and kissed his cheek. *I love you*, she thought but didn't have the strength to speak the words aloud.

Chapter 14

What had he done? Byron stared into the blackness
above the bed, too dazed to think straight. They'd
slipped beneath the cover and Amy had drifted to
sleep with her head on his shoulder. Her hand rested
on his chest right over his heart. He toyed with her
hair, afraid he'd wake her but unable to stop touching her. She'd given herself so trustingly, so freely . . .
to a man who didn't exist.

How could he have taken what she offered? Why
hadn't he stopped this? It wasn't as if he'd been so
caught up in the rush of passion that the act was
over before he came to his senses. He'd had plenty
of time for his conscience to kick in while he'd been
bringing her up the stairs. Had it, though? No. Not
one word of sanity had registered to stop him. And
even if it had, he wasn't sure he would have listened.
He'd wanted her too badly.

He'd wanted to hold her, to touch her, to give her
pleasure. Or was it that he'd wanted her to hold him?
To have someone good and sweet touch him? To be

with someone who didn't expect something in return?

He'd had no right to take that gift.

He wouldn't trade it now to save his soul.

When he'd joined his body to hers, when she'd welcomed him with such clear happiness, some secret chamber inside him had cracked open. Emotions more intense than anything he'd ever felt had poured out. For the first time in his life, he'd felt the sparkling wonder of being alive.

Of being in love.

He loved her. The breadth of the emotion staggered him. He'd never felt love before. Never realized how it overwhelmed everything else. He loved her.

And he could never let her know who he was.

Not after what had just happened. The experience had been shattering for her as well. He thought of how she'd laughed. How she'd held him. How innocently she'd kissed his cheek when it ended.

If she ever found out she'd shared all that with Byron Parks—shallow, jaded Byron Parks, who she wouldn't date for all the money in the world—he couldn't imagine how hurt and angry she'd be. Learning the truth would turn something special into something she regretted for the rest of her life. He'd honestly rather die than hurt her like that.

So he'd be sure she never found out.

Tears rose unexpectedly in his eyes. He pressed the heel of his hand to his eyes to stop them, to push back all the pain and fear rioting inside him. He used to do that so easily—but now that she'd unlocked the Pandora's box inside his chest, he couldn't seem to stuff everything back in. No wonder he'd gone through life refusing to feel. It hurt to feel. It god-damn hurt!

He took a deep shuddering breath.

And Amy woke with a gasp. He felt her glance about, disoriented. Her moment of panic snapped his own emotions back into place.

"Amy, shh, it's okay." The words came out roughly through his tight throat. "You're all right."

"Guy?" She sagged in relief. "I forgot where I was."

"You fell asleep." He cleared his throat and prayed she dismissed his hoarseness as him falling asleep too.

"I did." She sounded quite pleased with herself as she settled back down, snuggling against him. Her mood shifted, though, from happy to troubled. "I think I had a dream."

"Was it a bad dream?" He arranged her as tightly to him as he could, with their legs twined together.

"I don't know." She fell silent a moment. He pressed his lips to her forehead and felt her frown. "Wait, I remember. I dreamed I was back home. I woke up in my own bed and realized all of this was a dream." She propped her chin on the hand that rest on his chest. "How nice to find that for once reality is better than a dream."

He traced her mouth with his fingertip and found her smiling. "How do you know you're not still dreaming?"

"Well, if I am, I hope I never wake up." Shifting upward, she gave his lips a quick kiss. "Now admit it. Aren't you glad you unlocked that door?"

"Very glad," he said, not sure if that was truth or lie. And if it was truth, would it remain so?

"This changes things, though, doesn't it?"

"It does," he agreed, knowing that now, more than ever, he had to find a way to send her away. Pain stabbed his chest at the thought.

"For starters," she said, "I'd like to turn in my resignation effective as of an hour ago. Actually, make that as of last night." She traced a finger through the hair on his chest. "Very little of what I've done over the last twenty-four hours has been appropriate behavior for a housekeeper. So I'm afraid my conscience won't let me stay on working for you for the next three weeks."

Her words delivered a second stab of pain. Even though having her leave would spare her hurt, he wanted to hold her tight and never let her go. "Yes, of course. I understand." He cleared his throat. "I'll have Lance drive you to the airport tomorrow."

"What?" Amy sat up in surprise. She could make out the shape of him lying against the sheets but that was all. Did he really think she'd walk out on him now? "No silly. I didn't mean I was leaving. I just meant I can't stay as your housekeeper. In fact, I don't want you to pay me for the past week. I'd feel awkward taking money from you after what just happened."

He ran a fingertip down her arm. "But you did work for me."

"Every bit of which was fun." She took his hand to keep him from distracting her. "Aside from my worries about Meme, I've enjoyed being here more than I can say. And as for us, I feel as if we've been heading for this moment since I arrived."

"You do?"

"Yes." She squeezed his hand. "I feel like everything happened the way it was supposed to. Me getting lost and coming here. Meeting you. I think—don't laugh—but I think that we were both sent here for each other. It's like a time out of time." She lifted his hand and held the back of it to her heart. "Guy, you have helped me so much with things I've grappled with for years. I'd already started that journey on my own, but you helped me take some big steps."

"I'm glad." He pulled their joined hands to his lips to kiss her fingers. "You deserve to see yourself the way you are, which is absolutely beautiful."

Her heart filled with gratitude. "Then hopefully you won't mind if I stay until my friends' shower. I know I have to get back to my real life, but I would like to have these next three weeks with you."

He sat up in a rush, and propped his free arm against his raised knee to brace his forehead in his hand. "Amy . . ." He took a ragged breath. "If you stay, I'm afraid you're going to get hurt. I can't stand the thought of that. I can't risk that."

She bit her lip, debating what to do. "If I ask you a question, will you promise to give me an honest answer?"

He managed a humorless laugh. "No."

"Well, see, you just did." The smile that tried to come to her lips didn't quite make it. "That was honest."

"That was easy. The only thing easy about this whole mess."

Mess? He thought what they had was a mess? She buried the prick of hurt over that. "Do you *want* me to leave? Honestly. Don't tell me yes because you're set on being noble and you worry I'll be hurt if I stay. I'm tougher than you think I am. I want to stay, to be with you for this little time out of time. No matter what happens when it ends, I will never blame you. I'm making this choice, taking this risk. I'm asking you to be brave enough to take it with me. Now, do you want me to stay or go?"

He turned into her, buried his face against her neck, and held on to her as a sob racked his body. "Stay. I want you to stay."

She wrapped him in her arms and kissed the top of his head. "Then I stay."

Amy's world became divided between her nighttime life and her life during the day. How fitting that her emotions were equally divided between the elation of falling in love and the agony of knowing it wouldn't last.

She and Guy continued to have supper the way they had during that first week, only with the door to the tower open. Since she preferred to have light while eating, she'd sit at Lance's desk until their meal ended; then she'd join Guy in his bedroom, where they'd make love and talk for hours.

During the day, she continued to cook—for the enjoyment of it, not as a paid duty—but she had a new chore that brought even more pleasure. On her second night with Guy, she mentioned that the empty rooms made her sad. The following morning, Lance announced he was off to buy furniture and asked if she'd like to go along. She jumped on the chance with glee.

Together they scoured shops all over St. Barts, buying rattan sofas and chairs to create a conversational grouping in the living room, end tables and coffee tables, lamps and vases. With each purchase, she looked forward to night and telling Guy about her day and what they'd found.

"You seem to be enjoying your shopping trips with Lance," he observed toward the end of her second week on the island. They lay naked on top of the dark satin comforter, she on her stomach, propped up on both elbows, Guy on his side, facing her.

"I am." Bending her knees, she crossed her ankles and moved her feet back and forth. The pendant on her anklet tickled at the movement. "It's been a lot of fun."

"He doesn't make you nervous anymore?"

"No, he really doesn't," she said, realizing how true that was. "Maybe I've simply gotten used to him. You stop noticing the phenomenal good looks after a while."

She thought about that as Guy lazily traced the outline of her tattoo. It was a barely visible dark shape on her very white bottom, but he seemed mesmerized by it. She'd pointed out more than once that if he'd turn on the light, he could really see it. He'd declined, of course.

"I think it's more than that, though," she continued. "I feel different about myself now. For that I have you to thank." Leaning over, she kissed his mouth. "You make me feel sexy."

"You are sexy." He ran a fingertip up her back,

sending a shiver of renewed desire through her. They'd already made love in a fevered rush that had them rolling over the bed, laughing and then gasping as pleasure overtook them. She couldn't get enough of touching him and letting him touch her. Any inhibitions she'd had about enjoying the act of love he'd obliterated in ways that made her flush with heat throughout the day.

And it was love. They might not say the words, but love underscored every touch as they explored ways to give each other pleasure.

Rolling onto her back, she let him draw circles on her stomach. Why he enjoyed her belly she had no idea, but she'd learned better than to suck it in, or he'd scold her. "I never dreamed I could be this comfortable being naked with a man."

"I'm glad you are." He kissed her belly button. "I adore your body."

"I'm learning to like it too."

He grew very quiet. "Does this mean . . ." He hesitated. When he continued, she could hear the frown in his voice. "Does this mean that you've changed your mind about marrying? Now that you know you can enjoy being with a man? When you go home, will you . . . look for that man you once wanted. The one to travel with and give you babies?"

Goodness, what a question. Did he want her to say yes? She searched within for the answer. "No," she finally said. "I promised Meme I'd never abandon her, and I won't go back on that. I can't fit a husband and family into my tiny carriage house apartment."

"That's ridiculous. You can take care of her without living right there."

"I've told you how she is." Amy sighed. "She gets horribly ill anytime I even mention moving away."

"Because of her fear of losing you."

"That doesn't make her heart problems, or her arthritis, or her other legitimate ailments any less real. If I moved and she died, how would I live with myself?"

"That's your fear talking." He poked her. "I thought your goal was to get over that. To stop letting it rule your life."

She didn't know what to say to that.

"Amy . . ." he seemed to consider his words carefully. "If you can be brave enough to face your fears, why is it asking too much of your grandmother for her to face hers so that you can have a life?"

"I never thought of it that way. To be honest, though"—she caressed his face—"I don't think I could ever be this comfortable with any man but you."

He rolled onto his back and stared at the ceiling. "I wish you would try."

She blinked in surprise. "You want me to be with another man?"

"No. I want to commit murder at the thought of any man ever touching you. But . . ." He growled, then exhaled loudly. "I want you to be happy." He cupped her cheek. "I'd like to think I'd given you the confidence to have that, even if I can't be that man."

"Is that any different than what I wish for you? I want to return home with the knowledge that before I left I helped you accept yourself? If I can be brave enough to be this open with you, why can't you be brave enough to let me see you?"

"No."

"Guy." She nearly punched him in frustration. "I hate the thought that when I leave here you're going to lock yourself away in this tower, alone for the rest of your life."

"I'm hardly 'locked away.' I'm the one who holds the key."

"You might as well be, if you never use the key to let yourself out."

"Is that any different than you locking yourself away in your carriage house."

"I'm not. I've started to travel."

"Alone."

"Why are we arguing about this?" she asked.

"Because you're being stubborn." A grin sounded in his voice. "As usual."

"I'm being stubborn?" She gasped playfully. "What about you?"

"That's different. I have a reason."

"Which you won't share." The amusement died. "Do you know how much that hurts?"

"Amy . . . you're leaving in two weeks. Can we just enjoy each other's company until then?"

She was quiet for a while. "Can I ask you something?"

"Oh, Lord."

"If I didn't have my situation with Meme, would you . . . would you want me to come back here, the way you once did?"

"Are we talking, 'If I could have anything in the world I wanted, would I want a life with you?' If so, then yes. I would give up everything I own to spend all my days with you. But that's not an option."

"I know." She said brightly. "You could come home with me. I'll lock you in my carriage house, turn out all the lights, and have my wicked way with you."

"Tempting. But also not an option. What about you? If you could have anything in the world you wanted, what would it be?"

"Other than you? Let me think. I'd write children's books for real, not just my own pleasure."

"Why don't you?"

"I don't know." She shrugged. "I've never thought about it too seriously. I guess because it's scary. My stories are part of my connection to my mother. I'm not sure I could handle having some publisher reject them."

He sat up in a rustle of covers. "But think of how thrilling it would be to see them published. To share with other children the wonderment of the world that you and your mother created. I know submitting work and risking rejection is terrifying, but the pay-off in terms of pride has to be one of the most rewarding things anyone can experience."

She thought about it a while and realized he was right. She wasn't sure she could do it, but he was right. Then another thought occurred to her, and she bit her lip. "Okay, I'll do it, but only on one condition. You have to let me see you before I go."

He growled. "You never give up, do you?"

"Never." She grinned. "I'll wear you down. You realize that, don't you?"

"That's what I'm afraid of."

"You should be afraid. Because every beast has a weak spot." She danced her fingers over his ribs.

To her shock, he gasped and jumped away.

"Oh, my goodness." She laughed. "You're ticklish!"

"Don't you dare!" he warned as she tickled him more.

Ignoring the warning, she went in for the kill and soon had him on his back writhing beneath her. Straddling his hips, she pinned his hands to the mattress. "See? It's useless to fight me. You should give up now."

"When it comes to fighting for you, I'll never give up."

"We'll just see about that." She leaned down and covered his mouth in a slow, deep kiss.

Chapter 15

When faced with an unsolvable problem, consider all possibilities.

—*How to Have a Perfect Life*

Amy was angry. Really, truly angry. Byron knew she'd been mad, frustrated, and ticked off at him many times in the last few weeks, but never like this. Never like tonight, when they had only one night left.

What he wanted to know, though, was how their time had evaporated so quickly. Where had the weeks gone? Tomorrow Amy would be flying home. He'd expected to spend their last night with her in his bed, as they had spent every night since the first night they'd made love. But, no, Amy had delivered his meal to the dumbwaiter, then told him if he wanted to be with her, he could come to her room.

She'd be waiting. With the light on.

He saw that she meant it as he stood in the courtyard, surrounded by the night sounds as he stared at the closed doors to her room. Light burned brightly inside, even though the hours had slipped well past midnight. She'd peeked out a few times earlier, and he'd wondered if she'd seen him, but she hadn't looked for a while. Had she fallen asleep with the light on?

He felt his own anger rise at her stubbornness.

Their last night together, and she decides to spend it like this?

He thought back over their time together. Not just making love, but sharing so many things—and she didn't even know half of it. She'd befriended him as Lance as they'd wandered all over the island buying furniture, then arranging it. They'd laughed and talked for hours, every one of which had nearly killed him. To be with her all day, aching to touch her, to kiss her, to tell her he loved her—no wonder he nearly devoured her every night when she came to him.

He wasn't alone in his insatiable hunger, though. She came to him so eagerly, she overwhelmed his senses. At times they came together in a clash of passion that left them both breathless. Other times they rolled and played with a childlike exuberance that amazed him. He hadn't even known such happiness existed. But after the ecstasy of making love to Amy came the despair of holding her while she slept and knowing he couldn't keep her with him forever.

Worse, though, far worse, was when she'd beg him to let her see him. How many times had he almost given in? How many times had he thought maybe she could accept who he was and how he'd deceived her?

Standing in the courtyard, staring up at the light burning in her room, he realize the truth behind the story of Pandora's box. The last thing to escape was the worst thing of all: hope.

He'd never understood that, until now.

Hope made everything else hurt more because hope kept all the yearning inside him alive. He couldn't accept that Amy would never forgive him if she learned the truth, because hope kept whispering "maybe" and "what if?"

A shape moved behind her door, and his heart skipped. She wasn't asleep. That thought pulled at him, made him long even more to go to her. To give in. To confess everything. He was going to lose her anyway, why not take the wild chance that she'd accept him?

Because what if she didn't? What if learning the truth tainted everything they'd shared, turned it into a source of anger and humiliation? He couldn't take the chance of hurting her that way.

Date Byron Parks? Not for all the money in the world.

Her door opened and she stepped out wearing only her short white nightgown and the gauzy robe that matched it. The light from her open door made her look like an angel. Some invisible force reached inside his chest and tried to pull him toward her. Fighting it, he shrank back into deeper shadows.

She looked directly at where he stood. "Are you going to stay out there all night? Or are you coming in?"

The sound of her voice, so soft and sweet, made the pull harder to resist. He gripped the tree trunk next to him for strength. "Are you going to turn the light off?"

"No."

The word was a dagger straight to his chest. He leaned sideways against the trunk, his arm wrapped around it, his forehead pressing into it. "Then, no, I'm not coming in."

"Very well." That stubborn chin of hers went up a notch. "I'll come down."

Panic seized him as she walked along the gallery, her robe floating about her as she headed for the steps that led to the courtyard. The bluish light from the swimming pool posed more danger than the moon, which had sunk behind the tower. He moved away from the pool into a sheltered area where low palms screened off a lounge chair that faced the bay. It was Amy's favorite place to sit and read or enjoy the view during the day because she could sunbathe without "Lance" seeing her in her swimming suit. The stairs led her directly to it.

They entered from opposite directions and stopped when they saw each other. Several feet separated them as she stood in a beam of light cast from her open door and he clung to the shadows.

"I have something to say to you." With her hair spilling about her, her face held both hurt and determination. "I was going to wait until you let me see you, but I guess I have to accept defeat on that. I know we can't be together, I have my promise to Meme and this is your world, but I refuse to leave without telling you . . ." She took a shaky breath, and when she spoke, her voice broke. "I love you."

"Oh, Amy." A lump rose in his throat as tears glistened in her eyes. He couldn't step forward and take her into his arms without stepping into the light. "Oh, God. Don't. Don't love me. Please."

"Why?" she demanded, swiping at her tears. "Because you don't love me?"

"Jesus. No!" Pain closed about his chest. He'd told himself he wouldn't say the words, that he wouldn't tell her how he felt, what she'd done to him. But no force on earth could have held the words back. "I love you," he admitted hoarsely. "I love you more than life."

With a sob, she rushed to him and flung herself into his arms, her face against his chest as she cried. He buried his face in her hair, his arms wrapped tightly about her. She smelled like sunshine and flowers.

"Then why?" she asked. "Why won't you let me see you?"

"I can't." The longing tore at him. "Please believe me. I wish more than anything that things could be different. But they're not."

She lifted her head and he made out the silvery glitter of tears in her eyes. "You said you don't want to hurt me, but you are hurting me by not trusting me."

"Letting you see me would hurt you more."

"You don't know that."

"I do."

"So what am I supposed to do, leave here knowing that I failed?"

"No." He closed his eyes as he forced out the next words. "You're supposed to go back to your real life and meet someone who deserves you and be happy."

"I don't want someone else. I want *you*!"

He squeezed his eyes tighter, because that right there was the problem. He wanted to shout at her, *There is no me! I'm nothing but a phantom who exists only when I'm with you. That's why you can't see me, because I'm not real.*

He felt her fingers on his face. "I want you." She

whispered it this time so achingly, he nearly cried. "I want you." Her lips touched his.

His restraint broke. He took her face in both his hands and kissed her back with all the desperation living inside him. His fingers plowed into her hair as his mouth slanted over hers. She kissed him back just as desperately, her hands racing over his shoulders and back. It wasn't enough. He needed her hands on his bare skin.

Still kissing her, he pushed off her robe, then worked the buttons down the front of his shirt. Her hands went quickly inside it. "Yes. Touch me, Amy. Touch me." *Make me real. One more time.*

His heart pounded as she brought him to life. He gathered her nightgown and broke the kiss long enough to pull it up and over her head. Then his hands were on her breasts, filled with all that soft skin. They moved together toward the lounger.

Scrambling out of his clothes and into a condom, he sat and pulled her to him. She slipped off her panties and climbed onto his lap, kissing him deeply, then arching her back to let him feast on her breasts. Need obliterated gentleness as his hands rushed over her body. As eager as he, she rose up and sank down over him, taking him so deeply into her body, she gasped in wonder.

He buried his face between her breasts, wrapped his arms about her, and breathed her in as she moved. The unbearable sweetness of it, of holding her, of being inside her, of having her make love to him built to a painful pitch. He moved with her as her breath turned ragged. Longing to please her, to give her this at least, he ran his hands down her back to grip her bottom as he thrust harder into her.

Yes, sweet Amy, let me please you.

He took her breast in his mouth and suckled her hard, the way she liked sometimes, the way she seemed to need right now. She wrapped her arms about his head, holding him to her, her fingers lightly scratching his scalp. He felt her hair spilling down her back onto his thighs and knew she had her face tipped to the sky. Her breath came in little sobs of need.

Yes, that's it, Amy. Angel Amy, fly for me.

With a gasp of pleasure, she went rigid in his arms as her climax took her.

Focused on her, his own release caught him off guard. The instant she tightened about him he exploded inside her with a force that had spots of light going off in his head. He pressed his forehead to her chest as shudders racked his body.

When he could draw air into his lungs, he lifted his head to see the outline of her bowed backward. Slowly her taut body went soft. Leaning back, he gathered her to him, tucking her head under his chin as they both struggled to breathe.

Amy went willingly into his embrace, spent emotionally as well as physically. Neither of them spoke for a long time. She simply lay with her ear pressed against his chest, listening to his heartbeat. Of all the times they'd made love, it had never been like that, that level of raw need. She felt a little shocked, but the tears had stopped, as if the act had drained all the hurt out of her and left her numb.

She could feel his hand stroking her back and hair gently now, in contrast to how he'd touched her mere moments ago. Then he kissed her forehead.

"No matter what," he murmured, "never doubt that I do love you."

She lifted her head to look at his shadowy face.

Light exploded from behind her.

Guy cursed and grabbed her head, then pulled her face against his chest. Another light flashed followed by more curses.

"What is it?" she asked, her voice muffled against his skin. "What's happening?"

"You're on goddamn private property," he shouted, covering her face with his hand.

She froze. He was shouting at someone else. Another flash went off. Oh, good Lord, someone was taking their picture! She curled into a ball, trying to hide her nakedness.

"Keep your head down," he ordered her, shifting beneath her. He draped something over her head. Somehow they were standing and he was pushing her. "Get inside! Keep your face covered!"

Her face? What about her naked body? She did as he said and raced up the stairs and into her room. The horror of it hit her. Someone had just taken pictures of her and Guy naked after just having sex. How long had they been out there watching. The second horror hit, this time on Guy's behalf. They'd taken pictures of his face. Unless he'd managed to hide it.

She didn't think he had, though.

Dear God. Who would do such a thing?

Her body trembled so badly she could barely

stand. Guy was still out there. What was he doing? Realizing that he'd covered her head with her night-gown, she pulled it on and wondered what to do. Should she go outside to check on Guy?

No, he'd gone to great lengths to be sure they didn't photograph her face. If she went out there, that might all be for naught. So she paced, chewing her thumbnail as she waited.

The light, she realized. Guy wouldn't come in if the light was on. She turned it off and paced some more.

Finally the door to the gallery cracked open and she saw a dark shape slip inside. She had one flash of fear that it wasn't him. "Guy?"

"It's okay. It's me."

"Oh, thank God." Rushing to him, she ran her hands over his body to be sure he wasn't hurt and found that he'd dressed before coming in. "Who was that? Do you know?"

"It was the goddamn paparazzi. One of them, any-way. I wasn't able to catch him."

"What?" She stepped back in shock. "Why would the paparazzi want to take our picture?"

After a short silence, he heaved a heavy sigh. "Amy, turn on the light."

She went still.

"I would give anything to not do this," he said. "But the choice just got taken out of my hands. Those pictures are going to hit the tabloids in a matter of days. The minute you see them, you'll see . . . me."

Pictures of her naked were going to be in the tab-loids? Pictures of her fat, naked body straddling a man's lap would be in the tabloids?

The rest of Guy's words registered. He'd told her to turn on the light so she could see him. After weeks of begging for exactly that, she felt fear swell inside her. Shaking all over, she moved around the bed to the lamp on the nightstand and turned it on. She saw him through the netting, a dark shape dressed in a dark short-sleeved shirt and black shorts standing by the door. He had short dark hair, but she'd suspected that already.

Her gaze remained riveted on him as she moved toward the end of the bed. With a deep breath, she took the final step. And saw him clearly.

Her dazed brain took a moment to register what she was seeing. He stood staring back at her with no expression on his face. He wasn't ugly. Or disfigured.

He was handsome.

Breathtakingly handsome.

He was . . . "Byron Parks," she whispered as her world tilted.

When he spoke, Lance's accented voice came out of his mouth. "I fear it is even worse than that."

With a gasp, she covered her mouth. "Lance?"

"*Oui.*" He cocked a dark brow as if in apology.

"Oh, dear God." She stumbled back a step, her mind whirling. "You're Guy?"

"There is no Guy," he answered in Guy's voice. Putting his hands on his hips, he stared at the floor. "There is no Lance. There's just . . . me."

"Oh, dear God." She stared at him. He was even more gorgeous without the wig or goatee. The beard must have been glued on. How had she not noticed? The dark lashes and brows went with this face. This very famous face with perfect bones, flawless skin, and riveting blue eyes. He had lips worthy of a marble statue and that chiseled jaw with the distinctive cleft in the chin.

She'd been sleeping with Byron Parks, a man who had dated some of the most beautiful women in the world.

The paparazzi had taken pictures of fat Amy Baker from Speck-on-the-map, Texas, naked with Byron Parks, International Playboy and World's Sexiest Billionaire.

"Oh, dear God."

"Now you understand why I didn't want you to see me."

"Understand? I don't understand anything!"

"You thought I was some hideous beast hiding his face from the world. Instead, it's just shallow, jaded me, hiding out from that for a while." He pointed his thumb toward the courtyard.

"How could you not tell me? How could you let me sleep with you knowing what I thought? What you led me to believe?"

His eyes beseeched her. "I tried to tell you."

"That day with the tabloid." Her mind spun. "That's why you bought it."

"Yes. You made it clear what you thought of me, and I don't blame you. I am all the things you said."

"I don't even remember what I said." She massaged her temples, trying to think.

"I do. You called me unappreciative, extravagant, shallow, jaded, and said you wouldn't date me for all the money in the world. That's why I tried to send you away. But you refused to go."

She remembered that day, and the ones that had

followed. She'd been so nobly determined to draw Guy out, assuring him his looks didn't matter—and all the while, she'd been talking to physically perfect Byron Parks! "How you must have laughed at me."

"I didn't!" he assured her, stepping forward. "Never."

She stepped back. "I threw myself at you." Hysterical laughter shook her, and she pressed the back of her hand to her mouth. "Well, I guess this proves it. Men really will sleep with anything that moves. Even their dumpy housekeeper if she's all that's available."

"No!" He looked frantic at her words and took another step toward her. "No that's not—"

"Don't touch me!" She scurried away.

"Okay." He held his hands up, palms toward her.

Tears of humiliation flooded her eyes. "Dear heavens, I made it easy for you."

"Trust me, you didn't make anything easy for me."

"And there you were, pretending to be Lance with that fake French accent. You spent every day with me, acting like we were friends—letting me believe—and all the while, you knew you were the one I was sleeping with at night. You had all those memories of *me* in your head, while I was clueless that I was talking the man I was sleeping with. Were you snickering to yourself the whole time?"

"Amy, no—"

She grabbed a pillow off the bed and threw it at him. "How could you make a fool of me like this? How could you!"

He twisted as the pillow hit him, then held his hands back up. "I realize you're upset—"

"Yes, I'm upset!" The scream scraped its way up her raw throat.

"If we could just sit down and talk."

"I don't want to talk. I don't know you! You're a total stranger to me! Get out of my room!"

"Amy, please—"

"Get out!" She grabbed another pillow. "Get out! *Get out!*"

"Okay." He backed carefully toward the door. "We'll talk in the morning when you've had a chance to calm down."

"Get out!" She throw the pillow.

He slipped out the door before it hit him.

When he'd gone, she collapsed cross-legged on the floor, her face in her hands, and cried. There was no Guy Gaspar. That, more than the humiliation, ripped at her heart. Because she'd never wanted, or needed, him more.

Chapter 16

Life takes courage.

—*How to Have a Perfect Life*

Amy didn't sleep at all. She thought about e-mailing her friends, but the hurt throbbed too near the surface for her to put it into words. She thought about fleeing. About walking into town in the dark and getting a hotel room until her flight home.

As the sun came up, though, she knew she had to face him, this stranger who had deceived her. She had to face him and ask why.

She rose and took a shower, scrubbing the scent of him from her skin. Memories from the night before, of how they'd been in the courtyard, flashed through her mind like snippets from a movie reel she couldn't stop.

As she dried off, she caught a glimpse of herself in the mirror and stopped to stare at her tear-ravaged face. Her wet hair hung down her pudgy naked body. He'd made her feel so beautiful.

Had all those words been a lie? How could someone so physically perfect look at her and feel desire?

Numbly she braided her hair the way she had before coming here. The way she had in her old life.

When it was done, she saw for the first time how truly unflattering the style was for her face. Some spark of pride refused to go back to that. Yes, he'd hurt her, used her, but she didn't have to revert to Amy the Mouse.

She didn't have the heart to fix her hair the way she'd been doing, but she pulled a few tendrils free to soften the effect of the tight braid. A little makeup helped hide the blotchiness from crying. Now, what to wear for this confrontation that was making her physically ill?

Clothes can be a weapon and a shield.

He'd once told her that. Was that how he used them? She didn't feel like donning either. She just wanted to get past this morning and be home. She picked one of her more subdued capri sets and left off the jewelry.

The woman in the mirror looked caught between who she'd been before coming to St. Barts and who she'd been since.

Turning away, she left her room.

She found him sitting in the kitchen on one of the bar stools at the center island. That drew her up short. She hadn't expected him to be there.

For a moment they just stared at each other. He looked exhausted sitting there in the same clothes he'd worn last night: the dark shirt and black shorts. She realized that in all the pictures she'd seen of him, he'd always worn somber colors. So even Lance's clothes had been a lie.

A memory flashed through her mind of the first day when "Lance" had opened the door. His bright tropical shirt, quick smile, laughing eyes.

How odd to see Lance's cheeks, nose, and expressive eyebrows on another man's face. The difference was startling. It wasn't just the lack of the goatee and the different hair. It was the guarded expression, the rigid posture. This was a different man.

She thought of times when she'd see an actor in a role, then see them interviewed and realize the real person was nothing like the imaginary one.

He noticed the change in her as well, and disapproval, or remorse, flickered in his eyes for the barest moment. Then he looked away.

"I made coffee," he said, his voice flat. "Would you like me to pour a cup for you?"

She shook her head. "I'll get it."

So Lance was gone too, she thought as she got down a mug. Her hand shook as she poured the coffee. She'd lost both a lover and a friend. The pain returned, filling her eyes with tears. "I feel like he died. I feel as if I fell in love with this wonderful man who made me feel things I've never felt before, who made me happy and alive. And last night . . . he *died*. But I don't even have a body to grieve over."

"Oh, Amy." She heard him come up behind her, and she tried to move away. "No, don't," he said, sliding his arms around her from behind. "Let me hold you. Please. For just a second."

"You have his voice," she choked out, laying her arms over his. "And you feel like him. With my eyes closed, I can almost believe—"

"Please don't cry. Please." He rocked her with his cheek resting against the top of her head. "I am so abominably sorry, I can't even begin to say."

"Hold me." She turned into him. With her eyes

squeezed tightly shut, she wrapped her arms around him. He held her tightly as she cried for long gut-wrenching minutes until the grief abated and she could breathe steadily again.

"Better?" he asked.

"A little." She straightened and whipped her cheeks. "So much for putting on makeup."

"You look fine." He added his thumbs to the effort.

She glanced up into his eyes. Blue eyes, not brown. They both froze. His gaze lowered to her lips, and she knew he wanted to kiss her.

Shaking her head, she leaned away.

He nodded, accepting her boundary. Then right before her eyes, his face lost all readable expression. It went from tender concern mixed with aching desire to . . . nothing. Just like that. He wore the same bored look he had in so many photos. She blinked at the transformation.

He turned and went back to his bar stool. He even walked differently than Lance, tighter, straighter. He walked like royalty, she realized, like a man used to having his slightest request treated like a command.

"We have a few things to discuss," he said, his voice as devoid of emotion as his face.

A few things to discuss? Well, that was putting it mildly. Okay, then, if he wanted to conduct this like a business meeting, perhaps that was for the best. Carrying her coffee mug, she dragged a bar stool to the opposite side of the island from where he sat. "Did you print up an agenda?"

Confusion flickered in his eyes, then vanished. "You have every reason to be angry. The only reassurance I can offer is that I'm reasonably sure the photographer didn't get your face. No one ever has to know that that was you with me last night."

The relief that came from those words loosened her chest. It didn't lessen the grief and anguish over losing Guy, but it gave her one less thing to add to her humiliation. Except that would still be her big, fat, naked body people stared at in the grocery store lines. The magazines would block out any private parts not allowed by the censors, but that left her stomach, her hips, and her dimply thighs. She didn't even want to think of the shots the photographer might've gotten of her butt when she ran up the stairs. The thought brought the tightness back.

"I am so sorry." He started to reach for her hand, then stopped when she pulled away. With a sigh, he went back to looking bored and regal. "You get through it, you know. It's embarrassing for a while. Then the rags find something else to focus on, and people forget."

"I won't," she managed in a small voice.

He looked away. "I can't take you to the airport the way we planned."

They'd planned for "Lance" to take her to the airport.

"I'll arrange for a driver to take you."

She nodded.

"A big enough tip should keep his mouth shut until you're safely away. Everyone on the island will know the truth about who lives here as soon as the pictures come out, and some of those photos could hit the Internet today. With all the curiosity over *La*

Bête that's bound to create a stir. In a town the size of Gustavia, word is going to spread fast."

Oh, dear Lord. Her eyes widened at the reality of it. Pictures of her on the Internet?

"It's okay," he rushed to reassure her. "We have a few things working in our favor for keeping your name out of this. No one has any pictures of you with Lance, and very few of the islanders who met you know your last name. In fact, I can only think of one. The woman at the employment agency."

"Plus the travel agent and the teller at the bank."

"Okay, that's not that many. I don't think it's a problem. The people of St. Barts are very protective of the celebrities who vacation or live here. With a few obvious exceptions, last night being one of them. Once you're off the island, though, you're safe."

A new thought made its way past her own mortification, and she looked at the man sitting across from her. "What about you? You'll still be here. How much of that will you have to put up with?"

"Here? Not too much. St. Barts isn't exactly swarming with paparazzi. That little weasel is a nuisance, but he's easy enough to avoid. He's a local who hangs out at the beaches mostly, hoping to get shots of movie stars sunbathing topless or report on who's hanging out with who." He massaged his forehead. "I should have seen this coming. I even know the moment my disguise was blown. It was two days ago, we were eating lunch at that café you love so much."

She knew the one he meant. It was an open-air café that overlooked the harbor. She couldn't remember what they'd been talking about, but they'd both been laughing so hard, she'd had to wipe her eyes. He'd given her an odd look, something akin to adoration, and he'd called her "enchanting."

But it hadn't been real. She hadn't been laughing with Lance. She'd been laughing with this man. She frowned over that, trying to imagine this man being relaxed and happy like that. The picture wouldn't come.

He shook his head, remembering it as well but most likely in a different way. "We were sitting there, next to the sidewalk. I know better, but you enjoy the view so much. Normally I'm careful to watch for people who might recognize me, but I was distracted. The little weasel walked by, scanning for celebrities, and I made a fatal mistake. When I saw him, I ducked. I didn't turn away slowly. I ducked. And he looked right at me. He seemed puzzled, but I didn't see any recognition in his eyes, so I thought I was safe. I guess not, huh?"

"I guess not," she said woodenly. How awful must it be to live like that, always ducking from people who wanted to invade your privacy?

He sat in silence a long time, before the bored expression cracked and anguish filled his eyes. "Jesus, Amy. Don't you want to yell at me? Call me a bastard. Say something."

She took a deep shuddering breath. "I just want to know . . . were you laughing at me?"

"No! No. Please—" He reached for her hand, but she snatched it away. With a curse, he rose and went to the sink, where he stood staring out at the pretty view. The blue sky promised another gorgeous day on this island paradise. "I fell in love with you."

Her stomach tightened painfully. "How can I believe you, when you've lied about so many things?"

He turned to face her, gripping the counter at his back. "Very little of what I said to you was a lie."

"You told me the man in the tower was hideous."

"No," he said slowly. "I told you the islanders believe the man living in the tower was a monster, and that some days I could barely bring myself to look at his face. Every word of that is true. Amy, I came here seven months ago because I didn't like who I was, and I needed to think about that. No one should have to go through life not liking themselves."

She frowned thinking about how much she used to not like herself—but that was physical. Other than her fears, she'd never disliked who she was on the inside.

Looking at him, at this beautiful man who seemed to have everything life could offer, she wondered what that would feel like, to feel ugly inside.

"Then you came along," he said, "and everything inside me changed. Actually, it was already changing. But you . . . you brought—I don't know—light back into my world. It's like you breathed air into me, and I was alive, really alive for the first time in my life. Is it any wonder that I fell in love with you?" His eyes pleaded with her to believe him. "I don't understand how any man can be with you for more than five seconds and not fall in love with you. How any man can hear you laugh, see you smile, just *be* with you,

and not love you. I don't like myself very much, but
I like who I am with you. I like who we are together.
And I wish I could be that man forever."

"Oh, my God." She covered her mouth and cried.
To hear all that in Guy's voice tore her in two. "I
wish you could be too."

"Unfortunately, I'm not. But I'm not who I was
when I came here either. I'm not sure who I am. I
just know I don't want to go back to my old life.

"Jesus," he swore, shaking his head, "if last night
hadn't happened—if you'd found out some other
way—I'd be begging you right now to come back
after the wedding and help me figure out who I
really am. Maybe the real me is somewhere between
Lance and Guy, and I just need to learn how to be
that without donning a disguise or hiding in the
dark. But last night did happen. And now there's no
way for us to be together publicly without everyone
knowing that that's you in the pictures. I know you
well enough to know how intensely . . . 'uncomfortable' that would make you."

She realized the extent of what he was saying. Not
only would her friends and family know, which was
horrifying enough, but if they stayed together, every
time he introduced her to one of his friends and she
had to shake their hand and smile, she'd know: *This
person has seen me naked.*

His friends. Wealthy, famous, beautiful people.
Most of whom had spa-fit bodies. Maybe Byron
hadn't been laughing at her—she still wasn't sure if
she believed that—but the rest of the world would.
People would see the two of them together and say,
"What is Byron Parks doing with Fat Girl?"

Even without the pictures, even if she lost the rest of the weight and wasn't Fat Girl anymore, she couldn't imagine fitting in with his friends. Living that lifestyle.

She shook the notion away. "Even if that hadn't happened, we couldn't be together. You have a very different life, and I have to take care of Meme."

"Ah, yes. Your duty."

A little smidge of anger joined the hurt. "Not everyone can do whatever they want with their lives. Some people have responsibilities that can't be ignored."

"I know, but I meant what I said about you asking your grandmother to face her fears so that you don't have to sacrifice your life for her."

She stood to face him, shoulders braced. "I don't think it's a good idea for us to talk about anything that I shared with you when I thought you were someone else. Someone I could trust. Not someone who was playing a game so he could hide out for a while. Someone who was sleeping with his housekeeper because she was the only woman he could have without blowing his disguise."

"That's not how it was!" he insisted, then rubbed his face. "What can I say to convince you that what happened between us was real? It wasn't a lie. There is no Guy Gaspar, but what we shared was real."

"I keep thinking of how many times I begged you to be brave enough to show your face." She gave a shaky laugh. "How many times I insisted that how you looked didn't matter. Do you know how much I ached for you? Worried over you?" Her hands balled into fists as she clung to composure by a thread. "I wanted so much to help you accept yourself so that you wouldn't have to live your life locked away by your fear of how people would react to your appearance. I think I would have ached for you the rest of my life, thinking of you up in that tower all alone."

"But you weren't even up there most of the time. You were out enjoying yourself, the happy-go-lucky Lance Beaufort." A tear slipped down her cheek. "What a lark that must have been. I guess I'm not the only one you laughed at. I bet you were laughing at the whole island over your little tale of the beast in the tower and how everyone believed it. Let me ask you this. How long did you plan to keep up your little charade?"

"I don't know. Not much longer." Byron studied her, wondering how much to reveal. After what he'd done to her she deserved total honesty. "I was toying with the idea of Gaspar selling the place to me so he could disappear and I could move in."

"I see." She looked at him with such accusation a physical blow would have hurt less. "So I would have gone through life aching for you, feeling like a f-failure"—her voice broke and she pressed the back of her hand to her mouth—"like a failure for not helping you accept yourself and you would have gone traipsing back to your old life of parties and movie premieres and dating stars." She stood before him, visibly shaking. "I am not a woman given to cursing, but Goddamn you for that. Goddamn you!" She dashed toward the door.

"Amy, wait!" He rushed after her, grabbing her arm.

"Let go of me!" She batted at his hand.

"Please listen." He held up his free hand in supplication. "Just listen."

"Let go!"

"If I do will you listen?" She stopped struggling and he released her arm. Turning her back to him, she cradled her arm to her chest. "You weren't a failure. If I had been Guy, I would have trusted you. The only thing that kept me from letting you see me was knowing how hurt you'd be. And this has hurt you more than if you'd never known."

"That's not true." She glared at him over her shoulder. "I'm angry and humiliated, but I was already hurting and would have hurt for the rest of my life for someone who doesn't even exist."

"But I do exist. I may not be Guy, but I was trapped before you came. Trapped inside myself. You helped release me. So, no, I'm not going to go back to my old life even if I return to LA. It's time I stopped hiding, but I'm not going to revert to who I was before I came here.

"I won't ask you to forgive me for hurting you, but I will ask that you not revert to who you were either. What we shared here changed both of us. So I only ask that you have the courage to continue being the woman you were with me."

She looked away and stood a long moment before shaking her head. Whether shaking off his words or telling him no, he wasn't sure. "I have to go pack."

She left him standing alone in the sun-washed kitchen. So in the end, he was the failure. This time, when the pain rose in his chest, he let it come, let it fill him until he dropped his face into his hands and wept.

Chapter 17

If you don't like the reality you have, look for ways to change it.

—How to Have a Perfect Life

Amy woke in her bed at home. For a moment it was like the dream she'd had after the first time she made love to Guy: she'd never left and none of the trip had been real. And then the memories crashed in and she grieved all over again.

Reality and dream had flipped and the dream had become true. Her time on St. Barts was an illusion. There was no Guy. There was only a stranger named Byron.

She rose sluggishly to face the task of unpacking— not from her flight home; after packing, she'd left it all behind, bringing nothing but the clothes she'd worn on the plane. She did, however, have the luggage the cruise ship had sent. Going through her clothes felt surreal. These were the clothes Christine had helped her buy before she left. She'd thought they were so cute at the time. Now they looked baggy and dowdy.

Did she really want to go back to dressing like that?

On the other hand, did she have the heart, or energy, to go shopping for new clothes? Clothes like what Lance had picked out?

His voice echoed in the back of her mind. *Have the courage to continue being the woman you were with me.*

The memory brought fresh tears to the surface, which made her angry. She had to stop crying. She could almost hear her mother saying, "Crying does no good. It doesn't change anything."

Don't cry. Don't complain. Be brave. Be strong. Endure, endure, endure.

The words didn't strengthen her this time as they normally did. They only added to her pain. In a fit of defiance, she sat down on the floor by her suitcase of dumpy clothes and bawled so hard and so long, she made herself ill. She bawled for herself. She bawled for her mother. She bawled for the loss of her grandfather. And she bawled most of all for losing Guy. She bawled until she had nothing left inside her. Until she felt utterly empty.

Drained of all emotion, she looked around her cheerful little apartment and thought, *What am I doing here?*

That thought jarred her. What an odd thing to think. This was where she lived. Where she belonged. She'd known all along she'd come back here so she could take care of Meme, which she needed to do first thing. She'd arrived so late the night before, she hadn't had the chance to even check on her grandmother.

The thought of dealing with Meme threatened to drain away what little energy she'd managed to muster. Even so, she rose and dressed by rote. Since the clothes from the cruise needed washing, she put on an old red T-shirt and denim jumper, both of which were several sizes too big. A glance in the mirror let her know that frumpy Amy had returned.

Not wanting to think about that, she left the carriage house and took the path through the garden to the main house. A thunderstorm had swept through during the night, full of all the flash and drama of any good springtime storm in Texas. This morning, though, not a cloud marred the sky. The garden sparkled with moisture and the air held a golden glow.

She passed flower beds that looked remarkably well tended, and wondered if Elda had taken on the task. She'd have to thank the woman later, when they met to go over everything that had happened in Amy's absence.

Birds chattered and squabbled in the big oak tree that shaded the main grassy area. As Amy stepped onto the covered back porch, she noticed the storm had left leaves piled up here and there against the white wicker furniture. She'd need to get out here with a broom before she returned to the carriage house for her first day back at work.

"Meme?" she called as she let herself in the sliding glass door. The smell hit her with a barrage of memories. Her grandparents' house always smelled the same: like cookies baking, lemon polish, and roses. She saw a vase of freshly cut blossoms on the cherry-wood coffee table in the back parlor.

"Amy?" First came the rattle and clunk of her grandmother's walker, then Meme appeared in the door to the kitchen dressed in a pale blue leisure suit. A smile lit up the wrinkled face topped by a blue-tinted beehive. "I'm so glad you're home!"

Amy hurried forward and enfolded her grand-mother in an awkward hug with the walker between them. Closing her eyes, she absorbed the familiar feel of Meme's small, soft body and the scent of per-fumed talcum powder.

"It's good to see you." Amy straightened to get a good look, to reassure herself that Meme was alive and well. Her grandmother looked good, with a bit a pink in her cheeks. She had the same flawless skin and pretty bones she'd passed on to her children and grandchildren. "Why are you using the walker?" Amy asked. "You were getting around fine before I left."

"Oh, my hip is acting up again." Meme sighed.

"Well, come, sit down."

"No, no, I'm in the middle of making a cake." Meme turned and hobbled her way back into the kitchen.

"A cake?" Amy followed her into the sparkling white room with lacy curtains and appliances that dated back to the fifties.

"I wanted to make something special for your homecoming."

"You don't need to do that," Amy said. Had Meme forgotten, yet again, that Amy was on a diet and didn't eat sweets.

"You know I don't mind." Meme struggled to hold on to the walker with one hand and pick up the spatula with the other. Chocolate batter filled the an-cient cast-iron mixer that was running on the white tile counter. Meme's gnarled, arthritic hand trembled as she scraped the sides of the bowl. "I'm afraid I'm not as up to this as I thought I was."

"Here, let me do that. You sit." Amy helped her grandmother to a chair at the breakfast table.

Meme grabbed one of her hands and squeezed it tightly as she settled in a seat. "I'm so thankful you made it home safe and sound. How dreadful this whole thing has been."

"Actually, it wasn't that bad," Amy said and realized that, other than how it ended, it had been wonderful. The most wonderful time of her life. "Do you want me to tell you about St. Barts?"

"Things have been total chaos around here," Meme proclaimed, then went on to list everything that had happened in Amy's absence.

Amy listened as she poured cake batter into two round pans and slipped them into the oven. She was thankful, actually, that her grandmother didn't ask about her trip, but the litany of burdens Meme had suffered seemed endless.

That annoyed her more than usual, as if five weeks away had weakened her tolerance for listening to Meme's woes.

Among them was a neighbor who had been diagnosed with prostate cancer. The wife was such a mess, it was all Meme could do to console the poor woman. These things were such a shock to everyone; people just didn't realize how their sorrows affected others. And then there was that tragic car wreck that had killed the son and daughter-in-law of one of Meme's deceased bridge partners. The funeral had been so difficult, what with the spring rains making Meme's arthritis ache. And the hip wasn't the only thing that had been acting up. Meme had had a near-

fatal heart attack right after Amy left, which she was
still recovering from.

"What?" Amy gasped in alarm, even knowing that
"heart attack" probably meant Meme had suffered
some angina. "Elda didn't tell me that!"

"Well, of course she didn't, dear." Meme sighed.
"I didn't want to ruin your vacation, so I asked her
not to say a thing."

"Meme, no." Amy sat down and took her grandmother's frail hand. "You can't keep things from me
like that. I have to know when I'm away that I can
check in and know what's going on. Otherwise traveling will be that much harder for me, and I've told
you how much I want to go places."

"Well, that's the problem with traveling, isn't it?"
Another sigh. "People always say 'everything's fine'
when you call home, but for all you know the house
has burned to the ground and they just don't want
to ruin your trip. But you're home now, thank the
good Lord. And I hope this whole ordeal has taken
care of your notion about going on any more trips."

Amy sat back as realization hit her. It struck with
the force of someone ripping tape off her eyes,
allowing her to see. Guy was right. Meme did it on
purpose.

Amy said traveling would be more difficult if she
couldn't count on honest reports when she called
home, and her grandmother counters like this?

On top of that, half the burdens Meme had suffered hadn't even been her own. She'd taken on a
neighbor's worries and the loss of someone she probably hadn't even seen in twenty years. Yet Amy was

still supposed to feel guilty for leaving Meme to cope with all that on her own?

"You know what, Meme"—she patted the table— "I need to go."

"But you just got here. And your cake isn't done yet."

Ah, yes, the cake. Let's get Amy home so we can fatten her up again.

No, no. She shook her head. This could not be as bad as she was thinking. Meme couldn't be that selfish. Her fears were real, and that's what drove her to be the way she was. She didn't mean to suck all the freedom out of her granddaughter's life by shackling Amy with her own fear.

If you can be brave enough to face your fears, why is it too much to ask your grandmother to face hers?

She shook Guy's words away. "I'm sorry, I really do have to go."

"Are you all right?" Meme struggled to her feet. "You look a little ill. You didn't catch anything on your trip, did you?"

"No." Amy hugged the woman, not knowing if she should laugh or cry. "I'm fine. I'll be back later to check on you."

"Very well." Meme squeezed her back. "Goodness, have you lost weight?"

"Yes I have. Quite a bit."

"Well, my word." Meme really looked at her and worry filled her pale eyes. "You need to be careful you don't lose too much, or you'll make yourself weak. But don't you look pretty? I like that dress on you. It's very flattering for a girl with your figure."

No it's not, Amy thought. The dress made her look huge. She shook her head. "I really do need to go."

"All right." Meme gave her another hug. "We'll talk more later."

"Yes. Maybe we will."

Amy left feeling on the verge of hysteria. How had she not seen Meme's manipulation more clearly before this? Actually, she had seen it—she just hadn't realized how blatant it was.

Why, though? Why had she looked at it through a filter of excuses all these years? Meme didn't mean to hurt her with her need to cling. Quite the opposite. She meant to keep Amy safe. But the clinging still did damage. Like a vine that wrapped itself around a tree until it choked the tree to death.

When she reached the carriage house, she found the door to the office downstairs open to let in the morning breeze. Apparently Elda had arrived while she'd been at the main house.

The woman sat at the desk talking on the hands-free phone, her fingers flying over the computer keyboard. In her early sixties, Elda radiated the kind of confidence and warmth that were the trademark of any good nanny. The moment she saw Amy, her face lit with a smile.

"Welcome home," she said after finishing the phone call. She removed the earpiece and came around to give Amy a hug. "So glad you're back. Tell me all about your trip."

Amy nearly burst into tears. Why couldn't this have been the greeting she got from her grandmother?

"Oh, dear." Elda clucked as she steered Amy to

one of the wingback chairs that faced the desk.
"What happened?"

"Nothing." Amy took a breath to steady her emotions as she looked about her pretty feminine office.
All the plants appeared to be watered, the Queen
Anne furniture polished. "I'm just feeling really tired
from the flight home."

"Then you should take the day off." Elda resumed
her seat behind the desk. "I can handle things here
for one more day."

"No, I've asked you to stay on longer than you
meant to. I can't ask you to do any more."

"Oh, pish." Elda snorted. "I've enjoyed it. You
have such a lovely place here. To sit and gaze out at
the garden while I work has been a pleasure."

"I noticed the garden has been tended. Thank you
for taking care of it."

"I didn't take care of it. Your grandmother did?"

"What? But . . . how? Her hip is acting up and she
says she had a heart attack—which I know is probably an exaggeration, but still, I really wish you hadn't
kept that from me. I know the two of you meant to
spare me, but I need to know these things."

Elda laughed. "Oh dear. That Daphne! She is
something. She didn't have a heart attack. She had a
little angina brought on by an excess of emotion, but
it wasn't even bad enough to take her to the hospital,
even though she wanted to call an ambulance and
the whole nine yards."

"Are you sure?" Amy asked, even though that was
exactly what she'd suspected. "Did it happen when
I got stranded on St. Barts?"

"Heaven's no." Elda waved that away. "It happened because she was upset with me. She lay on the sofa the first few days you were gone, expecting me to cook for her and clean because she was feeling so poorly. I told her I'd do no such thing, that she was perfectly capable of taking care of herself.

"So she did a little drama—and I ignored it. That's one of the things I've learned from dealing with spoiled children. If you ignore their tantrums, they quit throwing them."

Amy blinked. Had Elda just compared Meme to a spoiled child?

"After the first couple of weeks, she started venturing out to the garden, pulling weeds in a very amusing show of making sure I could see how much she was struggling. I ignored that too."

"You ignored her while she was struggling to pull weeds?" Anger flared as Amy wondered what she'd done leaving her grandmother in this woman's hands. "What if she'd hurt herself?"

"Amy." Elda fixed her with a stern look. "I had my eye on her, and if anything had happened that warranted attention, I'd have been out there in a snap. But the truth is, Daphne needs to get up, get some exercise and fresh air. I think it did her a world of good."

"Then why is she back to using her walker?"

"Well, goodness, I can't imagine." Elda raised a brow that said quite clearly that Meme had pulled out the walker for her granddaughter's benefit. "If you want my opinion, she needs to be more active socially. Maybe have her friends over for bridge."

"Most of her bridge-playing friends have passed on."

"They can't all have passed on. And surely she could make new friends. I have a scrapbooking group that meets every Thursday. Maybe you could encourage her to accept one of my invitations to join in."

So now it was Amy's fault that her grandmother didn't have friends? She rubbed her temple and wanted to cry. Or scream.

"Dear, are you okay?" Elda asked, leaning forward.

"I'm sorry. I'm just really tired."

"Well, then you do as I say and take the day off. I'll take care of everything here."

"No, we need to go over the assignments pending."

"I have everything under control." Elda put the earpiece back on. "You go rest."

Amy thought to argue. She never took days off or left someone else to pick up her slack. Exhaustion pulled at her, though, until she felt ready to keel over. "Are you sure?"

"Absolutely. You go on. Let me get back to work."

Amy went back outside and climbed the stairs that led to her apartment. Needing the comfort of dark, she left the draperies closed, when she normally would have flung all the windows open on such a gorgeous day; then she set up her laptop to check in with Maddy and Christine. For once the thought brought dread. How would she tell them what had happened? Their last e-mail exchange had been her telling them about her ultimatum to Guy to get him to show her his face before she left. They'd wished her luck and expected her to report back.

Could she possibly tell them what had happened?

No, she realized. She couldn't bring herself to put any of it into words, not with the shock of it still so fresh. She had to let them know she was home, though. And that she was okay. Okay? A bubble of hysteria rose up at that, but she swallowed it down and booted her e-mail.

She found several new posts from both her friends, the usual handful of spam.

And an e-mail from Guy.

She froze when she saw the address. They had used the direct connection between their computers most of the time, but they had used e-mail enough for him to know her address and her to recognize his. Except there was no Guy. So the e-mail was from Byron Parks.

Subject: *Please Read.*

Did she dare open it? What would he have to say? With fingers that shook, she opened the e-mail.

Message: *I just want to make sure you made it home safely. I don't want to bother you. This next week may be a little rough, though, depending on how many of the tabloids pick up the photos, and if they make the front page. I'm hoping they get buried inside or don't make it in at all. But if it's bad and you need someone to talk to, vent, whatever, I'm here.*

She started to tell him she had friends—real friends—for that but remembered her decision not to tell them everything. Plus, what had happened had happened to both her and Byron. Perhaps going through the fallout together would make it a little easier. Bracing herself, she typed a polite but cool response: *Yes, I'm home. I appreciate your concern and will keep your offer in mind.*

She'd just returned her attention to reading the e-mails from her friends, when a response from Byron popped up. Apparently he was online. She imagined him sitting in the tower with his laptop, the way she had so many times, only now she knew what he looked like.

Byron: *I'm glad you made it home without incident. I noticed you left your clothes, though. I meant for you to take them. I'll be happy to box them up and ship them.*

Amy: *I don't want them. You can keep them.*

There, that should take care of him. But again, he responded before she could move on: *I doubt they'd look good on me. I'll send them to you. What you do with them is up to you. I'll repeat my plea, though. Please, don't go back to hiding yourself. You're a beautiful woman, Amy. One of the most beautiful I've ever known. Don't hide yourself away.*

Anger had her fingers flying over the keyboard: *Considering your last girlfriend was Gillian Moore, I find that a little hard to believe. I think I'm handling enough here. Please don't make everything worse with false flattery.*

Byron: *You still don't believe me? That's starting to tick me off. You believed me when you thought I was ugly. Do you think only an ugly man would find you beautiful? Amy, I could choke you for that. You need to go take a good long look at yourself in the mirror. Or maybe not. Since you're back home, and therefore dealing with your grandmother, I bet you're sitting there in your old clothes with your hair scraped down in a tight braid. Don't do that to yourself. Don't lock yourself away like that.*

She stared at the words, realizing that was exactly what Guy would say. He was right too. She looked down at her jumper and made a face. She'd been back less than twenty-four hours and she was already reverting to who she'd been before.

Exactly what Guy would say.

That thought shook her. He'd told her while standing in the kitchen that maybe the real him was somewhere between Lance and Guy. That gave her something to think about. In fact, she had a lot of things to think about, like the fact that Elda had handled Meme quite well apparently. The house hadn't fallen down. The gardens hadn't shriveled up and died.

Amy had been gone a month, and everything had been fine. Better, actually, than when she was there. Definitely something to think about. She responded to Byron's plea by promising to do her best on the clothing front. Then she turned her attention to Maddy and Christine. Christine was in Colorado again since her schedule at the hospital allowed her to fly up for three or four days at a time. Amy put off their questions about what had happened in St. Barts by saying she'd tell them when they arrived for the bridal shower. That gave her a few days to decide how much to tell them.

With her friends appeased—well, not really; they were issuing threats demanding she fill them in on everything, but they were at least held at bay—she closed the laptop with a snap, took up her car keys, and headed for the mall.

Chapter 18

The right road is often the one most easily traveled.
—*How to Have a Perfect Life*

Amy actually enjoyed her shopping trip. She approached the mall with shoulders braced, determined to find some clothes similar to what Lance had picked out. Well, Byron. That was really strange to think about. She'd gone clothes shopping with Byron Parks, the son of a world-famous fashion model. How many women would like to claim that?

As luck would have it, while heading for the department store where she normally shopped, she stumbled onto a really great boutique that had comfortable clothes that all mixed and matched.

She managed to buy the foundation of a whole new wardrobe in that single store, including lots of fun, chunky jewelry.

The minute she got home, she started to e-mail Guy—but caught herself. She was so used to telling him about her day, it felt natural to shoot him an e-mail. Except he wasn't Guy. He was Byron.

Even so, something in her still felt compelled to follow up on their earlier exchange. As angry as she was, she remembered how he'd begged her not to revert to being a frump. If he felt half as strongly about that as she'd felt about wanting to draw Guy out, she should extend the courtesy of easing his worry.

After a lot of debate, she wrote: *I wanted to let you know I went shopping today and bought some very attractive clothes in styles I think would meet your approval. So it really isn't necessary for you to send the clothes you bought for me.*

Byron: *You went shopping? Really? I wish I could have been there. I love shopping with you. What did you buy?*

Amy frowned at the screen. Okay, that felt weird, to get a distinctly Lance kind of response but written in Guy's American way of speaking. She thought about ignoring him, but that seemed rude, so she told him about the store she'd found.

He answered with: *I know exactly the store you're talking about. It's a small chain. A friend I met through my mother models for their catalog. She says they have the most comfortable, flattering clothes she's ever worn, and the photo shoots are always in fun places.*

Amy: *You've never talked about friends or family before, or anything to do with your personal life.*

Byron: *I couldn't when you didn't know who I was. Now I can. If you want me to. You can ask me anything.*

Amy told herself she shouldn't. This man was not someone she wanted to know. Liar. She desperately wanted to know him. She'd spent the most incredible four weeks of her life with him. So he wasn't who she'd expected when the mask came off, so to speak, but she wanted to know who he was.

And so began four straight days of e-mailing back

and forth. The conversations were endless and lasted well into the night. Amy fell asleep with her laptop, and woke to a "Good morning" message every day.

He answered every question, telling her about his childhood being shuffled back and forth between his famous parents, spending the school year in California and his summers at his *grand-mère*'s house in southern France.

Amy: *Is that the grandmother whose kitchen inspired yours?*

Byron: *Exactly. I loved spending time there. She lives in a tiny house outside Narbonne and raises her own chickens and goats. My mother thinks her simple roots are embarrassing, but I always enjoyed my summers there. It was the only place I ever felt I could just relax and—I don't know—be myself.*

She found that sad, that he'd adopted his bored mask at such an early age. And she was sure now that the face Byron Parks showed the world was a mask. She remembered him saying that he might not be Guy, but he had been locked away. So he really was the scarred man hiding in the tower—but the scars were emotional. Not that it excused what he'd done to her, but it helped her understand.

Then came the morning the tabloids hit the newsstands. Byron greeted her with: *I hope you've done your grocery shopping for the week, because you might want to avoid the checkout lines for a while.*

Amy: *How bad is it?*

Byron: *We made the front page of* The Sun. *Actually, the picture on the front isn't that bad. You're going to hate the ones inside, though. God, I'm so sorry about this.*

I wish I could get my hands on that little weasel and choke him with his camera strap.

Of course, she had to go and see. With her stomach in knots, she approached the checkout line and saw the photo. It was a close-up of Byron mostly, holding her against his chest with a look of rage on his face. He had one hand over her face, his other hand raised toward the camera as if to block it or grab it.

With people standing in line behind her, she didn't have the guts to open the tabloid and see what other photos they'd used, so she bought it and brought it home. All she could do was stare in numb shock at grainy pictures of her naked body running up the stairs. The headline made her even more queasy: BYRON PARKS CAUGHT WITH HOUSEKEEPER.

Would anyone who knew where she'd been and what she'd been doing put that together? Fortunately, St. Barts wasn't mentioned on the cover, so the handful of people who might figure it out— Maddy, Christine, Elda, and Meme—would have to read the article inside. Since none of them read tabloids, she felt relatively safe.

As for the article, she cringed over that too. They claimed Byron was so heartbroken over his breakup with Gillian Moore that he'd turned to his chunky housekeeper for consolation.

When her nerves settled, she e-mailed him: *Well, they're nothing if not predictable.*

Byron: *And inaccurate. I was hardly heartbroken when Gillian dumped me. It just woke me up to the fact that I didn't like the way my life was going. As for the "chunky" crack, I find that insulting to women everywhere. They're*

*implying that the only way a woman who doesn't meet
their definition of sexy could get a man is on the rebound.
I could kill over that. What about you, though? You handling this okay?*

Amy: *I don't know. I feel a little shaky, but it doesn't
quite seem real. I can't imagine how I'd feel if you could
see my face. How are you?*

Byron: *Pissed, mostly. It'll pass, though. I got a few
raised brows when I went to the market to buy a copy,
but then, I've been getting a lot of stares and whispers
since I ditched the wig and goatee. Having La Bête come
out of the tower has been the big news in Gustavia this
week. I have to say, I miss Lance. I really enjoyed being
an average joe. I've never had that before.*

Amy cringed as she typed: *So I guess all the men
who worked at the fort know that's me, even if no one
here knows. That's embarrassing to think about.*

Byron: *I am so sorry, Amy. Not just about this, but
about everything. Do you think you can ever forgive me?
I never meant to hurt you. I know we can never be together, that I'll never be the man you thought you fell in
love with, but do you think we could somehow be friends.
Just friends. I won't pressure you for more.*

Amy thought long and hard about that as she
moved through her day. Having the photos hit the
newsstand didn't affect her life other than making
her cringe inside. She worked in the office, the way
she had for years, taking calls from people wanting
nannies, listening to their travel plans, and thinking
of the places she'd like to go. That afternoon, she
coaxed Meme outside to help her get the garden
ready for the party.

Elda was right, Meme needed fresh air and exercise. And Guy—no, Byron—was also right that if Amy would be as firm with her grandmother as she was with him, they'd make progress. So when Meme complained that she felt too poorly to do more than sit and watch, Amy plopped a low stool next to one of the beds and thrust a pair of clippers in her hands. Meme had been stunned at first, and then she'd obsessed about an age spot on her arm that surely had to be cancer from the sun, but Amy forced herself, with a lot of strong willpower, to ignore her.

Thinking about Byron provided a good distraction. Of all the things he'd said, the two things that stuck out most were his comment about enjoying being an average joe and that his favorite times growing up were spent at a tiny house with chickens and goats where he could be himself. He'd spent his whole life being the son of legendary producer Hamilton Parks and famous fashion model Fantina Follet. How many people used that? How often did people befriend him because of his connections?

No wonder he'd gone into hiding to think things through on his own. He probably didn't have anyone he trusted enough to turn to in the midst of an emotional crisis. She thought about Maddy and Christine and imagined how much harder life would be without them. In this one instance, though, she couldn't turn to them. She could only turn to Byron. He was the only one who truly knew what she was going through.

That night, after a good long cry in front of the computer, she finally typed: *I do forgive you. And yes, we can be friends. I've thought about everything that happened, and I can see that you did try to protect me. I wouldn't take no for an answer, though, so I have to accept that I am partially to blame. I still feel as if the man I fell in love with died, though, and that's hard, because I can't share that grief with anyone here.*

Byron: *You can share it with me. You can share anything with me. I wish I were there to hold you, if you'd let me.*

Would she let him? He wasn't there, though, so it was a moot point. Instead, she asked: *What are your plans now that you've come out of hiding? Will you go back to California?*

Byron: *No. I'll keep my house there, but I've decided to make this my main residence. I've thought about it, and I can do a lot of my job from here.*

Amy: *You have a job? I mean, I sorta know you do something in the movie business, but it always looked to me like all you ever did was go to parties with a lot of famous people. I have a hard time picturing you going into an office and working.*

Byron: *Actually, the parties are my office in a way. I'm a script packager.*

Amy: *A what?*

Byron: *Agents send me screenplays or books they'd like to option for film. When I find one I like, I buy the option, then I go to parties where I can pitch it to big-name actors, get a director and/or producer interested, then sell the whole thing to a studio for a tidy profit.*

Amy: *Sounds like a fun job.*

Byron: *It is. The part I like, though, isn't actually going to the parties. It's the thrill of discovering a really great story, then seeing it get made into a movie. It'll ruin my reputation as a bored cynic—although I'm pretty sick of that, so who cares—but going to a premiere for a movie I packaged and seeing it brought to life is indescribable.*

Amy: *You're kidding? I mean, I imagine it would be*

amazing, but how do you manage to not show that? I've seen pictures of you at premieres, and if you're not on the verge of yawning—well, all I can say is, you're a better actor than most of the ones up on the screen.

Byron: *Yeah, well, I'm tired of acting. That's what I figured out during all these months sitting in this tower. I'm sick to death of acting. All my old friends are just going to have to get used to the new me. As for working, I can easily read scripts here, then do the preliminary work over the phone or invite people down for meetings. I don't think I'll have any trouble getting actors and producers to fly down to the Caribbean for a weekend party. If it weren't for those damned photos, I'd ask you to come play hostess with me. The fort could be like your grandparents' house, where we let the world come to us.*

Amy thought that over as she continued preparing for the bridal shower, which seemed strangely appropriate. The shower would be the first party in her grandparents' garden since her mother's death. She badgered Meme once again into helping. They planned the menu together and actually had fun pouring over cookbooks, discussing decoration, and reminiscing over past parties. The reminiscing seemed to be good for Meme. They usually avoided talking about Amy's mother, so it was nice to remember happy occasions.

"You know what I think you should do?" Amy told her grandmother. "I think you should go with Elda to one of her scrapbooking parties and do an album of Mom's life.

Meme insisted she couldn't handle it emotionally or physically. Amy held firm, though, and finally won a promise that Meme would try it one time.

The only damper on the day was having to listen to Meme's endless worries over everything that could possibly go wrong the day of the shower. And then there were the jabs that put her teeth on edge.

"Maybe now that you've lost a little weight, I'll be planning a wedding for you someday," Meme would say. "There's always hope, even if you never have been one for attracting boys."

That nearly sent her diving for the plate of sweets that always sat within reach, but she resisted. Did she really want to live with that for the rest of Meme's life, though? And then what? Continue living here alone for the rest of her life?

That brought her back to thinking of Byron's last e-mail. She remembered her first day at the fort, when she'd imagined turning the place into a bed-and-breakfast and how that would be the ultimate lifestyle. What he described sounded even more thrilling. The photos, though, weren't the only things keeping her from jumping on the idea. She'd have to leave Meme. Plus, living at the fort with Byron would be completely different now that she knew the truth.

Would they go back to being lovers?

The idea made her flash hot and cold as memories assailed her. What would it be like to make love to him with the lights on? Had she forgiven him enough for that? Would she be as comfortable with him now that she knew how gorgeous he was? Could she handle letting him see her, not just touch her in the dark?

The questions made her head spin. Finally she answered him with the simplest objection: *I can't imag-*

ine hosting a party for celebrities. I love cooking and entertaining, but I wouldn't know what to say to people like that.

Byron: *You'd get used to it. I grew up around celebrities, but I've watched a lot of actors and writers who come from very different backgrounds adjust. Some adjust by turning into arrogant assholes, but others stay grounded and real. Speaking of writing, have you thought any more about selling your children's books?*

Amy: *I have, actually. I read back over some of them and picked out one I think could be good with some polishing, but I don't know anything about how to sell a story. I don't even know how to format it so it looks professional.*

Byron: *Shoot, I can help you with that. Why don't you e-mail it to me, and I'll tell you what to do.*

Amy: *Oh, goodness, you mean let you read it? I'm not sure I'm ready for that.*

Byron: *If you're going to submit it to any agents, you're going to have to let them read it. Besides, you've let me read your work before. And I have to say one more time, you definitely have a way with words.*

Amy: *Oh, God, I'm trying to forget that. I blush every time I think of it.*

Byron: *Yeah, I get a little flushed too.*

She blinked at that response. Was he flirting with her? All her questions from earlier came pouring back.

Byron: *Now I've embarrassed you, haven't I? I apologize. I forget sometimes that we're supposed to be just friends now. I miss you, though, Amy. I really miss you.*

Tears sprang to her eyes as she answered: *I miss you too.*

Byron: *Except it isn't me you miss. It's Guy.*

Amy: *I'm not so sure anymore. I'm so confused. I think at times it is you I fell in love with. I wish there was a way to find out.*

Byron: *But there isn't. Not unless we hide from the world, and I can't ask you to sneak around that way. Besides, no one can hide forever. The minute we're seen together in public, everyone will know you're the woman in the photos. God, life can be cruel. I finally fall in love for the first and last time in my life, because I can't imagine ever feeling for anyone else what I feel for you, and I can't be with you without hurting you.*

Amy thought about that on the final day before the shower as she and Meme baked for hours. Maddy and Christine would both be arriving in Austin later, but not until after dark, so she wouldn't see them until the party.

For the first time she thought about telling them everything and begging for advice. Could she handle dating a man like Byron Parks with all that would entail? He said he planned to make St. Barts his main residence, but he'd still be going to Hollywood, the land of the paparazzi. Would he want her to go with him?

Good heavens, was she actually thinking about moving to the Caribbean and living with him? Could she really leave Meme?

She glanced at her grandmother, who was rolling out the sugar cookie dough they'd made the day before. In spite of all her worrying and complaining, Meme seemed steadier these last few days. Having the party to focus on seemed to help her. Elda had been so good with her, maybe they could work out something long term. In fact, Elda had even hinted at buying the franchise.

Turning back, she stared out the window at the garden. As much as she loved this place, did she really want to spend her entire life here?

She remembered Byron begging her not to let her sense of duty lock her away. Odd how in the last days, when she remembered their time together, in her mind she'd started picturing Byron instead of the image she'd formed of Guy. It was Byron she'd shared all that with.

And it was Byron she wanted to be with.

He was right, though. The minute they went public, her family and friends and everyone would know that was her who'd been caught having sex with him.

For some reason, the thought didn't horrify her quite as much as it had at first. Wouldn't Meme have a cow, though, if she found out her shy, frumpy granddaughter had been sleeping with one of the most sought-after men in the world? And she hadn't merely slept with him; she'd won his heart.

He loved her. He thought she was beautiful and sexy, and he loved her.

The amazement of it blossomed inside her. Even more amazing, she realized that she believed him. Because she was beautiful and sexy and smart and strong and talented. Why wouldn't he love her?

And why should she have to give up her life to ease the fears of a woman who had kept her from seeing those things about herself?

If you can be brave enough to face your fears, why is it expecting too much to ask your grandmother to face hers?

Was Amy brave enough, though, to take this step?

Her heart raced all that day. When night came, she sat before her computer, shaking inside as she typed: *What if I were willing to be seen with you, to let everyone know? What if I agreed to hire a nurse for Meme and move back to St. Barts?*

Byron: *Are you serious? Please, be serious, but also be sure. You told me once that you wouldn't want the lifestyle that comes as part of dating a man like me. You said, not for all the money in the world. And even though I want to minimize my time in Hollywood, I still want to go on packaging deals. Are you up to attending premieres on my arm? Having pictures of us appear in magazines and tabloids—although with our clothes on? Going to the occasional Hollywood party, where, yes, there will be people you don't like along with people you do? I know people who would give anything to have what I'm describing, but I know you're not one of them. I'd be there with you, though, every step of the way. But please be sure.*

Amy bit her lip to hold back the joy building inside her as she answered: *Maybe what I should have said is I wouldn't do that for all the money in the world—but I would do it for love. I asked you to have the courage to show your face. Can I demand any less of myself?*

Byron: *Are you saying you love me? Me, not Guy.*

Amy: *I think you are simply different facets of the same man. That you are Guy and Lance and Byron. The best parts of all three. And yes, I do love you. I have to warn you, though. I'm an old-fashioned girl who's just changed her mind about never getting married. If I'm going to do this, I want at least the possibility of family and forever. So if you're asking me to be sure, I'm asking you the same thing. Are you sure I'm what you want?*

Several minutes passed as she waited in agony for

his response. Maybe she had asked for too much up front. Maybe she should have simply said she was willing to be seen with him and then taken it from there. But she really did suddenly and quite desperately want marriage and babies and the rest of her life with this man.

Byron finally responded with: *I'll give you my answer tomorrow.*

Her stomach dropped all the way through the floor as she stared at the screen. She'd gotten up the courage to do something as terrifying as bring up marriage, and he was going to make her wait until tomorrow for his answer? How could he do that to her? Didn't he know how scary this was?

And why tomorrow, of all days, did her life have to be hanging in the balance? She needed to pull herself together enough to host a bridal shower. How would she ever make it through the day without a complete meltdown?

Chapter 19

Dreams don't come true on their own. We make them come true with faith, courage, and determination.
—*How to Have a Perfect Life*

"Amy, it's so good to see you!" Maddy exclaimed the minute Amy opened the front door to the main house.

Amy had only a glimpse of her friend's bright smile and saucy red hair before she found herself pulled into a tight hug. She squeezed back with equal enthusiasm. "I'm so glad you're here."

"Let me get a look at you." Maddy stepped back to arm's length, as colorful as ever in a gauzy orange shirt she wore belted at the hips over a wildly patterned hippie shirt. She beamed in approval over Amy's ecru capri pants and tank top covered by a colorful silk shirt that draped to midthigh. The playful necklace and earring matched the tropical design. "You look gorgeous!" Maddy proclaimed. "And I love your hair clipped up like that. Look at all those sexy ringlets, and highlights too."

"Thank you." Amy released a laugh and prayed it didn't turn into tears. Byron's e-mail had left her emotions wound so taut, anything could happen.

"Oh." Maddy turned to the two older women behind her. "You know my mother, Mrs. Howard, of course. And this is Joe's mother, Mama Fraser."

"Hello." Amy greeted both women. Maddy's mother looked so drab and shy, Amy always had a hard time understanding where Maddy came by such fire.

"So good to finally meet you," Mama Fraser, Joe's adoptive mother, said with a friendly smile. She might hobble along with a cane, but the lively twinkle in her eyes said she'd gladly take on the world. How very different that was from Meme, even though the two widows were about the same age.

"Please come in," Amy said. "The party's out back."

"Is Christine here?" Maddy asked as they made their way through the living room.

"She arrived just a bit ago. She said something about Alec and Joe spending the day together to finalize the wedding plans?"

"Yep," Maddy confirmed. "Those two have gotten really tight over the last few weeks, which is so great. I like the thought of our husbands being friends."

"That is nice." Amy offered a sincere, if distracted, smile. Could she slip away to check her e-mail and see if Byron's answer had come through? But what if it had and he said he had no interest in marriage ever? What if he said he didn't want anything more serious than living together with no commitment? She'd have a complete breakdown and ruin the shower.

The sound of laughter and female voices grew louder as she opened the sliding glass door.

"Oh, wow," Maddy said as they stepped onto the

patio and saw the crowded garden. "Amy, you've outdone yourself."

"Thank you." She looked around to be sure everything was as it should be. She'd been such a wreck while setting things up, for all she knew she'd forgotten something major like the tablecloth and napkins. Everything appeared to be in order, though.

Several small round tables with white cloths and white folding chairs sat on the lush green lawn, surrounded by the colorful garden. On each one was an arrangement of fresh flowers in old-fashioned coffee- or teapots. Strings of tiny white bells danced from the limbs of the sprawling oak tree that shaded the area. Two larger tables had been set at the edge of the grassy island against the tall hedge. The refreshments Amy and Meme had made—mini scones, fanciful pastries, and finger sandwiches cut in the shape of hearts—covered one, while presents covered the other. Most of the guests had already arrived, friends and family of both brides.

She spotted Christine talking to one of the women from the ER. Dr. Christine Ashton looked cool and classy, as always, in gray slacks and a cream blouse. Her blond hair hung down her back, shiny and straight. The minute she saw them she hurried over to hug Maddy. "You're finally here."

"Sorry we're running late," Maddy said. "Our flight got in so late last night, it was kind of hard to get moving this morning."

"Same here," Christine answered, then held her hand out to Maddy's mother. "Hello, Mrs. Howard. It's good to see you again. And you must be Mama Fraser." After the older women returned the greeting, Christine turned to Amy. "Now that we're all here, the three of us need some serious girlfriend time. Tonight."

"Definitely," Maddy agreed and gave Amy a pointed look.

The expression in both her friends' eyes told her they planned to grill her about "Guy." Her stomach tightened at the thought. "Let me introduce everyone."

She guided the little group to the table where Meme held court with Christine's mother and sister-in-law. Seeing them, Amy felt as if a faded and aged version of the old Meme, the queen bee of her social set, had come back to life. Meme had her blue hair piled high and wore her best pink dress with lace at the collar and cuffs.

"So tell me more about this wedding," Meme said once Mrs. Howard and Mama Fraser were seated.

"I need to check the refreshments," Amy said.

"I'll help," Christine offered, sounding slightly desperate. The two of them moved toward the refreshment table.

"I swear," Amy said, "if I hear Meme ask, 'What if it rains?' one more time, I'll scream. She's positively horrified that you two let the men plan a whole outdoor wedding on their own."

"She's not the only one," Christine said. "My mother is still pouting that I didn't let her throw some huge, formal society wedding at the country club. My father, on the other hand, is still trying to talk me out of marrying a younger man who grew up in a trailer home. But you know what?" Christine shrugged and happiness lit her eyes. "I don't care what they think. I'm finally through living my life to please them."

"Goodness, you really mean it, don't you?" Amy eyed her in surprise. Christine had expressed the same sentiment over the last few weeks, but hearing her say it—easily rather than resentfully—Amy could tell she really did mean it.

"I do." Christine smile. "I'm learning, with a lot of help from Alec, to let it go."

"I'm glad," Amy said and glanced back at Meme. "How does it feel? To let go of something you've clung to so long?"

"Fabulous." Christine laughed more freely than Amy had ever heard her laugh. "And very liberating."

Maddy joined them, suppressing a grin. "You guys are missing the entertainment."

"What do you mean?" Amy asked, eyeing the table where the mothers sat.

"Meme was fretting about the weather and the caterer and the flowers and insisting that men couldn't possibly handle all that on their own—a statement I find interesting considering that Meme's husband designed all this." Maddy waved a hand at the garden. "And Mama Fraser looked her dead in the eye with that expression that always puts the girls at the summer camp into their places, and said, 'Frankly, I'd trust my son to plan anything.' Then she looked at Mrs. Ashton and said, 'Aren't we fortunate that he came up with the clever idea of having the ceremony and reception someplace fun like the Wildflower Center instead of something boring and stuffy like so many formal weddings?'" Maddy covered her mouth briefly. "You should have seen the look on both their faces. Shut them up, just like that."

"Really?" Christine raised a brow. "Okay, that settles it. From everything you've told me about Mama Fraser, I've decided that's who I want to be when I grow up."

"The woman has so much spunk," Amy said. "I wish Meme could be like that."

Maddy and Christine exchanged a meaningful look, and Amy knew what they were thinking.

"Don't say it. Please." She held up her hand. They'd both told her more than once that Meme didn't have spunk because no one ever expected her to. Her husband had pampered her their whole married life, and when he died Amy had slipped right into the role. No matter how Byron responded, she was determined to change that, because she was starting to see that playing Meme's game was hurting her grandmother, not helping. "You'll be happy to know I'm going to be making some changes around here. I'm not exactly sure what yet, but things are going to change."

"Really?" Maddy lit up. "I think that is the best wedding present you could have given me."

"It's not going to be easy, though." Amy pressed a hand to her stomach. "But I'm going to have a long talk with Meme about hiring a nurse. And this time, I'm not going to take no for an answer."

"Amy," Christine said. "She doesn't need a nurse. She's not as feeble as she pretends to be."

"Well, think of it as a companion then. And the woman I have in mind will be a lot tougher than me."

Maddy laughed. "I'm not sure there is anyone tougher than Mother Amy."

"Watch it, Gypsy Girl," Amy said, using Maddy's nickname from college. They were quite a threesome: Gypsy Girl, the free spirit; Mother Amy, the nurturer; and the Pristine Christine, the brainy ice princess.

How on earth had three such different woman become so close? And what would her life have been like without them? Her eyes prickled with emotion, letting her know the only way she'd make it through the party was if she kept moving. She busied her hands arranging refreshments on a serving platter. "I need to pass these around and check on our guests. And you two need to mingle."

As if on cue, one of Maddy's former neighbors from when she lived in Austin came up to say hi.

Amy passed out sandwiches and scones and refilled the delightful hodgepodge of dainty teacups. She chatted with people she knew and people she didn't, playing hostess as she had so often as a child. How wonderful it felt to be entertaining again, in this garden that held some of her happiest memories. It was time to move on, though. To create a new magical place with Byron. If he wanted what she wanted.

Had his answer arrived?

Her nerves stretched a little tighter. She laughed and talked and poured more tea.

"Okay, everyone," she finally called. "Time for Maddy and Christine to open presents."

The guests shifted in their chairs to face the table piled with gifts, where Maddy and Christine sat in the chairs she'd decorated like thrones. As the maid of honor, Amy sat nearby, writing down who gave what to whom. Excitement bubbled all about her as women *ooh*ed and *ahh*ed over kitchenware, dishes, and novelties that ranged from tasteful to silly.

Maddy purposely broke several ribbons, a traditional wish for children. "Joe wants at least two kids," she explained. "At our age, I figure we better get busy."

"Hey, maybe you'll get pregnant on your honeymoon," Christine suggested.

"What about you?" Maddy asked. "You haven't broken a single ribbon."

"You got it," Christine laughed. "Alec and I are having too much fun, just the two of us."

Amy watched her friends glow with happiness and felt a little stab of envy through her joy.

When the last gift had been opened, she helped pick up wrapping paper and made streamers of bows for keepsakes. "Nobody go," she called. "I have more tea and some of my grandmother's sugar cookies coming."

Several people moaned, complaining they'd gained at least ten pounds, but no one left.

Amy circled the garden with a platter of cookies and the teapot. Another half hour, she told herself. That's all she had to hang on; then she could race upstairs and check her e-mail. Depending on what she found, she could either fall into a sobbing heap on her friends or announce that she and Byron might not be far behind them in walking down the aisle.

Her hands shook as she refilled Mrs. Howard's teacup.

"Amy, I meant to tell you," Maddy's mother said

in her quiet voice, "you look lovely today. Have you lost weight?"

"Yes, I have. Thank you."

"Maddy tells me you just returned from the Caribbean. Did you have a good time?"

"I had"—she thought of everything that had happened, and warmth filled her cheeks—"a wonderful time."

"Well, I love that outfit on you." The timid woman eyed it with obvious longing. "Did you buy it there? It's very young and stylish."

"You don't think it's too flashy?" Meme asked before Amy could answer. "I've always thought once you reach a certain age, the latest fashions make a woman look silly, and even older than she is."

Amy froze, staring at her grandmother in disbelief. In her heart, she had to believe the digs weren't intentional. But they still hurt. Meme had picked at her confidence all her life. For the first time she didn't try to swallow anger over that. A whole flood of resentment burst through the dam she'd built through years of overeating.

"Old?" Mama Fraser snorted before Amy could let her tirade loose. "Why, Amy's no older than Maddy and Christine. And look at them? Christine getting married for the first time. Maddy and Joe starting a family, the good Lord willin'."

"Yes." Meme sighed and patted her chest. "That does give me hope that someday my Amy will find a nice man who appreciates the shy type. He'd be getting quite a catch since she is a very good cook."

Amy tightened her grip on the teapot. When she spoke, her voice came out strong and level, contrasting sharply with the tremors assailing her insides. "I happen to think I have a lot more to recommend me as 'a good catch' than my talent in the kitchen."

Meme frowned at the sharpness of her words. "Amy, are you sure you didn't pick up some tropical bug on your trip. You've been acting very strangely since your return."

Words that had been suppressed for decades built up inside her chest. The only thing that stopped them from bursting free was knowing she stood in the middle of her friends' bridal shower, and she refused to ruin that. But that couldn't stop the words completely. "The only thing I picked up in the Caribbean is a backbone."

"What an odd thing to say." Meme looked taken aback.

"Well," Mama Fraser said, apparently sensing the tension crackling around Amy. "As much as I do love everything you cooked for the party today, I have to agree that you have a great deal more than that to attract a man."

"Thank you." Amy lifted her chin. "As a matter of fact, I do have someone special that I met during my trip, and he would definitely agree with you."

"Oh, how delightful." Mama Fraser clasped her hands together. "Tell us all about him. Do I hear wedding bells in your near future."

"Quite possibly, yes."

"Oh, dear." Meme patted her chest harder. "I think my angina is acting up, and I left my pills inside. Oh, good heavens!" She gasped in pain, clutching her left rib cage.

Mrs. Ashton's eyes went wide with alarm. "Christine!"

Mrs. Howard leapt up to help as Meme slumped in her chair, her eyelids fluttering.

Amy watched as if from a distance as Christine raced over to examine her grandmother.

Christine checked the eyes, monitored the pulse. "Where does it hurt?"

"My left . . . side," Meme panted.

"Here?" Christine probed her ribs.

"Yes!" Meme gasped. "I need my nitrous glycerin tablets. They—they're in the house."

"Try her pocket," Amy said, setting the teapot and platter of cookies down with a clatter.

Christine dug in the pocket of Meme's dress. Finding the bottle, she shook out a pill and slipped it into Meme's mouth. "Take a deep breath for me, to help you stay calm."

"The doctor said my heart could go at any time," Meme said.

"Mrs. Baker." Christine enunciated every syllable. "You are not having a heart attack. I only gave you the nitrous as a precaution."

"Oh, dear. Oh, my. Amy?" Meme reached a hand toward her. "Hold my hand. Has anyone called an ambulance?"

"You don't need an ambulance," Christine said, still monitoring the pulse. "You're having indigestion, not a heart attack. You ate too many sweets."

"I most certainly am not having indigestion." Meme gathered enough strength to scald Christine with a look. "I've had heart palpitations before. I know what they feel like."

Mrs. Ashton pulled a mobile phone from her purse. "I'm calling your father."

"Fine." Christine rolled her eyes. "That's exactly what we need to do during an acute attack of dramatitis. Call the head of cardiology in the middle of his golf game because a lowly trauma specialist isn't qualified to treat theatrics."

"Must you always be so impertinent?" Mrs. Ashton asked.

"Actually, I must." Christine smiled sweetly at her mother. "It's a burning need inside me I just can't control. Sorry."

Amy giggled. It was all too funny, really. Just too funny. All the guests had gathered around, looking on with a blend of confusion and concern.

Maddy came up behind Amy and took hold of her shoulders, straining to see the action. "What happened?"

Amy pressed the back of her hand to her mouth, battling laughter. "I told her I'd met a man."

"Well, that explains it." Christine gave another eye roll.

"You mean Guy?" Maddy asked.

"Yes and no," Amy said.

Maddy turned her by the shoulders to stare at her face. "What do you mean, yes and no?"

"Oh, my God," someone in the crowd said. "Who is *that*?"

"He looks familiar," another woman said.

"He looks gorgeous" came a third whisper. And then, "Wow, that's what's-his-name. Byron Parks. His picture was all over this week's issue of *The Sun*."

Amy turned with a gasp. The world fell away as she saw him standing on the walkway that led to the front of the house. He'd appeared as if by magic, looking suave and casually sophisticated in gray slacks and a black short-sleeved shirt. Everyone around her fell silent. Even Meme.

His eyes went to Amy, and she saw a shock of longing followed by uncertainty. He looked over his shoulder, toward the street, then back at her. "I, um, I may have the wrong address. I was looking for . . . someone."

His eyes told her he hadn't expected to stumble onto a party. He'd come, though. He'd come! All the way from St. Barts to deliver his answer in person.

Which meant it had to be yes. He really did love her, and he wanted a life with her.

From the apology and need filling his eyes, she knew he'd wanted to talk to her privately first—not thrust her into the middle of a public scene that would link them together forever.

The apology turned to a plea. "Perhaps someone could tell me the correct address for . . . the woman I'm looking for."

Amy stepped forward, smiling as she answered in a clear voice. "You have the right address. And I'm exactly who you're looking for."

"Oh, thank God." He hurried toward her. She met him halfway and leapt into his arms. He crushed her to him and buried his face in her hair. "Are you sure about this? Are you really sure?"

Leaning back, she beamed up at him. "Yes. I'm very sure."

"Okay. Then here goes." He cupped her face in

his hands and stared into her eyes. "I want you looking at me when I ask you this."

"I'm looking." She drank in the sight of his face. This beautiful, wonderful, complicated man loved her.

Fear wrinkled his brow. "Will you marry me?"

"Yes!"

"Yes!" He shouted in triumph and lifted her off her feet to twirl her about. Throwing her head back, she laughed at the sky.

When he set her down, Amy turned to the crowd, gripping his hand. "Maddy, Christine, everybody, I'd like you to meet—" She hesitated, wondering how to introduce him. She looked at him, then back to her friends, laughing in disbelief. "My fiancé, Byron Parks."

Meme did a classic swoon while everyone else stared.

"Maddy, Christine," Amy clarified, "this is Guy."

"That's Guy?" Christine stood, motioning one of the nurses to take over with Meme. A chaos of questions followed as Maddy and Christine came forward.

Amy explained the best she could, through laughter and tears. She held on to Byron the whole time, shaking with happiness.

Finally Maddy waved all the questions away. "We'll sort it out later, when you can talk. For now"—Maddy hugged her—"congratulations, Amy!"

"Thank you." Amy found herself in Christine's arms next.

"Yea you." Christine squeezed her tight.

Then they each hugged Byron. He looked startled

at that. She laughed at his expression, knowing he probably wasn't used to having strangers hug him.

"I know." Maddy smiled. "We'll make it a triple wedding."

"Oh, no, we couldn't," Amy protested. "The wedding is only a week away. That's too soon." But when she looked at Byron, hope sparked inside her. "Isn't it?"

He kissed her hand, smiling into her eyes. "Considering my plan was to drag you to the nearest courthouse the instant you said yes, I'd say it's not soon enough."

Amy looked at her friends. "Are you sure? All the plans are set. Goodness, I'd need a dress."

"We can handle that," Maddy insisted.

"Are you sure, though?" Amy asked again. "I was supposed to be the maid of honor."

"Personally I'd love to have you be a bride," Christine said. "Are *you* sure, though?"

Amy looked at Byron.

Conviction shone in his eyes as he said, "I've never been more sure of anything in my life."

Amy threw her arms around her friends. "Then yes. Yes, I would love a triple wedding!" Leaning back, she grinned at them, the three of them joined by their hands. "I love you guys so much. This is just too perfect."

"It is," Maddy and Christine agreed. "Absolutely too perfect."

Epilogue

"Here we go," Amy said as she carried a tray of drinks onto the gallery just outside the living room. "Time for our anniversary toast."

Maddy and Christine sat in the rattan chairs she and Byron had picked out. Potted palms provided some welcome shade, even though the day was mild with just the right amount of breeze coming up from the bay. Over the past year, they'd built several guest suites on the upper floor of the fort and turned the lower level into entertainment space with a poolside bar, game room, and changing room with showers. They'd had a lot of people come to stay, but nothing as special as the company they had now.

"I have to say, Amy, when you decide to break free, you really break free." Maddy shook her head in wonder at the view. "As much as I love Santa Fe, this has to be one of the most beautiful places on earth."

"You haven't seen Silver Mountain yet," Christine

countered. "I agree, though, this is pretty spectacular."

Down in the courtyard, Joe and Alec were doing laps in the pool while Byron sat in a lounge chair nearby, his ever-present mobile phone pressed to his ear. After the wedding, they'd all agreed to spend their anniversaries together, rotating between St. Barts, Santa Fe, and Silver Mountain. Amy was glad she'd pulled the short straw to play hostess first.

"I can't believe it's our first-year anniversary already," Amy said as she set the tray down on the coffee table, then fussed a bit with the fruit and tiny paper umbrellas that garnished the three hurricane glasses. Satisfied, she took a seat between her two friends, then frowned at the men. "Are Alec and Joe still racing?"

"Yep," Maddy confirmed, adjusting her sunglasses. "Joe can't stand it that Alec can swim faster, so I think his strategy is to wear him out."

"Fat chance." Christine shook her head at the two men. "He has no idea what he's up against. Joe may be a former Army Ranger and one of the fittest men I've ever seen, but Alec has enough adrenaline to fuel a space shuttle. Although, can I just say, *yum* to all the eye candy down there?"

"Absolutely!" Maddy said as they all took in the sight of three gorgeous buff men in swim trunks. "What's Byron doing, though? Does that man ever get off the phone?"

Amy bit her lip, wondering if she should tell them now or wait until her news was for sure. "He's working on a deal to have my children's books turned into a series of animated movies."

"Your *Flying Ship* books?" Maddy asked. "Amy! That's fantastic! Why haven't you told us?"

"It's not a done deal yet."

"With Byron Parks putting it together?" Christine gave her an arched look. "I'd say it's pretty done. And I'm so proud of you for everything you've accomplished." Christine hugged her. "Dealing with Meme. Publishing your first book with more to come. Finding a really wonderful man who clearly adores you."

Down in the courtyard, Alec sent a spray of water over Byron on the lounge chair. "Yo, dude! Get off the phone."

Byron ended his call and did a cannonball into the swimming pool, making all three woman laugh.

"I'd say we all did well," Maddy observed. "So let's make that toast."

"Okay, here's Maddy's drink." Amy handed an alcohol-free one to the expectant mother. "And here's Christine's." Taking up her own drink, she said, "So here's to our one-year anniversary."

"Actually, second anniversary," Christine said.

"What?" Maddy asked as they all lowered their glasses.

"The challenge," Christine explained. "Today isn't just our wedding anniversary. It's the second anniversary of when we went to Jane's book signing and made our challenge."

"Goodness," Amy said. "A lot can happen in two years' time."

"No kidding." Maddy patted her round belly. At six months' pregnant, she absolutely glowed with happiness. "Two years ago, I never would have predicted any of this. Life can certainly get interesting when you decide to face your fears and go for it."

"It certainly can." Christine nodded.

"How are you feeling?" Amy asked Maddy.

"You mean aside from exhausted and emotional? Fabulous!" Maddy laughed and rubbed her baby. "As thrilled as I am over how the art career is going, I'm a thousand times more thrilled over this."

"I imagine Joe's beside himself," Christine said.

"He is." Maddy smiled. "And he nearly collapsed in relief when the sonogram said girl, not boy. I think he was terrified he'd get some big cosmic payback for what a hell-raiser he was. So are we ready to make that toast? I'm parched."

"Wait," Amy said. "I'd like to make one more announcement before we do."

"Oh?"

"Maddy's drink isn't the only one that's alcohol-free."

"Oh?" Maddy lifted a brow.

Laughter spilled out along with Amy's news. "Byron and I are expecting a boy five months from now."

"Oh, my God!" Maddy leaned over to hug her.

Christine came next. "That is fantastic. By this time next year, I'll be an auntie twice. Too cool."

Amy pressed a hand to her nearly flat tummy as wonderment filled her. "To think I worked so hard to get skinny, and now that I am, I'm completely elated at the thought of ballooning up again."

"But in a totally different way," Maddy pointed out.

"True. So, what about you and Alec?" Amy asked. "Still no interest in kids?"

"Our lives are very full, and we're completely happy," Christine said. "I'll be tickled just being an aunt—in a manner of speaking."

"Well, good." Amy nodded. "Everyone has a different definition of their perfect life, and I think we each found ours."

"I agree, but Christine being an aunt is more than a manner of speaking," Maddy said. "I've thought about this a lot lately, about how each of us had to overcome baggage from our families to accept ourselves and find happiness. And I've decided there are two kinds of family. The one you're born into, and the one you choose." She looked at them, then at the men frolicking in the pool like a bunch of kids. "So I'd like to make a toast, to the family of my heart."

They all raised their glasses.

"To family," Amy said.

Christine grinned. "And each of us finding our own perfect life."

Caribbean Rum Punch

While researching *Too Perfect*, my husband and I went sailing in the Caribbean aboard the *Star Clipper*, scoping out the perfect island for Amy and Byron. Along the way, we sampled a lot of rum punch, and noticed each islander seemed to have their own family recipe. But we also learned a little ditty for how to make this drink the traditional way. It goes like this:

One of Sour
Two of Sweet
Three of Strong
And four of Weak

In plainer terms, that means one part this to two parts that. So here's the original recipe for the drink that has inspired so many variations.

Ingredients:

3 oz lime juice
6 oz simple syrup
9 oz rum (Use a good quality dark rum like Mount Gay. *Not* a spiced rum, just a good dark rum.)
12 oz water
a few dashes of Angostura bitters
grated nutmeg

Directions

Blend first five ingredients in a jug and store in a cool place. (The islanders almost always make this in gallon batches and drink a little at a time.) Serve over lots of ice and grate fresh nutmeg over the top. I like to garnish mine with fruit, like cocktail cherries and pineapple wedges.

Warning

This drink tastes so good and goes down so easily, you barely taste the alcohol. But trust me, they call it "punch" for a reason. So savor slowly, and as they say in the Caribbean, "Don't worry, be happy!"